A FOG OF FEAR HAD DESCENDED ON THE CITY

No one was safe.

No one knew who the next victim would be.

No one knew what horrifying force could control the mind and destroy the body.

No one except whoever it was who had the power to make puppets of the entire population.

No one except the one other person who suspected the blood-chilling truth and had to find a way to defeat it before he, too, succumbed to—

THE SCOURGE

Impossible to fight . . . unthinkable to surrender. . . .

More Suspense from SIGNET

The
SCOURGE

by

Nick Sharman

A SIGNET BOOK
NEW AMERICAN LIBRARY
TIMES MIRROR

PUBLISHED BY
THE NEW AMERICAN LIBRARY
OF CANADA LIMITED

NAL BOOKS ARE AVAILABLE AT QUANTITY DISCOUNTS
WHEN USED TO PROMOTE PRODUCTS OR SERVICES. FOR
INFORMATION PLEASE WRITE TO PREMIUM MARKETING
DIVISION, THE NEW AMERICAN LIBRARY, INC., 1633
BROADWAY, NEW YORK, NEW YORK 10019.

 SIGNET TRADEMARK REG. U.S. PAT. OFF. AND FOREIGN COUNTRIES
REGISTERED TRADEMARK—MARCA REGISTRADA
HECHO EN WINNIPEG, CANADA

SIGNET, SIGNET CLASSICS, MENTOR, PLUME, MERIDIAN
and NAL BOOKS are published in Canada by The New American
Library of Canada, Limited, Scarborough, Ontario

PRINTED IN CANADA

COVER PRINTED IN U.S.A.

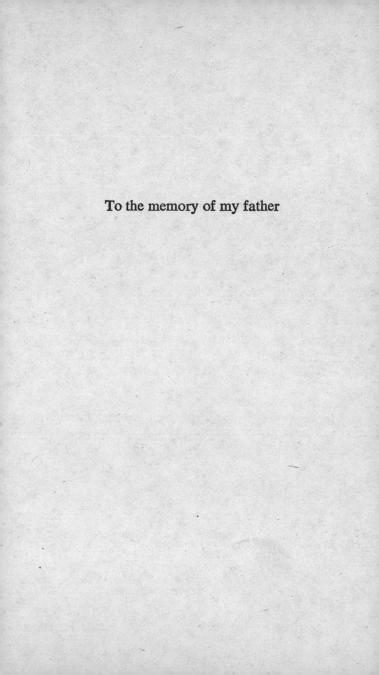

To the memory of my father

He cried in a whisper at some image, at some
vision,—he cried out twice, a cry that was
no more than a breath—
>"The horror! The horror!"

—Joseph Conrad, *Heart of Darkness*

Once meek, and in a perilous path,
The just man kept his course along
The vale of death.

—William Blake,
The Marriage of Heaven and Hell

Chapter One

When he awoke, Kiley was aware of three distinct areas of discomfort: a series of dull, throbbing hammer-blows in his right temple, a muffled, suffocating sensation around his nose, and the promise of agony in his lower lip.

He opened his eyes cautiously. Overhead a necklace of lights streamed by in the darkness. He shifted his gaze and discovered that he was sprawled in the reclining passenger seat of a Triumph TR7 sports car. He moved his head cautiously. A woman was driving. She was in her mid-thirties, with features a little too masculine for beauty, but handsome nonetheless. Her long, flowing hair shimmered in the glow from the dashboard. It looked as if it might be honey-blond in the daylight.

Kiley closed his eyes and tried to piece together the events of the previous evening, conscious of the engine's gentle thrum and the warm air from the heater wafting against his legs.

He had been at a party given by Marcus Daricott, the producer of one of BBC Television's top children's programs and until recently a client of Kiley's ailing one-man detective agency. The case, which had taken two weeks to wrap up, had earned Kiley a handsome fee, and an invitation to one of Daricott's star-studded show-business parties as an additional bonus.

He had gone down by train to Daricott's Oxfordshire mansion, where he had proceeded to get blind, raving drunk, his way of celebrating being solvent again.

Kiley opened his eyes again but didn't feel well enough to speak. He stared out the side window for a while. His mouth tasted as if an ashtray had been upended into it, and his stomach warned him against any sudden move-

1

ments. The pain in his skull was worsening with increasing consciousness.

Outside, rain was pouring down from a starless, moonless sky. The car headlights illuminated pools of water on the two lanes of highway and spotlighted bedraggled trees standing by the roadside, wintry, leafless, and glistening with rain.

Kiley could recall the first hour of the party with relative ease. He had wandered around like a star-struck teenager, chatting happily with various television personalities, all the while despising himself for being impressed by the glamour of the occasion. They, in turn, had treated him with patient amusement. Then the discotheque had started and there had been more drinks and he had been desperately trying to make it with a beautiful actress and . . . the rest of the evening fragmented into a series of flickering images, like those cast by a malfunctioning movie projector. There had been a lot of laughter and dancing and an endless supply of whiskey, and then, around two o'clock in the morning, there had been an argument, and the last thing he could remember was dropping onto the floor.

He groaned.

Beside him, the driver inclined her head slightly in his direction. "Welcome back to the land of the living, Mr. Kiley." Her voice was husky and humorous.

"Not so fast. I'm not sure I've rejoined it yet."

She laughed; it was a nice sound, throaty and natural. "I don't suppose I need ask you how you feel."

"There are no words to describe it." His speech sounded muffled, as if his mouth had been stuffed with cotton. He wondered, with a twinge of hope, whether he had made a pass at her, of which this ride home was the successful outcome.

She seemed to read his thoughts. "I was one of the few people sober enough to drive back and, as we live quite close by, I elected to drop you off at your place."

He swallowed his disappointment. "Was I really outrageous, then?"

She gave a shrug. "No more than most of the guests. Actually, I'd say you were doing fairly well until a certain husband took violent exception to the amount of attention you were giving his wife."

"Did he hit me?"

"Several times. In fact, everyone wondered how you managed to stand up for so long, Mr. Kiley."

"Professional pride, I suppose—and please, just call me Kiley."

"Don't you have a first name?"

"I try to forget it—it was just one of many sadistic impulses my parents gave in to."

He found the lever by the side of his seat and hoisted himself into a vertical position. She turned to look at him with a lopsided smile that managed to convey both sympathy and censure. He couldn't place her face but there was something very familiar about her.

"Is there a bruise about the size of a football on my forehead?" he asked.

She had turned her gaze back to the road. "No, but if your nose doesn't stop swelling, you'll have a great career impersonating W. C. Fields." He raised his fingers to touch it and winced. "Don't worry," she continued. "There was a doctor at the party who said it wasn't broken. There's also a small split in your lower lip which he said wasn't bad enough to require stitches. It's starting to bleed again. You'll find some tissues in the glove compartment."

She switched on the car radio and Musak tinkled out of the speakers set in both doors. Her index fingers tapped out the beat on the steering wheel and she hummed along tunelessly.

By the time Kiley had managed to stem the thin trickle of blood from his lower lip, the early morning sky had lightened to a dirty, industrial brown. The cloud cover was dull and complete, and the rain seemed gentler. Traffic had begun to thicken around them. The countryside had flattened out and was defaced by neat rows of suburban dwellings, drab and lifeless in the morning gloom.

Kiley shifted in his seat and watched his chauffeuse for a while. She drove with a detached, professional competence. Kiley noted with satisfaction the absence of a wedding ring on her finger. Their relationship had hardly enjoyed the most auspicious of starts, but the thrill of challenge only added to the natural attraction he felt for her. Whether it was her soothing presence he couldn't tell, but he was definitely feeling better. His various pains had begun to ease and he no longer felt nauseous.

She sensed his sidelong gaze and gave him a glance. "Do you always behave like that at parties?"

Kiley shrugged. "Make a fool of myself, you mean? Not really. I only get totally plastered about three times a year, either when I'm depressed or elated."

She smiled. "Only three times a year? I would have thought your life was more exciting than that. What was it this time?"

"Elated. I'd just completed a job for . . ." He paused, deciding it would be impolitic to discuss the Daricott case. The impression that he knew her from somewhere had been getting stronger as they talked. "I know this sounds like the oldest line in the book, but haven't we met someplace before?"

She nodded. "At a party last night. So you're a private detective?"

He decided to go along with the conversational sidestep. "They exist, I promise you . . . and if you're one of those movie buffs who can recite Lauren Bacall's lines about private eyes from *The Big Sleep*, please spare me. I've had them recited to me once too often."

She laughed throatily. "Don't worry. I wasn't even going to say how glamorous private detection must be. I was just interested in how you got into it."

Kiley shrugged. "I was with the police for years—the job just got to me after a while. Ex-coppers either become security advisers, publicans, or private detectives. I thought I'd try my hand at being my own boss for a while."

"Has it worked out for you?" The professionalism of her questioning technique matched that of her driving. She managed to sound genuinely interested, as if they were having a conversation rather than just passing the time.

"Great," Kiley responded. "If business goes on booming this way I'll soon be able to eat every other day." He groaned inwardly as he realized protestations of poverty weren't the best prelude to asking an obviously well-heeled woman for a date. "Seriously, it hasn't worked out too badly. Every now and then a juicy case comes along that pays the rent."

"Marcus Daricott was telling me how well you'd handled something for him. In fact, he spent the whole evening telling everyone they should hire you whenever they had any problems the police couldn't handle."

Kiley allowed himself a triumphant smirk but was brought up short by the pain of his cut lip. He watched the rain spattering off the hood of the car for a while. The rhythmic clacking of the windshield wipers was making him pleasantly drowsy. On the road the other vehicles were beginning to switch off their dimmers.

"What do *you* do for a living, besides helping lonely drunks?" he asked finally, more to keep himself awake than to elicit information.

"I'm one of those disgusting people who live off their investments," she replied sardonically.

Unfortunate, Kiley thought, now any advance he made might be construed as gold-digging. "I'm suitably disgusted. I just . . . look, I *do* know you from somewhere."

"I think I would have remembered if we had met before," she said and gave him a slightly worried glance.

"I know!" Kiley suddenly chuckled delightedly. "You're Anne Warren!" He wondered now why it had taken him so long. Anne Warren had been the biggest sensation on television: the first female talk-show host. She had been excellent—incisive questions, interesting guests, none of the usual show-business pap. Then there had been some personal tragedy, he couldn't quite recall what, except that she had abandonned her career as a result.

"Okay," she responded stiffly, "I'm Anne Warren." Her reaction made him feel as if he had invaded her privacy.

"I'm sorry," he murmured. "I did that rather clumsily." When people faded from the television screen it was as if they had died. Coming into contact with them again after years of obscurity was uncomfortably like being faced with a ghost, and Kiley realized she must be only too aware of that.

She gave him a reassuring smile, but he could feel that discovering her identity had changed everything at one stroke. The atmosphere in the car was noticeably cooler. Kiley cursed his lack of discretion.

To fill in the awkward silence his words had produced he sat back in his seat, rummaged in his jacket pockets and lit a cigarette, careful to keep it as far away as possible from the split in his lip. He coughed after the first drag.

The highway was beginning to climb into the air on squat pillars. Ahead of them, on either side, rose the concrete tower blocks of the main West London housing complex, mute testimony to an architectural dream gone disastrously wrong. Instant slums, Kiley thought. He felt the good mood that had previously triumphed over his hangover begin to evaporate as the music faded on the car radio.

"You're listening to Capital Radio, and now it's over to the newsroom for the latest news headlines . . ."

Kiley was wondering whether there was any way of resurrecting the bond that had existed between himself and Anne Warren when the newscaster's voice broke through his reflections:

"This is the Independent Radio News, eight a.m., Friday, November 18th . . . Trouble has once again broken out in the Middle East. Reports have been received of a Syrian bomber attack on . . ."

Kiley had just composed an ice-breaking crack about the husband who had slugged him when he heard Anne Warren gasp. He looked over at her, surprised. She was staring blankly ahead, white-knuckled hands clenched on the steering wheel. She was mouthing something to herself and her whole body, which had been relaxed, was suddenly tense.

Kiley stared anxiously through the windshield. Everything seemed normal. Traffic was moving smoothly along the glistening highway. He could see nothing to explain Anne's apparent alarm.

"Miss Warren, you all right?" The formal approach was something that had been inbred into Kiley during his years of police work. She didn't seem to hear him. He reached out and touched her arm. She shrank away from the contact, startled.

"Anne, what is it?" He tried again, louder.

Her mouth had stopped working and her jaws were clamped tight. The veins on her neck had started to bulge and she was breathing harshly through flaring nostrils. Kiley stared at her helplessly. She was having some kind of a fit. He glanced at the speedometer, which was hovering around seventy. She couldn't have chosen a worse time for an anxiety attack, or whatever the hell it was she was going through. At least she was staying in her lane.

"I think we'd better slow down a little, Anne," he suggested gently but firmly. A car directly in front of them, noting their approach, swerved into the middle lane. The TR7 wobbled unsteadily. At first Kiley put it down to their being caught in the wind currents that tend to make overpasses dangerous in bad weather, but when he looked he saw that the motion was being caused by the spasmodic movement of Anne Warren's hands on the steering wheel.

Her mouth formed a silent "No." She craned forward suddenly. Her eyes were bulging madly, peering through the murky windshield. The light was bad, Kiley thought, but not that bad.

"There's nothing there!" he yelled.

Anne Warren opened her mouth and screamed, turning the wheel sharply. The car veered into the next lane.

"Slow it down!" Kiley bellowed, thoroughly scared now.

A horn blared behind them. Their speed was up to eighty and increasing. She gave the wheel another turn. With a shock, Kiley realized that they were heading at a forty-five-degree angle for the concrete retaining wall of the overpass.

With a bleat of panic he grabbed the wheel and tried to twist it back. Anne was still screaming. Her grip was like iron and it took all his strength to shift the wheel. The car whiplashed into a four-wheel skid. The back bumper slashed into the narrow concrete wall, the only barrier between them and the road below. The impact slammed Kiley's head into the door on his side. He lay still for a moment, stunned, trying to collect his thoughts. Aware that the car was moving again, he forced himself back into a sitting position.

They were now headed in a direct diagonal across the road. Cars squealed to a halt around them. Anne's mouth was still open, but no sound issued from it. Kiley screwed his eyes shut as the car shaved the rear of a Lotus Elan in the fast lane. The TR7 shuddered as the vehicles touched, and suddenly they were sheering through metal railings separating them from the three lanes of oncoming traffic.

The needle had crawled back up past eighty. Kiley made one last, despairing attempt to gain control of the wheel, but Anne's grip was steel tight. He pushed his door open and flung himself out into the rushing wind as they hit the center lane. He got a brief impression of astonished faces peering at him from windshields as he rolled himself into a fetal ball and hit the ground, his left shoulder inches away from a moving car.

A moment later, he heard the sound of a collision.

He looked up just in time to see the blue sports car, Anne Warren still clutching the steering wheel, twirl through the air in a complete somersault. Then it crested the concrete edge of the overpass and disappeared.

Kiley scrambled to his feet and limped over to the side of the overpass. The TR7 lay shattered on the ground below. The sound of breaking glass and crumpling metal had been followed by a dull boom as the engine exploded.

The car that had collided with the TR7 was lying on its side by the concrete barrier, the engine spewing out of a rent in its hood. Kiley stumbled round it to get a closer look at the flaming wreckage forty feet below. Shards of metal were still winging through the air, and strange, twisted shapes were flaring amid the remains of the car. Kiley realized with horror that they were human bodies. The car had ploughed into a bus queue.

Suddenly a figure appeared out of the conflagration and for a split instant Kiley held his breath—but it was a young girl, about eight years old. She ran frantically down the road away from the holocaust, her clothes and curly hair spurting flames. Kiley wasn't sure whether it was her screams he heard or the echoes of Anne Warren's cries of terror reverberating in his mind.

He felt waves of nausea, and everything began to weave in front of him as his legs gave way and he sank slowly to the ground.

Chapter Two

The tall, burly man closed the door of the small private room softly, walked across to the foot of the single bed, and stared down at its apparently sleeping occupant.

Aware of the scrutiny, Kiley opened his eyelids slowly and, with an effort, focused on the intruder. Small, brown, piglike eyes gazed back at him unwaveringly from an impassive slab of a face roadmapped with ancient scar tissue. The visitor was enveloped in a shabby camel-hair coat that was speckled with fresh droplets of rain.

Kiley recognized his species immediately: archetypal copper. The sort of man who did as he was told and got annoyed when the rest of humanity failed to follow his example.

The big man hardly opened his mouth when he spoke. "All those bandages make you look like The Mummy." He made a dry, wheezing sound that might have been construed as a laugh but gave no other indication that his statement was to be taken as a joke. Kiley knew that thirty years of trying to hide feelings while interrogating suspects robbed a man's face of the capacity to express emotion.

"I'm Detective Inspector Withers. I'd like to ask you a few questions concerning the statement you made to my men yesterday." His voice was deep but blank and noncommittal, like his face.

Kiley groaned. He had spent most of the previous day being interrogated through the haze of shock, and he wasn't sure he was up to another session. The Gestapo had been sadly mistaken in using physical force to extract confessions; the British police method of wheedling questions endlessly repeated was far more effective.

"Are you charging me with anything, Inspector?"

9

Withers's eyebrows made a tiny, upward movement. "Not at the moment. Why, do you need a lawyer?" The offer contained a thinly veiled threat.

Kiley shifted until his back was against the pillows. His ribs and upper arms were swathed in bandages. The doctors had assured him that, miraculously, there had been no damage beyond severe bruising and, as far as they were concerned, he was free to go whenever he felt well enough. Now he just had to convince the police.

"I think we understand each other, Inspector. I know the routine well enough by now. I'm willing to cooperate."

Withers gave an almost imperceptible nod, fetched a steel-and-canvas chair from the corner of the room, pulled it up close to the bed, and sat down.

"I have a problem, Kiley. At six fifty yesterday morning you were carried in a drunken stupor from the home of a Mr. Marcus Daricott, whose all-night party you had been attending, to the car of a Mrs. Anne Warren, who had offered to drive you back to London. You were, by all accounts, in a bad way; you had been drinking heavily and you had been involved in a fight. At eight five yesterday morning, Mrs. Warren's car, minus you, pitched off the Westway overpass at Shepherd's Bush, killing four people and seriously injuring four others."

"Don't forget Anne Warren; she died as well."

Withers paused to light a cigarette, tossed the match onto the spotless floor, exhaled smoke softly, and continued: "My problem is, Kiley, was it an accident or suicide . . . or manslaughter? You could probably plead that."

Kiley was aware of an involuntary stiffening in his back and a certain difficulty in breathing. He wondered if all the innocent suspects he himself had interrogated in his time had felt the same quiver of fear. He continued to stare ahead at the door of the room. Behind him, rain pattered against the window. An ambulance siren blared somewhere in the distance.

Withers waited just long enough for what he was saying to sink in. "You yourself have stated that it wasn't an accident. The car was functioning normally and the only collision with another vehicle took place after the TR7 was already headed for the edge. We'll leave suicide for the moment and consider manslaughter. You woke up still drunk, found a pretty woman sitting beside you, and made a pass at her. She rejected your advances. You persisted, used physical force. She struggled. The car went out of control . . ." He let the allegation peter out. "Well?"

"Well what?" Kiley growled.

"Is that what really happened?" It was strange, Kiley reflected, how Withers's deep, quiet voice was so loaded with menace.

"Fact: I had *not* been aggressive earlier in the evening. Anne Warren told me that I had been paying too much attention to another man's wife. He hit me and I didn't retaliate. Maybe I would have had I been sober, but, then again, I wouldn't have been pestering his wife unless I'd been drinking. Fact: although I was definitely drunk at the party, I was stone-cold sober when I woke up. The fight must have taken place around two o'clock. I'd had six hours to sleep it off. Fact: I have never used physical force on a woman in my life. I admit I was physically attracted to Anne Warren, but in the condition I was in yesterday morning I couldn't have made love to Raquel Welch."

Withers shrugged. "Okay, so it wasn't manslaughter." He dropped his cigarette on the floor and stamped on it. "That brings us back to suicide."

"It wasn't suicide!"

"You sound very sure of that, and yet you said in your statement that no words passed between you and Anne Warren after she started acting up. How can you be positive that she didn't intend to kill herself?"

"Nothing before or during the event pointed to it being a suicide attempt. Why would she drag me along? And why engage in twenty minutes of cheerful conversation beforehand?"

"Perhaps you depressed her."

Kiley decided that this time it had to be a joke. He laughed and turned his head to look at Withers, who was lighting another cigarette.

"Inspector, have you ever been surrounded by a bunch of thugs looking to beat you up?"

Withers thought for a moment, then traced the scars on his face with the tip of his index finger. "That's how I got these," he said quietly.

"Obviously you remember how you felt. Well, that's how Anne Warren seemed. She was scared stiff, literally scared out of her mind. She saw something out on that road that horrified her so badly that she was willing to do anything to get away from it. She didn't take her own life; she gave it rather than face whatever the hell she imagined was lying in wait for her."

Withers studied the tip of his cigarette. "An hallucination?"

"How should I know? I'm just guessing."

"And maybe you're just trying to sell me a pack of bloody lies."

Kiley groaned and turned his head away. Withers levered himself out of his seat and walked to the window. He gazed out at the gray, rainy day.

"So, you used to be on the force," he said softly.

"You manage to make that sound like an accusation."

"Why did you leave?" Kiley was getting used to the question. He had been asked it three or four times on the previous day by other policemen.

"The pay, the hours, the working conditions, the amount of asskissing I had to go through to get anywhere. Besides, the gray men were taking over—the administrators, the paper-pushers, the accountants. Not my scene." He glanced over at Withers, who was eyeing him from his vantage point at the window. "And don't tell me you feel any different."

Withers turned back to the window. "Some of us had the guts to stick it out. I checked up on you. They said you were a good cop, with a discipline problem. Too much of a maverick. Seems a waste." He paused. "What were you handling for Marcus Daricott?"

"None of your business!"

Withers let his cigarette butt drop to the floor where he mashed it with the toe of his shoe. "Something sleazy, no doubt. Always is with you private boys." He sighed. "Okay, Kiley, that'll be all for now. I'm not charging you. You're free to go when you feel up to it. There's a bunch of reporters downstairs waiting for you. You'd best slip out the back. Seems a lot of people still remember Anne Warren. There'll be an inquest next week," he added. "You'll be informed about it."

Withers continued to hover by the window, not saying anything.

"Is something wrong?" Kiley asked after a while.

Withers shrugged slightly. "I might as well tell you. You'll read about it in the papers. Yours wasn't the first crash Anne Warren was involved in. A few years back she and her husband were driving back from Scotland. A car going the other way went out of control and came straight at them. There was a head-on collision. Anne Warren was driving that time too."

Kiley whistled softly between his teeth. "Was she badly hurt?"

"No, but her husband was killed instantly." Withers walked to the door, opened it, and turned. "I offer you a friendly word of advice, son—don't get involved in this. I don't want to hear that you've been pestering people. Remember, you're not one of us any longer." He exited, closing the door with a bang.

As soon as he was gone, Kiley moved out of bed, groaning and clutching at his ribs. He felt dizzy when he finally managed to stand up straight but put that down to the effect of the sedatives the nurses had administered. He dressed slowly, wincing with pain, then stood by the window for a long time, watching the rain pelting down from a sky that was almost black with clouds. Ten stories below him, matchstick figures scuttled across the courtyard of the West Central Hospital.

Kiley was surprised to find his nose suddenly clogged and his eyes blurred with tears. He drew in a deep breath and dismissed the reaction as delayed shock.

The air of mystery that clung to Anne Warren's death was haunting. He tried to fit the information that Withers had just given him into some sort of pattern. Had a terrible vision of her husband's death flashed across Anne's mind in the seconds before the crash in which she died? But why then? There had been no build-up, no indication that she was troubled by anything. That was what made it all seem so odd. It was as if her mind had switched tracks in a split instant . . .

Kiley shook his head. It was pointless of Withers to tell him to leave well enough alone. He was already too personally involved to drop everything. Besides, Anne Warren had done him a good turn when he needed it. In a way he was now in a position to return the favor.

Lightning flashed close by, followed a second later by an ominous roll of thunder that reverberated through the corridors of the vast hospital. Kiley wondered briefly if it was some kind of sign.

Police Constable Labran smiled grimly as he turned off Oxford Street and headed into Soho. He crossed Soho Square and entered Greek Street, keeping close to the shop fronts to avoid the freezing rain that sheeted down from the early evening sky. His helmet was tipped forward, shadowing his steady, pale gray eyes. The light from the street lamps shimmered on his drenched raincape.

Despite his discomfort, he welcomed rain on Saturday nights. It washed the grimy pavements clean and sent the street vermin scurrying underground for protection. Rainy nights meant less trouble, and that was something for which Labran was always grateful.

Two years before, when he and a number of other recruits had arrived at Vine Street Police Station as part of a "Get the police out of the cars and back on the streets" campaign, he had reveled in the excitement of the area. Now he loathed everything about it—the massage parlors where a quick hand-job set clients back twenty quid; the down-at-the-heels strip clubs; the tatty rooms rented for an hour by northern girls who had come south for "a bit of excitement" and had found that prostitution was the only way of scraping by; the dark Victorian pubs filled with petty criminals and psychotically violent men; the dope pushers plying their trade in Gerard Street; the emaciated kids with empty eyes and suppurating sores from rusty needles. And Labran hated the sounds that filled the streets—the harsh thudding rhythms of underground discos; the laughter of garishly dressed blacks punctuated by occasional cries of anger or despair; the thrum of idling motors as drunks cruised, eager for pickups; the masked night noises floating up from dark doorways where leering club owners stood, beckoning gullible pedestrians inside.

For Labran the excitement had given way to fear, the fear to loathing. Tonight he appreciated the rain all the more; his regular beat partner had reported in sick at the last moment and there was no one else available to make the rounds with him. There were never enough uniformed constables to go round, and it was when you were on your own that it became really dangerous. He reflected sourly that most of the recruits he had been friendly with were now deployed to protect foreign diplomats from the violent results of their own domestic policies.

Outside a discotheque, a gang of football fans was creating a disturbance. Labran halted near them until they noted his presence and quieted down. He waited, however, until the group had dispersed before heaving a sigh of relief and moving on.

He was praying for a quiet night—no knife fights, no drug overdose victims, no tourists whining about prostitutes stealing their money, no drunks waking up in alleyways covered in blood and bruises because they had knocked over the wrong man's drink at the bar, no prostitutes sliding out of doorways with their faces slashed by a dissatisfied pimp, no Chinese Tong fights around the illegal gaming clubs in Brewer Street. The rain was all he had going for him. It calmed and controlled everything, like a slap in the face of an hysteric.

Labran paused outside the Gay Hussar restaurant. The bottoms of his blue serge trousers were soaked, and water had already seeped into his boots. He touched the walkie-talkie clipped to the front of his jacket under the dark blue raincape, wiped the moisture from his face, and began walking down toward the theaters on Shaftesbury Avenue.

On the whole, most pedestrians were intent on getting to their destinations as quickly as possible, but here and there knots of tourists stood bunched around the windows of strip clubs, eyeing the photographs on display and forcing Labran to keep to the center of the pavement. Despite the drenching downpour he maintained a stately pace. At the corner of Bateman Street his progress was halted by a Salvation Army band belting out a mournful hymn. The girl beating the tambourine was pretty, in a pure, scrubbed way. Labran smiled at her and she turned her earnest gaze on him and smiled back.

Labran was still smiling when he caught sight of something out of the corner of his eye. He shifted his gaze from the girl he had been studying appreciatively and rose up on his toes to get an unobstructed view. Under the blinking neon signs of the Old Compton Street intersection he could make out someone jostling pedestrians off the pavement, coming toward him against the flow of the crowd. One bobbing head was visible, like a stranded dinghy in a sea of people.

Before Labran could react, a man burst out of the crowd. He was huge, some six inches taller than Labran himself and weighing a good sixty pounds more. The giant ran down the center of Greek Street, careering off car bumpers and knocking against the sides of braking vehicles.

With a start, Labran recognized him. The electric-blue mohair suit was an unmistakable trademark. It was Max Bronson, a pornography-dealing gangster with a well-deserved reputation for personal violence. Labran couldn't see what Bronson was running away from, but he noticed he was clutching a gleaming metallic object in one hand. By the time Labran had the walkie-talkie unclipped it was too late to contact the station. Bronson was almost abreast of him, his speed increasing.

Labran stepped out into the road and stood legs apart, arms outstretched, poised to grab the fleeing man and force him to the ground. At the last possible moment, he shouted for Bronson to halt, and as he did, he got a brief glimpse of the giant's terror-stricken face. Labran threw himself forward, but the tackle was badly mistimed and he found himself heading for the gutter, his helmet bouncing along the pavement. Labran heard an explosion near his unprotected head. It was several stunned seconds before he realized that Bronson had shot at him.

Conscious of the crowd's squeals of fear, Labran got to his feet and looked around for the walkie-talkie, which he had dropped. He discovered it had been crushed by a passing car, and with a curse he set off in pursuit, praying that a police car would appear soon. Gun or no gun, Bronson had to be stopped before he managed to kill someone.

Labran had a good fifteen years on the gangster and was in excellent physical condition; he was gaining on him by the time they were halfway across Soho Square. The giant looked around every few seconds with wild, unfocused eyes. Twice Bronson tripped and fell, but his momentum kept him going; he was no sooner splayed on the ground than he was up and running again, his torn, sodden suit flapping around his bulky body.

As the sound of pounding feet approached, people halted and turned to stare in astonishment. Labran was a mere five yards behind when Bronson attempted to vault the hood of a car that was inching across Soho Street. The gangster's tree-trunk legs buckled as he hit the pavement on the other side. He slipped sideways off the edge of the curb and there was a loud crack as his skull met the road. His gun skidded off across the street. Labran scrambled over the car hood in pursuit. He bent down and dragged the shaken man to his feet, then started to reach for handcuffs. However, Bronson looked so stunned that the cuffs seemed an unnecessary precaution. Blood gushed from a deep cut across his flaccid cheek, and an ugly, blue-black welt was swelling on his forehead.

"You bloody idiot!" Labran shouted. "What are you playing at?" The very loudness of his voice betrayed his fear, but Bronson seemed not to hear him. Instead he stared over the cop's shoulder. Labran guessed he had a bad concussion. As he became aware of the crowd moving in on them, Labran turned his head and snapped, "Go on about your business! Nothing to see here." The crowd halted but did not retreat. Labran was wondering just how to get Bronson back to Vine Street Station when he felt the gangster quiver in his grip. He turned back to face his captive, already sensing that he had made a dreadful mistake in not using the cuffs.

As he did, he caught a fleeting glimpse of Bronson's knee rising and then felt the crushing force of it in his groin. With a moan, Labran let go of Bronson's arms and toppled forward, clutching his testicles. For a few seconds, he lay face down on the road, feeling the chill wetness of the asphalt against his cheek and fighting back waves of pain and nausea. He knew he had to get up. No walkie-talkie, no backup patrol car. It always happened when you were on your own. He rose up on all fours and remained like that for a while, trying to regain his breath. By the time he managed to stand up, a crowd was gawking at him foolishly but keeping its distance. No one stepped forward to help.

He focused with an effort. Bronson had run the length of Soho Street and was turning the corner into Oxford Street. Labran looked around for the gun. It was nowhere to be seen. He hoped to God that Bronson hadn't retrieved it before he had bounded away.

Labran took off with a roar of anger, shouting at people

to get out of his way. He hit Oxford Street too fast. A double-decker bus missed him by inches as he went sliding to the center of the avenue. Bronson was tearing down the sidewalk like a wounded elephant, bulldozing his way through pedestrians.

Labran checked to make sure there were no patrol cars within sight, then began running once more. Up ahead, Bronson slipped and fell against a shop window. The glass wobbled alarmingly as he caromed off it and continued his hysterical flight. Labran was beginning to draw abreast as they approached Tottenham Court Road. Suddenly the gangster disappeared from view. Labran skidded to a halt and looked up at the sign over the open stone entrance-way: TOTTENHAM COURT ROAD UNDERGROUND STATION.

The policeman managed a quick, humorless smile. As long as he didn't get to another exit, Bronson would be trapped in the station.

Labran began fighting his way through the crowd on the pavement, using his fists to clear a path. When he reached the long alleyway leading to the main part of the station, it still echoed with the metallic click of Bronson's heels. Labran raced along the passage to the ticket machines. He came hurtling out just in time to see Bronson high-jump the automatic barriers and head down a long escalator leading to the train platforms below. Labran followed suit, ignoring the ticket collector's shouts. By the time Labran had reached the top of the first escalator, Bronson was about halfway down it, shoving people aside, sending them sprawling and filling the station with their panicky screams.

"Let him through!" Labran shouted; he saw that the gun was back in Bronson's hand. The policeman ran to the top of the central stairway. He took the first few steps too fast, felt his foot slip off the serated edge of one of the stairs, and was suddenly sailing through the air. He crashed to a halt some thirty yards down, heaved himself up, and began hobbling down, teeth gritted against the throbbing agony in his crotch, hoping that whatever damage had been done wasn't permanent.

Bronson leaped off the last step of the escalator, then halted, arms outstretched, twisting his head from side to side, confused by the choice of passages leading to the train platforms. Labran took the last five steps in one leap, letting out a yell of pain. Bronson turned. The big man shrieked, aimed his gun haphazardly, and fired. Labran froze. As Bronson veered off to the left, the policeman heard a groan behind him. Someone had been shot. Heart hammering against his ribs, breath rasping in his throat, Labran began staggering toward the thirty-yard-long curved passageway down which Bronson had disappeared. He reached the entrance in time to see the gangster career into the wall as it curled into the last stretch leading at right angles onto the platform.

Labran felt the rumble of an approaching train beneath his feet. He halted. There was no way he was going to catch up with Bronson. He watched in mute astonishment as the gangster vaulted into mid-air over the tracks, his massive body twisting as he neared the advertising posters on the facing wall. The big man let out a wail of fear and fired the gun at the same time. The twin sounds were swallowed by the train, which thundered across Labran's line of vision. Bronson was already falling toward the rails when the first car hit him and carried him down the track like a matador impaled on the horns of a bull.

The high-pitched squeal of the train's brakes rang in Labran's ears as he walked slowly and painfully toward the edge of the platform. There was no longer any need to hurry.

A black woman in her early twenties ran past Labran, her white silk dress spattered with blood, her open-mouthed face a mask of horror.

Labran guessed there wouldn't be much left of Bronson. He was right.

Chapter Three

Kiley found the house he was looking for about halfway round Marlin Crescent, a quiet Victorian street. He backed up twenty yards to park between a tan Lamborghini Miura and a mudspattered Range-Rover. Since the invasion of London by Arabs, property values had skyrocketed. Even the modest two-story dwellings of North London's tatty Camden Town were now well beyond the reach of anyone bringing in less than fifty thousand pounds per annum.

Kiley killed the engine, lit up a cigarette, and indulged in a huge yawn. He had been hard at work ever since he sneaked out of the hospital earlier in the day. He had driven straight to the Fleet Street offices of the *Daily Express* where a reporter friend from the old days, who owed Kiley several favors, had arranged for him to use the newspaper's clipping files.

The coverage of the crash in which Anne Warren's husband had died was extensive, as befitted her status as a major television personality. They had been returning at two o'clock one morning from a week's stay in the Scottish Highlands, when a car driven by a drunk, joyriding teen-ager hit the verge between the north- and southbound lanes, took off through the air, and crashed straight into Anne's car. Her husband, Frank Warren, asleep in the passenger seat, was killed instantly, as was the teen-ager. It had taken firemen an hour to cut Anne free from the mangled wreckage of her car. She had been conscious throughout the maneuver, unable to move. Her husband's corpse had been wedged against her. Kiley wondered what effect such a gruesome experience would have on a sensitive person's mind.

The press clipping file also contained reports on Frank Warren's funeral, as well as Anne's long convalescence and her decision to quit television.

Anne Warren's sister, Dr. Mary Blake, a practicing psychoanalyst in whose Camden Town house Mrs. Warren has been staying since the tragedy, said earlier today: "Anne's decision is linked to her ghastly ordeal. Her doctors feel that a long period of time will be necessary for full recuperation. However, although she is not ready to face the cameras again at this moment, there is always a chance that she will return some time in the future."

After his stint at the *Express,* Kiley phoned Daricott to explain what had happened and to find out if there had been anything unusual about Anne Warren's behavior at his party. Daricott suggested that Kiley speak to Anne's sister, with whom Anne had continued to live up until her death.

"Mary Blake is a bit of a fire-eater," Daricott added by way of warning. "Be careful how you approach her."

Kiley had called her number several times during the afternoon, but her phone had been left off the hook. It was obvious that the only way he was going to get to speak to Dr. Blake was face to face.

He crushed out his cigarette in an overflowing ashtray and stared out at the street. In the foggy light of the street lamps, skeletal tree branches twisted up toward a pitch-black sky. The rain sheeting down on his '72 Jaguar made it look as classy as it had six years before when he had purchased it secondhand.

The news on the radio interrupted his musing. "Reports are just coming in that, due to an unidentified body on the tracks, no underground trains are in service at present on the Northern line. London Transport suggests that alternate routes—"

Kiley switched off the radio. He thought about lighting another cigarette but instead opened his door with a determined gesture and stepped out into the rain. Some jobs were an unpleasant necessity, but he had learned early in his police career that putting them off for the moment invariably meant canceling them altogether.

Head down, he walked to the front of the house, then stood for a few moments, allowing the water to trickle down the neck of his short leather jacket. He opened the waist-high wrought-iron gate and walked up four steps to the front door set in a stucco facade painted a bilious green. He pushed the bell and waited, listening to the rain thrumming against the glass canopy over his head. After a minute he heard footsteps approaching from inside. There was a peephole in the door and he felt himself being scrutinized.

"I don't care if you're a reporter or a fan, I'm not talking to anyone." The woman's voice was clipped and forceful. Its owner was obviously used to being obeyed.

"I'm neither, Dr. Blake. My name's Kiley. I was in the car with your sister right up until the accident."

There was a moment's pause, then he heard a chain being disconnected and bolts being shifted. An eye peered out at him suspiciously. "The police told me you were being held for questioning."

"I wasn't being held. I was flat on my back in a hospital. Besides, they've finished with me. You can phone Detective Inspector Withers and check."

"What do you want, exactly?" He hadn't expected such a frosty welcome.

"My first priority is to get in out of the rain. Do you have any idea what the temperature is out here?"

The door opened abruptly. "You'd better come in."

Mary Blake wasn't at all what he had expected. She was tall, only some three inches shorter than his six feet, with wide green eyes that were red-rimmed as if she had been crying, a button nose, and a pert mouth. Her rounded, kittenish face, framed by a helmet of auburn hair, seemed strangely out of place on her long, slender body. He would never have spotted her as Anne Warren's sister.

He followed her down a narrow hallway into a living room. Her slender torso shaded into ample buttocks and long legs, both shown to maximum advantage by a tight-fitting black knee-length skirt that had a vaguely Fifties air about it. Her manner was brisk and businesslike. Kiley guessed she was, like him, somewhere in her early thirties.

The living room, which stretched the length of the house, was tastefully decorated in a blend of old and new, with subtle lighting that brought out the restful quality of the predominantly beige color scheme.

She pointed to a black leather Chesterfield couch near the window. He sat down and she perched on a chair opposite him. A low smoked-glass coffee table stood between them. The cream silk shirt she was wearing clung to her small breasts, outlining the nipples quite distinctly.

"Now that your first objective has been achieved, perhaps you'll tell me why you're here." Her tone was still glacial. "Have you come to say how sorry you are?"

"I wasn't aware that I had anything to apologize about. I came to speak to you about Anne."

There was a moment's pause. Mary Blake's gaze remained steady. She reminded him of a schoolmistress he had once suffered under and for whom he had always retained a secret passion.

"Why, exactly?" The words were fired at him rather than spoken.

Kiley shrugged. "My first motive is purely selfish. Yesterday I came close to losing something that's very precious to me—my life. I feel I have a right to know why. The second motive is quite simple. I only knew your sister for a very short time, but I liked her. I liked her a lot. She didn't strike me as the kind of person who deserved or wanted death. Thirdly, I have a professional interest. I'm a private detective and my work entails the uncovering of rational explanations for events. I haven't yet found one for Anne's death."

Mary Blake slumped back in her seat as if a puppeteer had cut her strings. She brought up a slender hand to wipe her eyes. The transformation was remarkable.

"I'm sorry, Mr. Kiley. The last thirty-six hours haven't been particularly easy for me."

"I can imagine. The police and the press aren't renowned as respectors of grief," he said gently. He could see she was trying hard to stop herself from falling apart. He wasn't sure he should have come. It seemed cruel to intrude.

"I don't really think I've accepted the fact of her death yet," she went on.

"Were you very close?"

"For the last two years, yes. If anyone was in a position to see something like this coming, it was me."

"How do you mean? Did she give any indication of being emotionally unstable? Was she like that?"

"Exactly the opposite."

She gazed at him. Her temporary collapse had halted. Her manner was brisker when she resumed. "Would you like a drink?"

"Sure, if it's no trouble. Whiskey, neat."

She rose, went to a cabinet near the front window, and fixed their drinks with a slightly shaking hand. She handed Kiley the Scotch and reseated herself, then took a long pull on her drink.

"Please, Mr. Kiley, could you tell me exactly what happened? The police only gave me a vague outline, and the morning papers were filled with such rubbish. One of them even managed to imply that Anne had been taking drugs at Daricott's party. I'd like to hear the truth."

Kiley shook his head. "Drugs had nothing to do with it for a start. It wasn't that kind of party—strictly booze, and Anne was quite sober. Incidentally, I'll promise to tell you everything if you'll call me 'Kiley' without the 'Mister.'"

She nodded and even managed a half-smile. He recounted his story briefly and unemotionally. He paused for a moment when he had finished it. Mary Blake was frowning, staring at her nearly empty glass.

"Dr. Blake, earlier on you said you should have been able to see something like this coming. Anne struck me as a happy, stable woman and yet I found out that she went through something dreadful a few years back. Did it affect her badly?"

Mary put the glass down on the arm of her chair and studied it contemplatively for a moment before she answered. "After Frank's death, Anne came here to live with me. We'd never been *that* close, but we always got along fairly well and it was obvious that she needed someone around to help her through a bad patch. Her marriage was childless, and both our parents were dead. She really had no one else to turn to. She spent six weeks in a hospital and moved here right afterwards. The arrangement worked out surprisingly well. I had just ended a long relationship with a man and was glad to have the company. I watched her carefully for signs of mental stress at first—

no one lives through an experience like that without getting scarred."

"She was in a bad way, I suppose."

"That's what was so remarkable. Oh, she was depressed a lot of the time, but that was only to be expected. I know she blamed herself for Frank's death in some way—she told me so. But Anne is . . . was strong, incredibly resilient. After six months she was back to her old self. I was amazed and delighted."

"What about her refusal to go back into television?"

Mary shrugged. "She needed a rest. She had been working hard for eight years. She wanted to relax and take stock of her life. For the past three months she had even been talking about going back to work. That was her main reason for going to Daricott's party—to get back into the swing of things, renew her contacts."

"So she'd been optimistic recently. That makes it even more puzzling. Look, do you have *any* idea what could have happened to her back there on the road?"

Mary shook her head. "Psychological events usually have a physical correlative."

Kiley grinned. "I'm lost already."

"Sorry. Let me put it another way. Psychological strain tends to manifest itself in a person's behavior over a period of time. I've been racking my brains trying to recall anything Anne did or said recently that might show she was undergoing some kind of trauma—heading for a breakdown. I can't think of a damn thing. Marcus Daricott phoned me yesterday and told me that Anne behaved normally at his party and now you tell me that she was quite cheerful during your drive."

"Happy as a lark. As for the accident itself, do you think she was hallucinating?"

"I just don't know. It doesn't fit the classic pattern. Hallucinations are usually experienced by neurotics and the effects are cumulative."

"What does that mean?" Kiley sipped his whiskey.

"A man suffering from paranoia won't just suddenly see someone following him in the street. He'll start with the feeling that he's being followed, then he'll imagine coattails disappearing into doorways when he turns to look, then, finally, his mind will *invent* someone to account for his suspicions. Instantaneous hallucinations, or the reliving of past events, except during sleep, are extraordinarily rare."

"Do you think Anne was imagining herself back in the car with her husband?"

Mary Blake shrugged. "If she was, then something must have been responsible for it. Every effect has a preceding cause." Mary sighed and brought the fingertips of one hand up to rub at her left temple. "But why now, after all this time?" she said softly, as if to herself. "Anne began driving again without a qualm two months after the accident." She shook her head slowly. "Poor Anne. I don't suppose we'll ever know what really happened."

Kiley gazed at her for a while. Mary Blake reminded him of a lot of professional women he had met—a mixture of soft femininity and cool detachment. Anne Warren had possessed this quality as well, but in her the contrast was not so obvious. It was a combination that intrigued and excited him, so much so that for almost a minute he had some difficulty concentrating on the matter in hand. He drained his glass. The bruise in his side was beginning to throb.

"I intend to find out what happened," he said quietly. "You said that every effect has a cause, and I agree. If there isn't an adequate psychological explanation for Anne's death, I'll just have to look elsewhere."

Mary looked up and gave him a wan smile. "You strike me as being a rather stubborn man, Kiley. And a little arrogant."

"Pig-headed and opinionated would be nearer the mark. Arrogance is the product of self-doubt. Besides, I thrive on dead ends."

"What do you intend to do now?"

He shrugged. "I really can't answer that. Let me ask you a few more questions and see whether we can dig something up. Did Anne go out with anyone?"

"You mean lovers? Not really. Men took her out to the theater every now and then, but it was never anything very serious. It sounds terribly corny, but Frank Warren was an extraordinary man. I don't think she believed she would ever meet his equal."

"Women friends?"

"One or two. Why do you ask?"

"I just want to know more about her. I'd like you to

give me an idea of Anne's movements over the past week. Maybe talking about it will help you remember something you'd overlooked previously."

"Please, Kiley, let's remember just who the psychiatrist is around here," she said, smiling genuinely for once.

"You'll have to forgive me. Detectives get used to treating people as if they were backward children."

Mary put her head to one side. "I'm not so sure they're always wrong."

She seemed to be more relaxed with him, Kiley observed. He got out his notebook. Things were looking up.

"You know, Kiley, I was ready to slam the door in your face. I'm pleased I didn't. You're a cathartic agent."

Kiley realized he felt the same way, and wondered if there was something ghoulish about being attracted to Anne Warren's sister.

"Start with last Sunday," he suggested.

Mary let her head rest on the back of her chair and concentrated. "We stayed in all day, doing nothing in particular, then in the evening we went to see the latest Clint Eastwood film. Anne paid for the tickets. Monday, she . . . no, nothing happened on Monday," she went on hurriedly. The slight pause worried Kiley.

"Dr. Blake, I'm sorry if I seem too suspicious—it's all part of my job—but why did you hesitate just then? Are you sure Monday was uneventful?"

"It has nothing to do with your question," she said bluntly, brushing imaginary specks of dust from the arm of her chair.

"Perhaps you'll let me decide that. What happened?"

Mary placed her hand back in her lap and frowned down at it. "She went to dinner with an old friend."

"Could you give me his or her name?"

"No, I can't. I can tell you it *was* a man."

Kiley tapped the end of his felt-tip pen against his teeth. "You mean you don't know who it was?"

"No, that's not what I mean," she answered firmly. "Listen, he's a married man. I don't want you bothering him. There was nothing in the least bit sordid about their relationship. Besides, it's his private affair."

"Okay, let's not fall out over it. I'll just put down 'an old admirer.' Tuesday?"

"Nothing—and this time I *am* being honest with you.

Anne felt tired after her evening out. She slept late and spent the afternoon reading."

Kiley made a note, humming the words he was writing under his breath. "That brings us up to Wednesday."

"Wednesday, Wednesday . . . yes, something did happen. Anne had a speaking engagement at the local branch of the Women's Institute. Now that *was* very strange . . ."

"What's so odd about that? People obviously remember her from the old days."

Mary frowned. "Anne *told* me she had been there—she even commented on how boring it had been. She hated that sort of thing, but had begun to accept invitations as a way of getting used to audiences again."

"Then what's the mystery?"

Mary rose from her chair and moved to an escritoire at the far end of the room. She returned with a letter and handed it to Kiley without speaking. He waited until she was reseated, then opened it.

It was dated Thursday, December 16th and was headed Camden Town Women's Institute. The letter was badly typed and ended in a fussy, flowery signature that looked like "Emma Maitland."

Dear Ms. Warren,
    May I say how disappointed we were that you failed to turn up at yesterday's meeting. Thirty of our members were disappointed as a result. I would appreciate some form of explanation.

Kiley looked up sharply. "Why didn't you tell me about this at once?"

"Now, don't be so accusatory. It had slipped my mind."

"Was Anne in the habit of lying to you?"

"No, but then she must have realized that I would be angry with her."

"Was she normally this unreliable?"

Mary shook her head. "Not at all, but anyone can get cold feet. I expect it was a last-minute decision." She yawned on the last word.

"I'm sorry, this won't take much longer, Doctor. Have you shown this to the police?"

"No, their investigations didn't take that direction . . ."

"Hmmm." Kiley folded the letter and handed it back across the coffee table. "That brings us to Thursday."

Mary nodded. "Anne went out in the afternoon to buy a new dress for Daricott's party, that was all. She left here about six o'clock to drive down." She yawned again.

Kiley decided to call it a day and let Mary get some rest. Despite her protestations, his visit couldn't have been easy for her. Besides, the pain in his side was worsening and hunger was gnawing at his guts—he had had nothing to eat since breakfast. The identity of Anne's mysterious dinner companion and an explanation for her absence from the meeting would have to wait for another day.

He folded his notebook and slipped it into his jacket pocket. "I've taken up enough of your time. You've been very kind . . . very patient," he said, rising and arching his back.

"I'm pleased you came, but I *am* a little tired. Have I given you anything to go on so far?"

Kiley caught a trace of subtle perfume as he turned to her. "I don't really know. I'll be able to think more clearly about it in the morning."

She reached up a hand to smooth a few strands of hair behind her ears. "I hope your injuries aren't too bad."

He smiled. "It only hurts when I make love."

They parted with a brief handshake. "I'll be in touch if there are any developments," he called back over his shoulder as he tripped down the steps to the front gate. He promised himself that he would be in touch in any case.

By the time Kiley turned into Ladbroke Grove, where his office was situated, he was having trouble keeping his eyes open, even though it was not yet eight o'clock. Whiskey on an empty stomach, he reflected, was not the best remedy for tiredness.

He drove slowly down the narrow West London avenue, the wipers sluicing water off the Jag's windshield. For once there was a parking space directly in front of his office. His ground-floor entrance was cramped between a Chinese take-out restaurant and a seedy massage parlor. He swung the Jag into the space, crunching over empty Coca Cola cans and Kentucky Fried Chicken boxes. A hunched shadow moved along the pavement beside him. Dull eyes stared at the car from a gray-black face. A junkie, an ur-

ban zombie. Kiley waited until the adolescent was safely
past, then ran the short distance to his doorway, almost
slipping on the pavement. Paint clung here and there to
his door, like the traces of a skin disease. He took his keys
out of his pocket and stepped inside, holding his breath
against the dank graveyard odor of the stairway leading
up to his office. The door with *Kiley Inquiry Agency*
printed across its frosted glass panel was jammed as usual
and he had to slam it with the palm of his hand to get inside. He crossed to his desk, switched on the lamp that
provided the sole illumination for the room, and levered
himself into his battered desk chair. It squeaked as he
eased himself into a comfortable position.

From his jacket pockets he removed a squashed Big
Mac hamburger, a late edition of the *London Evening
News*, and his notebook. He chomped on the 'burger while
he went through the notes he had made at Mary's place.
Then, interlocking his fingers behind his head, he stared
for a while around the dilapidated, boxlike room. The
walls needed plastering. Bare floorboards showed through
disintegrating linoleum. His eyes came to rest on a Victorian hat-stand just inside the door. There was something
about its busy, curving lines that helped him focus his
thoughts when he puzzled over a difficult case.

There were already two mysteries for him to contemplate. First, the identity of the gallant gent who had escort-
ed Anne to dinner—Mary would have to reveal it sooner
or later—and, second, what Anne had done during those
missing hours, the ones she should have spent in the company of Emma Maitland's ladies. Perhaps, as Mary had
suggested, Anne had just backed out at the last moment
and hadn't bothered telling Mary for fear of her sister's
censure.

His mind was too far gone to concentrate any further.
Sitting upright he reached for the newspaper, and read the
sports pages carefully, then leafed through to the front
page. Much of it was taken up by a photograph of a ge-
nially smiling man, homburg tipped jauntily to one side of
his bald head, one wrist braceleted by a handcuff. Kiley
read the first two paragraphs under the screaming banner
headline and pursed his lips disdainfully. He couldn't bring
himself to feel sorry for Bronson—he knew the kind of
pornography the gangster dealt in and it turned his stom-

ach. He read the account of his death through twice before realizing that something was missing: the object of the gangster's fear, the thing that had made him run to his death. From the police statement it was clear that Bronson had already been running away from something when Constable Labran gave chase. It had to be something truly terrifying to make Bronson lose his head and fire into the crowd that way, Kiley reflected.

He put the paper down and went back to staring at the hat-stand. After five minutes he became aware that something was bothering him. He snatched up the paper and reread the account of Bronson's death.

Police admitted they were baffled as to the cause of Bronson's panic . . . One witness told reporters: "He was possessed. You'd have thought the devil himself was after him."

A connection was beginning to form in Kiley's mind.

Chapter Four

The alarm clock on Kiley's bedside table rang shrilly. Groaning, he reached out one arm from the depths of his quilt and bashed it with a clenched fist to stop the ringing. The events of the preceding forty- eight hours slowly began to edge into his consciousness. Now fully awake, he spent a few moments separating image from reality.

He got out of bed and dressed quickly, his breath forming jets of steam in the small room. Putting on a black shirt, leather jacket, and Levis over his bandaged limbs, he walked to the basin, splashed cold water onto his face, and brushed the foul residue of cigarettes from his mouth. Kiley turned to stare at his room. Brilliant sunlight stabbed through the dusty windows, emphasizing the starkness of his surroundings. Outside a street sweeper treated the residents of Portobello Road to a shrill, tuneless whistle.

Apart from a row of paperbacks on a makeshift shelf above his bed, the room was free of personal associations. Four years of disastrous married life had put an end to clutter and ties. Spartan. It was the way he wanted it for a while. Lighting his first cigarette of the day, he clattered down the stairs and strode out into Portobello Road.

He stopped and drew in a lungful of crystal air. The freshness would be gone soon enough, but at that moment the air was sparkling with the kind of cold that cracks the skin on your lips and hands if you are not used to it. Kiley took off up the street toward the corner newsstand. The street sweeper called out a cheery "Hello" and Kiley waved to him. He marveled at the way the sun managed to dispel the sense of hopelessness which normally permeated his sector of West London; the Island of Lost Souls, he had christened it privately. Even the piles of lit-ter left by the Saturday morning street-side antique stalls appeared neat and orderly.

Clutching a copy of every national Sunday newspaper, a packet of cigarettes, and a chocolate bar, Kiley walked back to his car and slipped into the driver's seat. He switched on the heater and began reading.

The reports on Bronson's death told him nothing he didn't know already. The police were putting it down to an attempted gangland revenge killing, but that was sheer nonsense. Nothing added up. Why would Bronson have run all that way, why hadn't the police constable seen anyone chasing him, and, if the gangster had wanted protection, why hadn't he simply asked the cop to take him into custody?

As if to reinforce the strange connection Kiley had imagined he detected between the two, the report on Bronson's death was right next to Anne Warren's obituary in the Sunday *Times*.

He lit a cigarette and tapped his fingers against the steering wheel. He needed to find out more about Bronson's death without getting his knee-caps blown away by one of the remaining members of the gang. There was only one man in the Bronson camp he could safely approach. Kiley gunned the Jag into life and roared up the empty street toward Soho.

Alan Brown felt something tickle against his lips. He opened his eyes. His wife, Erika, was kneeling by the sofa, her long, serious face close to his, smiling. "I'm off to the pool with Chloe."

He stretched his neck and kissed her chastely.

"There's plenty of coffee in the percolator," she continued, reaching out to wipe a dab of marmalade from her husband's chin, ". . . and dishes in the sink."

"Slavedriver," he muttered and let his compact body sink back onto the warm couch.

Erika moved out into the hall. He listened to her bustle around for a while, then heard the front door open.

"Bye, bye, Chloe," he called out. "Don't fall in the water." The child gurgled back, making him laugh.

He listened for the familiar crunch as Erika shifted the car into gear, then winced despite his preparedness and wondered once again how such an intelligent, educated woman could have so much trouble with a simple mechanism like a car clutch. He smiled happily as the engine roar faded along the elegant South Kensington street. Through the first-story window of their spacious apartment he could make out an icy winter sun piercing gold out of a light-blue marble sky. A perfect Sunday morning. It was a welcome respite from the continuous rain of the preceding week. All that water made him nervous.

Alan reached down by the side of the couch for the Arts Supplement and leafed through it listlessly, more to check on the advertisements than for the contents, then laid the paper against his chest where it crushed a mass of curling blond hairs. He ran the palm of his hand over the stubble on his square jaw. A wisp of light, curly hair fell across his eyes. He swept it back into place over his high forehead. It was nearly time for his bath and shave, but first he would allow himself a few moments of relaxation in the all-too-temporary peace of the apartment.

The birth of their daughter had come late in the Browns' marriage—Erika had been thirty-two at the time—and the event had been all the more important to them because of that, cementing an already caring, solid relationship. Naturally it had meant sacrifices; the little girl demanded her fair share of attention and could be raucously noisy when she chose. Sunday mornings, when Erika took Chloe for her weekly swim, provided the only true break that Alan ever got. The rest of his week was given over to managing an advertising agency. The boosting of his power-crazed clients' egos left him drained.

Sunday! Alan closed his eyes, snuggled his head into the corner of the couch, and began drifting back into contented sleep. Screw the dishes! A car horn blared in the street below. He sighed. There were always traffic problems with cars coming out of the damned garage across the way.

Fully awake now, he felt a familiar twinge of guilt. It was, he knew, a father's job to escort his children to the swimming pool. He had often thought of making the effort; perhaps it wouldn't be so bad once he got his trunks on and actually stepped out by the poolside, but no, the very thought of it made his skin crawl. He had only to think about any expanse of water and his breathing became labored and cold sweat broke out on his forehead.

He knew how unreasonable his reaction was, but that didn't help him to control it.

During his first term at boarding school, when he was still a shy, sensitive thirteen-year-old, some fellow pupils, discovering his inability to swim, had lured him to the pool and had proceeded to push him in, fully clothed, at the deep end. The memory of those ghastly, suffocating moments was still fresh in his mind—he had relived them often enough in nightmares. Only the timely intervention of a prefect who just happened to be passing had saved him from certain death. Three of the boys who had organized the dangerous prank were expelled. With the twisted logic typical of children, Alan had been blamed for everything by his fellows and a systematic campaign of persecution had made the next few years of his school career totally miserable.

He shuddered. No! He would never consent to visiting the pool. It was the one weak spot in a psychological makeup characterized by bulldoggish strengths and determination.

Annoyed with himself for giving way to morbid reflections, he sat up straight, folded the Arts Supplement—full of nonsense anyway; brick sculptures and fringe theater events organized by out-of-work communists—and turned to the sports section, scanning the pages for the Rugby Union results. His old school had been soundly beaten. The news cheered him up. He glanced at the date near the top right-hand corner of the page and placed the paper on the carpet by the side of the couch with a thoughtful expression. He swung his legs off the cushions and stood up.

It was then that he noticed the pictures staring up at him from the front page. Two photographs side by side—he bent to pick up the paper, stared at it for a few moments as if trying to remember something, then let it fall back on the floor, where it fanned out into its various sections.

The silence in the apartment was suddenly oppressive, even vaguely threatening. His body felt dirty with stale sweat. He scratched his stomach through the robe he was wearing. He felt as if he had not bathed for a long, long time.

With a grimace of distaste, he moved out into the hall and through it to the bathroom. He found himself wishing that Erika and Chloe had stayed behind. A great weight of loneliness was crushing in on him. It was like being back at school, during the years of persecution . . .

There were no pretensions about The Dug Out, Kiley thought as he parked his car across from the club's Old Compton Street entrance.

It was a dive, pure and simple; a drinking club for businessmen to stumble into after four-hour expense-account lunches when a reappearance at the office might have had worse consequences than an afternoon's truancy; a no-nonsense boozer's hangout where the respectable could get a cheap thrill by rubbing shoulders with London's underworld. Kiley wondered how many armed raids had been arranged in that dingy room, how many bribes had changed hands, how many villains' fates had been sealed by a quiet nod and the ordering of another round of drinks. He knew that it was a main contact point for Soho's dope pushers, small arms' peddlers, and pornography dealers. It was the kind of place your wife wouldn't like you visiting. Kiley shrugged. He didn't have a wife to worry about anymore.

He stepped out onto the pavement and glanced at his watch. Approaching midday. Once, during his year with the Serious Crime Squad, he and a partner had organized a watch on The Dug-Out for a week. Nothing had come of it, but he remembered now that Sunday morning was the time for Willie the barman to replenish the booze stocks. Kiley strode across to the entrance door, hoping nervously that the remnants of Bronson's gang had not decided to hold an emergency meeting there that morning. If they had, there would be little chance of him getting out without at least one broken limb.

The door was ajar. He opened it and walked down a flight of wooden stairs that gave onto a narrow, dingy passage hung with photographs of Max Bronson posing with various politicians and show business personalities. He looked carefully at the photographs but didn't find the one he was looking for.

Kiley paused and peered over the chest-high swinging doors that gave access into the main clubroom. A light was on over by the bar. He sniffed the air—a foul mixture of sweat and stale whiskey—and shoving open the

Western-style doors, moved noiselessly through the empty tables to the bar. He reached over, picked up a bottle of Britvic orange and pried off the cap, using the edge of the bar.

"Anyone home?" He drank from the bottle, then hoisted himself up onto a stool and swung round to face the room, elbows on the bar top.

A door next to the Gents toilet on Kiley's right was pushed open a few inches.

"Hey, you, we're closed. Beat it!" The door remained slightly ajar.

Kiley smiled in its direction. "Is that any way to speak to an old mate, Willie?"

"Oh, aye, and who might this old mate be?" There was a trace of fear behind the aggressive suspiciousness. Glasgow, Kiley decided, produced the ugliest regional accent in Britain.

"Don't worry, Willie, I'm not one of Max's enemies come for a reckoning."

The door was kicked open and a small, wizened man with unnaturally white hair stepped out. He was dressed in a bow tie, white shirt, black trousers, and a striped apron. Swaying between the tables with practiced ease, he approached cautiously and halted in front of Kiley. His gaunt face had a corpse's gray pallor; a razor scar dissected one cheek.

"Aye, I remember you. Kiley. Used to be a copper. Well, you'd best be on your bike, sonny, 'cos you'll no get anything frae me."

Kiley continued to smile and stood up slowly. There was almost a foot difference in their heights. The barman's eyes were narrow, suspicious slits.

"How about a drink, Willie, for old time's sake?"

"Looks like you had one already. Do you need a hearing aid, sonny? I said we're shut and I have nothin' to say to you."

Kiley reached into his pocket and brought out a ten-pound note. "I'd like a half pint of lager . . . and keep the change."

Willie stared at the note fluttering in front of his eyes. His tongue darted out, snakelike, leaving his thin lips wet where it had touched. He shrugged and walked behind the bar. Kiley kept his back to him as he heard the drink being poured, then swung round to take it, flicking the note on the bar.

He sipped and made a face. "Jesus!" he said with a shudder. Willie was standing staring at him impassively, the banknote crumpled in his bony hand. Kiley edged the glass away across the counter. "Have the police been around, Willie?"

"What if they have?"

"Cut up about your boss, are you?"

"I'll find another."

"Sentimental bastard, aren't you?"

Willie shrugged his thin shoulders. "Bronson wasnae a bad type—as that type goes."

"Not unless you object to pictures of ten-year-old girls being interfered with by full-grown men. Bronson was a pig. King of the porkers."

"Maybe. Anyway, it's none of my business . . . and none of yours."

"Oh but it *is* my business now, Willie. That note in your hand makes it my business."

"What do you want. I havenae got all day."

Kiley traced a pattern with his index finger on the chipped wood of the bar top. "Just tell me what happened."

"Why do you want to know?"

"Let's just say I have a personal stake in the affair. You must have been here when he ran out."

"Aye, I was." Holding the apron flap aside the old man slipped the note into his pocket. "He came in early yesterday evening, about five or so. He was in a hell of a state, hungover. Only just out of bed. Like a bear wi' a sore head. He had a couple of gins, large ones. He was snarlin' at everyone. I left him alone. He asked for the TV to be switched on." The barman yanked his thumb in the direction of the set perched above the bar. "I think he wanted the racin' results. He usually had a few bets on—'specially when he'd arranged the result. The place was pretty empty, just a few of the boys hangin' around the tables. Bronson was watchin' the news. He began runnin' his hands over his face, like he was nervous or somethin'. I thought it was just the hangover. Then he said: "Willie, gie us the gun.' "

"You keep one here?" Kiley asked.

"Oh aye, below the bar, just in case of trouble. Been a few bad fights in here lately. The office blokes sink a few too many and get mouthy. One of Max's boys usually sorts them out, but I keep the piece just in case. A shooter's a handly old thing, right enough."

Kiley frowned. "So you gave it to him, just like that."

"Aye, he's the boss. He took it and put it in his pocket. He was staring around the room, looking worried about somethin', as if he was expectin' trouble. Then he let out a wee cry, jumped up, and ran out the room. Two of the boys tried to stop him, but he was too fast. Almost knocked over a couple of blokes by the front door. Next thing we hear, he's brown bread, dead." Willie shook his head. "Bloody strange, so it is."

"Give me a whiskey." Willie poured one and handed it to Kiley. "Was Bronson in any trouble with any other gangs? The Chinese, for instance. I hear he was having a row with them a while back."

"Naw, it's nice and peaceful at the moment. Bronson came to an understanding with the Tongs."

Kiley sipped his drink. "So he wasn't worried about the Chinese, no one spoke to him, he didn't receive any phone calls, and there was no one in here who could have frightened him?"

Willie nodded. "That's about the size of it."

"Has anything else happened during the last week or so—anything out of the ordinary?"

A cunning look came into Willie's eyes. His tongue made a brief reappearance. "Maybe," he said cryptically.

"What the hell does that mean?"

"The sight of the Queen's portrait on a piece of paper tends to refresh my memory."

"Maybe the tip of my boot would help it along just as well."

Willie shrugged. "Aw, come on, Kiley. Inflation's gettin' to everyone these days."

Kiley frowned and extracted a five-pound note. "And don't tell me it's the wrong color, 'cause it's the only one you'll be seeing."

Willie pocketed it swiftly. "You know every Wednesday Bronson used to visit his old mother in Bermondsey. He never misses. Always takes along a present—box of choco- lates, flowers, something like that. Very fond of his mum, he was. Anyway, he took off last Wednesday about four o'clock. An hour later we got a call from his mother askin' what had happened to him . . ."

"Hang on, Willie. Didn't Bronson travel with a body-guard?"

"Not since the agreement with the Chinese. Anyway, his mother was no sooner off the phone than the boss walked in here. I told him about his mum's phone call. He just laughed. 'Daft old bitch!' he said. 'Her mind's goin'. I've been there all afternoon.' I didnae argue wi' the boss, but it struck me as odd at the time. I'd spoken many times to his mother and she was as sharp as a razor."

Kiley levered himself off the stool, feeling a slight tingle in his spine. He wondered if Anne Warren had been living under the delusion that she had visited the Women's Institute that Monday afternoon, just as Bronson believed he had paid a visit to his mother. Mary's theory lay in ruins.

"Have you told the cops about this?"

"Your old firm?" Willie sneered. "I wouldnae give them the time of day . . . and if anyone asks you, you didnae hear any of this from me."

Kiley nodded. "Thanks, Willie. You've been a big help!"

"Aye, sure, and next time you're passin', just pass."

Erika Brown had chosen aquamarine as the main color for the bathroom. Alan's aesthetic sensibility was suffi-ciently stunted for him not to object to any color scheme, but the blue-green tiles reminded him unpleasantly of chlorinated water. Today, he noted as he entered, locking the door behind him, the association was particularly strong.

Hooking the robe onto the back of the door, he slid his feet across the shaggy blue carpet and stepped onto the bathroom scales. He peered down over his thickening waistline. Ten pounds overweight, at least. Disconcerted, he stepped off and watched the needle swing back to zero. The trouble with advertising was the amount of entertain-ing it involved; endless expense-account lunches and post-prandial brandies were an accepted part of the job. After a while it began to play havoc with your weight.

An unpleasant image flashed before Alan's mind's eye: himself in ten years' time, grossly overweight, standing in the same spot looking in the full-length mirror next to the scales, feeling the pains shooting up his arm and across his chest, clutching at his heart and crumpling to the floor, dead from a massive coronary.

He shook his head angrily. Being an eminently practical man, morbid thoughts annoyed him.

He leaned over the bath, inserted the rubber plug and opened both cloverleaf taps with a twirl. The pipes that led from the old-fashioned enamel tub up the length of the wall behind him groaned slightly. There was an almost human splutter as air was expelled and water gushed freely into the bath. He watched it for several seconds, then bent to check the line he had recently etched in the enamel to represent the danger mark. When water flowed above the mark, it tended to splash onto the floor and cascade down the walls of the sitting room of the apartment below. Alan was tired of apologizing to the old lady who lived there. He reached down to extract some of Chloe's plastic toys. Water swirled around his wrist and he cursed; it was freezing cold. It always took time to warm up, especially during the winter.

With a long-suffering sigh he turned from the bath to the wash basin on the wall opposite the pipes, removed his razor from the mirror-fronted cabinet above it, turned on the hot tap, and shook a plastic container of shaving foam. He squirted white lather onto his hand before transferring it to his face, then passed his razor under the tap and dragged the edge of the blade down over his upper lip. He winced as a small dot of blood began to spread through the lather like red ink on blotting paper. The water issuing into the basin was as cold as that pouring into the bathtub. For a few moments he considered boiling a kettle in the kitchen, but decided not to. During his last year at school he had often been forced to shave with cold water, and his skin could take it.

With a shrug he wet the razor blade again and drew it carefully across his face. He dried himself with a towel, splashed on some aftershave, sucking in his breath as it stung the three flesh wounds he had inflicted on himself. He applied dots of tissue paper to the bloody areas, then turned the tap off.

The water continued to gush out. He stared down impassively for a few seconds, then tested the tap. It was locked tight in the "off" position.

At the same moment he became aware of a thunderous rumble emanating from the bath. He turned. The tub seemed to be filling at an unbelievable rate. He noticed with surprise that the waterline was already hovering near the scratched danger mark. With a groan he threw his towel to one corner of the bathroom, marched over to the tub, bent over and twisted both taps.

No change. The water continued to pour out. Alan's mouth fell open in surprise and a tiny, questioning sound caught at the back of his throat. He opened the taps again, then closed them. No effect. Still gushing.

He stood for a moment, hands on hips, a frown on his face, lower jaw jutting out fiercely. Bloody stupid machinery. It was always going on the blink. Nothing was built to last anymore. Cheap materials and shoddy workmanship—and he spent his whole life promoting crap like this to gullible bastards like himself.

He watched helplessly as the water edged inexorably up past the danger mark. He turned to the door and reached out for the key. He would have to phone a plumber.

He halted. The key was gone.

With a disgusted sigh Alan got down on his knees. He ran his hands over the rough carpet, waiting for some reassuring contact with cold metal. He felt a spray of water on his back, then heard the first rivulets of liquid lap over the edge of the bathtub.

Cursing, he stood up and tugged at the door handle. It was stuck.

Water was now running over the edge of the bath in steady waves. The pipes were groaning again. He walked over to the bath and plunged his bare arm in up to the shoulder and pulled at the plug. The metal chain disconnected in his hand. He gouged at the plug with his fingernails, but it refused to budge.

Alan stood up, his arms limp by his sides, and gazed down stupidly at the water pouring over his feet. It was soaking into the wall-to-wall carpet and edging toward the door. He massaged his shoulder thoughtfully and shivered. The water showed no sign of heating up and the air in the bathroom was decidedly chilly. He had no desire to catch a cold just before the major winter round of business presentations. Brown, White and Holgate needed new clients, and Alan was the only man who could get them.

He realized that he had no choice but to break the door down. His sense of urgency was increased by the fact that the pipes, now massively overloaded, were groaning louder and louder. The washbasin was filled to the brim.

Alan made a sudden charge at the door, feet splashing through the water. He pulled up a split instant before impact and hit the door with a soft thud. It remained fixed.

He stepped back, annoyed at his own cowardice, and was just preparing himself for a braver effort when the rumbling of the pipes took on a new and sinister quality. It was a high-pitched squealing sound, like metal grinding against metal. He glanced in its direction.

The pipes were moving, bucking, scraping against each other, dislodging pieces of plaster. As Alan watched, the squeal reached an unbearable pitch. He brought his hands up to cover his ears. A crack appeared in the main pipe. Water jetted from it up the tiled wall behind the bathtub. Another, wider crack appeared, sending a fine spray of water clear across the room. It soaked him.

Alan felt his annoyance give way to a tiny tremble of fear. He told himself gruffly that there was no need for panic and turned his attention back to the door.

The water was up around his ankles. There was no chance of finding the key now. He hunched over and made a run straight at the door, this time making contact with his full weight behind his shoulder. He let out a yell as he bounced back off the unyielding wood and clutched at his elbow; probably sprained, possibly broken, he thought.

Alan turned round, his firm jaw slack. The corners of his eyes were wet with unshed tears. Water was creeping up around his knees; the spray from the pipes hung in the air like blue mist.

He had to find the key! Alan knelt down, keeping his damaged arm close against his side. He began splashing about in the water with his good arm, his face completely immersed.

Something jabbed into his back; something sharp. He lifted his head and saw that splinters of metal from the pipes were ricocheting around the room. As he watched, the pipes tore loose from the wall and a gaping hole appeared where they had been.

The water was at his crotch, moving up and up, freezing cold, enveloping his testicles in an icy grip. Now it was at the level of his navel. The tub and basin were completely submerged. He began to splash about helplessly, tears of fear and frustration flowing freely. The water rose up to his chest, past his nipples.

Alan opened his mouth and bellowed with terror; a raw, inhuman roar. He was back in the pool at school, head bobbing frantically above the waterline, shrieking for help: "Save me! Can't swim . . . Save me!"—and the water was pouring into his mouth, flooding his throat, cutting off his shouts; he was unable to breathe and every effort to save himself was just making it worse . . .

No, not back at school. He made a last desperate attempt to get his mind back under control. He was in his own bathroom, water filtering into his nostrils as he stood on tiptoe, bubbles pouring from his mouth to explode on the surface as he emitted soundless shrieks. When the water reached his eyes he could see towels, bars of soap, plastic shampoo bottles, fragments of pipes, Chloe's toys, all floating around in front of him like the random remnants of some natural disaster.

His whole body was jerking spastically, his good arm thrashing, his legs kicking as he tried to keep his head above the waterline. His strength was going fast. And then his eyes were covered and the world all of a sudden looked strangely peaceful through a blue haze. Familiar objects swirled lazily through the bubbling atmosphere. The scene was disturbed only by a hint of churning violence around the hole in the wall where the pipes had been.

The adrenaline which had been pounding through his body faded to a thin trickle. Finally, dark edges began to move in on his mind and he floated gently through the water. He gave a resigned half-smile, air dribbling from the corners of his mouth. It would be all right. He would wake up soon, by the poolside, face-down, rough hands kneading his back while jets of water spurted out of his slack mouth . . .

Erika Brown struggled out of the car onto the pavement and stood for a few moments blinking against the wintry sun. With one hand, she held Chloe, slumbering peacefully, against her chest, while the other clutched a beach bag and water wings. She eased the car door shut with one hip, then ran across the road to their block of apartments. As she walked up the plushly decorated stairway to their first-floor apartment and scrabbled in her bag for the key, she noticed that the place seemed strangely quiet, the silence broken only by the distant hum of Sunday morning traffic.

"Alan?" The sleeping child woke, yawned, stretched out little balled fists, and blinked her eyes clear of the wet rat-tails of hair straggling over her forehead.

"Alan!" Erika tried again, walking across the hall to the sitting room. Perhaps he had gone out for a lunchtime drink. She placed the child in a corner of the couch on which Alan had been resting and walked back across the hall. She glanced at her watch. It was time to start prepar-ing lunch, husband or no husband. First she would dry Chloe's hair properly. She tried to open the bathroom door. It seemed to be locked. She rattled the handle, con-fused.

"Alan, darling, are you in there?" Silence. "Alan, come on, Chloe's soaking wet. I need a towel." No response. Erika rapped her knuckles against the door, then banged on it petulantly with the side of her fist. With a stamp of her foot she moved across to the bedroom in order to get the spare set of keys. As she walked back, Chloe, who had somehow managed to make the perilous descent from the couch onto the floor, came crawling out through the sitting room doorway, then stopped and watched her willowy mother. The child, wide-eyed, mouth dribbling, gurgled happily.

Erika sorted through the keys hurriedly, experiencing an odd tremor of panic; she found the right one and tried it. At first it refused to go all the way in. "Damn!" she mut-tered, skewering it in farther, then twisting it and pushing the door open.

It took several seconds to take it in. Then her hands flew to her face.

"Alaaaannn!" she wailed, the sound echoing through the apartment.

Chloe watched her mother with frightened eyes for a few seconds, saw her crumple to the floor, then turned and crawled back into the sitting room.

In the apartment below, the old lady wakened from her doze and scowled up at the ceiling. Strange family, the Browns. She was convinced that all that bathing did no one any good at all.

Chapter Five

Mary Blake agreed to see Kiley at her office the next day at four o'clock. He had spent most of Sunday afternoon and all of Monday morning wrapping up a sordid divorce case he had been working on for several weeks. It was grubby work that left a bad taste in his mouth and he was pleased it was over. Photographing lovers sneaking out of apartment houses in the early hours of the morning when the husband is away was not Kiley's idea of a manly occupation. The check he had received for his labors was not overly large but, together with Daricott's contribution, it would allow him to spend a few days on Anne Warren's death.

Mary's office was situated on the third floor of an elegant building in Harley Street. To get to her office, Kiley had to fight his way through crowds of black-robed Arab women visiting the gynecologist whose practice occupied the first two floors. Abortion, he decided, had to be the in-thing with the oil-rich set.

Mary Blake's office was everything a psychoanalyst's place should be; cool, shaded, restful. Double-glazed windows reduced the traffic noise outside to a faint whisper. The walls were adorned with signed documents testifying to her professional stature, interspersed here and there with a few abstract paintings that couldn't have done harm to even the most fragile psyche.

Mary was back to being the brisk, rather starched young lady she had impersonated at the start of their previous interview. Perhaps the professional setting helped. She motioned him to a seat on the other side of her desk.

"Coffee? Or something stronger?"

47

He shook his head on both counts. "I tried to get you several times yesterday. What happened?"

"I decided to spend the day in the country with friends."

"You look well, more relaxed."

"Country air works better than a course of my treatment . . . but for God's sake don't let my patients know that." She was being overtly friendly, but something in her manner struck him as brittle. Perhaps she hadn't really recovered yet.

He opened his mouth to speak, but Mary cut in: "I've been thinking about our conversation on Saturday, Kiley, and I've come to the conclusion that we were both rather overwrought. I think we were still in a state of mild shock." Her pert mouth twisted into a quick, false smile that was almost like a facial spasm. "The mind, you know, tends to overheat at times like that."

He lit a cigarette to avoid looking at her. The tremor of nervousness underlying her voice could not be accounted for by mere embarrassment. "I'm sorry you feel that way; there have been some developments."

"I'd prefer not to hear them."

"Your sister never attended the Women's Institute meeting," he said softly.

Mary frowned. "I thought we'd already agreed on that."

"Yes, but we didn't get a chance to sort out *why* she didn't attend."

"I told you, maybe she didn't feel up to facing a sizable audience. It's a terrible pressure after you've been away from it for a while. My God, I freeze up if I have to address more than five people at a time—"

Kiley cut in: "Anne *thought* she had attended that meeting, but she hadn't."

Mary frowned. "Kiley, you're making no sense at all!"

"Anne was under the impression that she *had* addressed Emma Maitland's ladies over lunch. When she spoke to you about it, she didn't realize that she wasn't telling the truth."

Mary shook her head. Her green eyes showed a trace of anger. "Kiley, this is pure conjecture—and pretty silly conjecture at that. Give me one real, solid fact to back up your theory and I'll consider it." Her voice was almost strident. She sat back in her seat and rearranged her hair fussily, trying not to meet his eyes. "I think we should leave it to the police," she added after a pause.

"Did you read about Max Bronson's death? He's the gangster who died on Saturday while we were talking."

Mary nodded vacantly and began fiddling with some files on her desk. Kiley went on: "A few days before he died Bronson went to visit his mother, as he did every week. Strange how sentimental villains get about their mothers. Only this time he never showed up at her place. When he returned to his club, The Dug-Out in Old Compton Street, he was convinced that he had spent the afternoon with her. Meanwhile the old lady had rung the club barman to ask where the hell her normally punctual son was." He paused to let the facts sink in.

Mary had stopped shuffling the files and was staring at a spot on her desk. "I'm very busy right now," she said quietly, her hands motionless on the arms of her chair. "Thanks for coming, but now I think you should leave. I really must ask you to go."

Kiley crossed his legs nonchalantly. "You're frightened."

"I'm not frightened, I assure you. I would just like to be left alone. You have no right . . ." She halted. Her lower lip quivered and she brought a hand up to wipe tears from her eyes. She sniffled, then straightened up and returned Kiley's gaze. "Leave me alone!" she pleaded.

"Mary, you *are* frightened. You realize that there's some connection between Max Bronson's death and Anne's. But it's more than that. You were scared when I walked in here. You've found out something that you feel you can't handle. Something about Anne? You'd better tell me."

She stared at him in silence for several moments, then closed her eyes and sighed. He could tell that she was struggling over a decision. Her shoulders slumped defeatedly. She opened a drawer, brought out a folded newspaper and slid it onto the desk top. Kiley reached out for it. Mary held her hand over her mouth and watched as Kiley read a brief item circled in red ink:

Alan Brown, the managing director of Brown, White and Holgate, Britain's fastest-growing advertising agency, was found dead in the bathroom of his South Kensington flat earlier today. Police reports suggest that he drowned in his bath. Foul play is not suspected. Mr. Brown, who was 36, is survived by his wife and 2-year-old daughter.

Kiley looked up, puzzled. "Why should this frighten you. After all, it's just a domestic accident . . . isn't it? Was he a friend of yours?"

Mary caught her lower lip between her teeth. "Do you remember I told you about Anne having dinner with an old friend a few days before she died, and I refused to tell you who it was?"

Kiley nodded.

"It was Alan Brown." Her wide green eyes looked at him imploringly. "What's going on, Kiley? There's something eerie about all this. I really am frightened, I don't mind admitting it. When I read this this morning . . ." She shrugged.

"Please don't keep anything else back from me," he said gently. "Where did Anne know Alan Brown from?"

"I've no idea. I don't think she ever mentioned anything about the start of their friendship."

"Were they sleeping together?"

"You don't believe in soft-pedaling, do you?"

"We've got beyond that stage. Three people are dead. There may be some connection. Now I'll repeat the question. Were they lovers?"

Mary nodded wearily. "I think they had an affair once, but it was before Alan's marriage. As far as I know, they were just friends toward the end. Alan was a great comfort to Anne after Frank's death—he visited her often in the hospital. Afterwards they used to meet for dinner every few months. I honestly don't think it was any more intimate than that."

"Have you mentioned any of this to the police?"

She shook her head. "It made me feel . . . scared, as if I was getting involved in something dangerous. I wanted to forget all about it. Funny, I've seen this kind of reaction many times with my own patients." She held her hand against her forehead for a moment as if to cool the fevered workings of her brain. "Physician, heal thyself!" she murmured.

"If it's any consolation, I don't blame you for feeling that way. There *is* something creepy about all this. I think one thing is becoming clear—Anne's death was no ordinary accident."

"You mean it was planned?" Her voice was a whisper.

"Let's just say there's more to it than meets the eye. If I can find some definite connection between these three deaths, then I'll do as you originally suggested and hand it all over to the police."

"How exactly do you intend to go about it?"

"I have to find out more about Alan Brown's death. Maybe it *was* just an accident. I don't want to go off to Withers half-cocked. I have a contact at the *Daily Express* who might know some more about it." He paused. "You know, reporters and private detectives have one thing in common; they're both considered a low form of animal life, yet members of both species can come in handy in tricky situations."

"Bitch! Cow! Loonyloonyloony . . ."

The old lady stood at the end of the hall, staring up the dark, narrow passage toward the door. She sagged against the banisters, the children's insults echoing in her ears. She gulped greedily from a tumbler clutched in her hand, then gasped.

The doorbell rang several times; sharp, insistent buzzes accompanied by the rhythmic clacking of the mailbox. Her head was throbbing. The noises confused her.

"Go away!" she yelled suddenly. "I'll phone the police!" The words slurred unsurely from slack lips. A chorus of humorless laughter greeted her plea.

"Go to hell!" she tried, louder. She stomped heavily up the hall in her ancient brogues. The children aimed a few kicks from outside the door at her approach. They shrieked in mock fear as she began turning the handle. She heard their feet racing away down the wet pavement and let the handle slip back. It was safer not to look. There was no guarantee that they had all left. They might just be waiting outside for her . . .

Little monsters! Why did they do it? The old woman shook her head listlessly. The world had changed so fast. Once everything had been so dependable, recognizable; there were structures, rules, customs. Then she had turned away for a few years and when she looked back it was all utterly different. The world had swiftly changed into something alien and dreadful. Care, kindness, charity, Christian ideals—all gone. These children of the materialistic post-war society seemed to have had all the humanity sucked out of them. There seemed to be no one to guide them, no one to set limits.

The taunting had gone on for about six months. At first it was limited to a few isolated incidents—the doorbell ringing, shouted insults, crude drawings left on the door-step. As they grew bolder, the torture had increased. Rubbish bins had been upturned in her tiny front garden. A piece of soiled toilet paper had been shoved through her mailbox. They followed her down the street, aping her shambling, arthritic walk. Once, when she was out, they had broken into the house—almost everything she possessed, and God knew it had not been much, had been destroyed. They had waited for her to return and then had tripped and kicked her in the darkened hall, laughing all the while. The police could do nothing. And the parents? It was all their loose talk about her drinking and "not being right in the head" that had fired the children's sadistic urges in the first place. Now the old lady rarely went out until she was sure the little fiends were off the streets for the night. If only Robert were alive, it would all be so different. He would have caught them and . . .

Emily Anstruther padded unsteadily into the small, dark front parlor, moved over to the window and pressed her cheek against the cold pane to stare out at the evening world. She massaged her cheek gently against the glass. Her breath formed small foggy ovals.

Outside the rain drizzled down out of a black, moonless sky. The yellow glow of the street lamps caught the drop-lets and seemed to hold them stationary in mid-air. Only the rivulets coursing down the gutters on either side of the mean, terraced suburban street showed that the water ever reached the ground; that and the sound of the rain against the pavements and rooftops, like a million fingers drumming on a million tabletops. It sounded tropical. For an instant it was like being back in Africa . . .

Tears welled in her tired eyes and she gave a sad laugh. It had been over thirty years since she and her husband, a dedicated Anglican minister, had foresaken their neat, or-dered English existence for a new home in the heart of darkness. Robert with his passionate, muscular idealism, ready to battle the three-pronged evils of ignorance, poverty, and disease; she, a frail, delicate creature in her early twenties, moving with quiet faithfulness in the immense shadow he cast, her head filled with notions of sacrifice and duty.

And then the reality—a run-down leper colony miles from civilization. She had been aware from the start that here at last was Robert's ideal environment. Here were a set of problems worth coping with. He had not even paused to rest after their arduous journey, but had sent Emily off with the native porters to the wooden shack perched on the hillside which was apparently to be their home, and had immediately started striding through the camp, fair skin sweating in the humid jungle air, seeking out officials, shouting orders, terrifying patients.

Emily had stood for a while in the dirt-encrusted living room of their crazily sloping house and had burst into tears, much to the amazement of the black porters. They drifted away at this sign of the white woman's weakness. The lilac rays of the tropical sunset crept through the dusty windows, enveloping her slim body in a warm glow. She had finally managed to control the sensations of strangeness and terror that had arisen within her. In the distance she heard Robert's booming, assertive voice echoing through the isolated outpost. It made her feel better. She was still listening when a noise behind her had made her turn. A figure was creeping through the dark shadows at the far end of the long room.

"Hello?" she had called uncertainly, thinking that perhaps one of the porters had stayed on.

A strange, low sound greeted her inquiry; an animal rumble from the back of the throat.

"Hello!" she had called again, stepping toward the shadows. There was a scuttling sound and a form shambled across the room to the door—a decrepit, bent body moving awkwardly on misshapen legs. Emily took another step toward the intruder.

"My name is Emily Anstruther," she had said loudly. The figure was hunched over the door handle, fiddling with it. "Please," she continued, forced kindness honeying her voice, "let me help you."

A last shaft of uneven sunlight had come flooding

across the room. The figure began to turn round, slowly. It advanced two shuffling steps toward her.

At first Emily had thought it was a trick of the light, a black face indistinct amid dark shadows. She had seen photographs of victims in the advanced stages of leprosy, but nothing had prepared her for this. Her mouth opened wide and a scream burst from her throat. The face had been unclear in the shadows because there was no face to speak of; a melted waxen apology for a face, a bad sculptor's poor effort abandoned soon after inception. It consisted of clumps of rotting flesh, the remnants of a nose, one half-shut eye, and a tiny aperture where the creature's mouth had been.

Still screaming, Emily had taken a step backward. The thing in front of her stretched out its arms. They ended in stumps at the wrists. To Emily they looked like mahogany clubs. As the creature moved toward her, she half-turned, then tripped and fell, lying stunned for a few seconds. She could hear the faint rasp at the back of the creature's throat, then felt its breath against her cheek. It smelled unutterably foul. She fainted.

Shuddering afresh at the memory, Emily separated her numb cheek from the windowpane and took a long pull at her tumbler of neat gin.

Across the way, a door opened in the line of tiny terraced houses. A man stood on the front step for a moment, silhouetted by his hall light. He looked up at the bleak sky, pulled on a raincoat, and, with a backward wave to his wife, ran down the path through his small front garden and exited onto the pavement.

Emily drained her tumbler and put it down on the windowsill. She pulled the dirty quilted dressing gown tighter around her puffy body and hugged herself.

For nearly thirty years she and Robert had slaved in that place. Emily's stark introduction to leprosy had been fortuitous in a way. Never again had she been so frightened by the ravaging power of the disease, but locked away deep in her mind in a secret compartment, which dear Robert had never been allowed to inspect, her fear of it had done nothing but increase over the years, fed daily by new horrors. Each morning and evening had found her checking her own body for signs of leprosy. She had always done this in private, rather guiltily, sensing there was something vaguely unchristian in her fears.

Soon, through Robert's almost superhuman efforts and with Emily's staunch support, they had begun to win the fight against the disease. With more funds and medical aid, and improved hygienic standards, they had actually started curing lepers, either by catching the disease in its early stages, or, in those cases where it had gone too far, by entirely halting its progress. It was fulfilling work, and the gratitude of the cured victims had given a sense of purpose to their lives.

Nonetheless, her thoughts would sometimes turn to her childhood in Bath, to gentle spring rain and softly sloping green fields, to tea parties on vicarage lawns, to the click of cricket bats in the haze of an English summer afternoon, to BBC radio programs and pleasant country lanes. Every now and then, she and Robert would return to England for a few weeks. They had loved those journeys home, but never for a moment did they consider leaving their adopted country. Their work had become their life and an existence without it would have been unthinkable.

And then came Independence and a new regime. Troops suddenly filled the streets, their work was interfered with, government funds were less easy to come by. Robert found himself in the peculiar position of having to beg the state for money to help its own people. The couple had suffered from harsh anti-Western laws and the government-controlled whipping up of racial antagonism. It was as if everything possible were being done to jeopardize their work.

Finally, the new regime's propaganda had taken effect. One night, a group of youths from a nearby village, fired up on gin and the memories of colonial repression, came storming through the leper colony armed with spears and wooden clubs. Hearing the disturbance, Robert had gotten up from the dinner table. Poor Robert! He had never understood diplomacy: "Waste of time, my dear. If you want something done, bark for it." He walked out of their house and down the hill toward the intruders. They halted momentarily as he approached. He barked at them, and they clubbed him to death.

Emily, watching the whole scene from the same window through which she had stared on the day of their arrival so many years ago, began shrieking. The blacks, hearing her screams, turned toward the house, eyes gleaming cruelly in the moonlight. Mercifully, her cries had alerted Robert's helpers in the camp and all the lepers. They came out of the shadows, a crippled army, to avenge their dead leader. Before the alcohol-befuddled youths had reached the main house, they were halted with incredible ferocity.

It was murder, just as Robert's death had been. This time Emily watched the killing with the sweet joy of revenge in her heart. The carefully constructed edifice of her beliefs collapsed at that moment. The teachings of Christ had paled to insignificance against more primal emotions.

Robert was buried in Africa. Emily traveled home soon afterwards. She was alone now; all her family were dead, and her marriage had been childless. With the little money she had managed to save during their African years she purchased the seedy terraced house in North London and proceeded to drink herself into a stupor, from which she had rarely emerged in five years.

Standing back from the window, she caught sight of herself in the small oval mirror hanging on one wall of the unlit room. Only her face was visible. She cocked her head wistfully to one side. The foggy glow of the street lamp shimmered off her unkempt white hair. For an instant she resembled an artfully painted Madonna; but then the lines on her face, the bloated cheeks, the sad, sunken eyes became apparent. In five short years, she had aged twenty.

A boiling kettle shrieked from the back of the house. With a sigh, Emily turned from the mirror and padded out into the hall and down to the kitchen where a glaring overhead bulb revealed a chipped enamel sink, a grooved wooden drying board, plaster walls in need of a coat of paint, an old coal stove that she had never used, a rickety kitchen table and two miniature stools that would have looked more at home in a kindergarten.

She tugged the kettle off the gas ring, poured water into a clay mug that one of the lepers had crafted for her, and spooned in coffee. She stirred it listlessly with a dirty spoon and drank quickly.

"Home, sweet home!" she murmured drunkenly, then giggled. She wondered if there was enough alcohol to get her through to the next day. Emily looked at the frayed fat-spattered calendar above the stove. What day was it?

She calculated carefully. Less than a week to go till the fifth anniversary of Robert's death.

Still clutching her coffee mug, Emily moved back to the front parlor, bumping into a chair as she returned to the window. She placed the mug down on the windowsill and reached for her tumbler. She needed a real drink. It was time to open another bottle. The past was still too fresh in her mind, like a livid, seeping wound.

It was then that she noticed her hands.

Mary had been standing by her office window while Kiley was busy on the phone. Reading about Alan Brown's death shocked her, coming as it had so soon after Anne's; it had temporarily paralyzed her with fear—a fear which Kiley's reassuring presence was helping to overcome.

She turned when he replaced the receiver. He stood for a moment, tapping his index finger against his lower lip, his eyes staring off into space.

"Who were you talking to?" she asked, more as a way of getting his attention than to find out.

He didn't answer for a second, and when he did, he still seemed far away. "What? Oh, yes. Prince, a crime reporter on the *Daily Express*. They call him the Prince of Darkness because he wears sunglasses and a black raincoat draped over his shoulders the whole time. He's Fleet Street's resident murder expert."

"Did you find out what you wanted to know?"

"I'm not sure." He shrugged. "According to Prince, Alan Brown's widow claimed her husband was terrified of water—wouldn't go swimming, wouldn't take a holiday on the coast."

"Mmm." Mary walked back to her desk and sat down. "That's my department. Was it connected with something in his past?"

Kiley nodded. "Apparently so, though Alan Brown refused to discuss it with her in any detail. He just said that something had happened to him at school, which he preferred to forget about."

Mary picked up a pencil and began doodling on a notepad. "Probably some accident in his youth. That makes two so far."

"How do you mean?"

"From the little we know, it seems likely that Anne was reliving her accident with Frank when she died. Alan Brown could have been repeating his original ordeal at school. I wonder if this Max Bronson character was going through a similar experience."

"It would make more sense than the official police explanation. Professional criminals tend to be afraid of one thing—violent retribution. Maybe Bronson fingered a fellow villain, got him put away, and has been waiting for him to get out of prison and come after him. It happens more often than you'd think. Prison provides an excellent opportunity for mulling over injustices."

Mary completed her doodle and looked up. "So far we have three people who appear to have died through some fear that was not a reaction to any actual physical danger."

"Does this match anything in your professional experience?" Kiley asked.

"No. The nearest I've come to it is in cases of mass hysteria, but this is different. Fear is communicable among people when they are together, but not when they're separated."

"Would it be possible for someone to engineer this type of death?"

"Totally impossible . . . unless they used brainwashing techniques and that's a process which can take up to six months."

Kiley shrugged. "And Anne and Max Bronson were only missing for a few hours. We'll have to think of something else." He gave a protracted yawn. "In fact, the cops can figure it out."

Mary gave him a surprised look. "You were so against going to them. I hope I didn't put the idea in your head."

Kiley gave a wan smile. "No, you didn't. I was unwilling to go to them before, when it was just a matter of professional pride and personal involvement. Now we're talking about three dead people. There might be more to follow. I just don't have the resources to handle something as complicated as this. I wanted to be sure before I contacted them. Alan Brown's death is the clincher!" He stood up.

Mary continued to stare at the desktop. "I can't think of

a single person who could have had a reason to kill Anne."

Kiley looked at her awkwardly for a few moments. "I'm sorry to stir all this up. It can't be easy for you. I feel as if I'm putting you through hell. Perhaps I should have left it alone from the start."

Mary looked up at him sharply. There was a trace of anger in her eyes and two red spots had appeared on either rounded cheek.

"That's how I felt when I read about Alan Brown this morning, but you've changed all that. If something was done to cause Anne's death, then I want to know who did it and how they managed it. If you hadn't kept at it, Kiley, we wouldn't even have gotten this far. I'm grateful to you for that." She stood up and extended her slim hand. Kiley took it and held it for several seconds.

"Thanks, that makes me feel better. I'll drive over to Scotland Yard and dump everything in Withers's lap. You never know; if we manage to uncover something, we might get invited to the Police Ball this Christmas."

Mary laughed and contemplated him with her head tilted to one side, as if he were an interesting painting. "You know, I can understand why Anne offered to drive you home."

Kiley was smiling to himself as he tripped down the stairs past the cluster of Middle Eastern women still milling about on the floor below.

He stood for a moment on the pavement, fingering his car keys. People slouched past in the murky darkness, coats drawn up over their mouths as if the evening air might contain contaminants. Kiley breathed in deeply to test it and began walking toward his car. He felt relieved and annoyed at the same time. He was stopping halfway through a case, something he had never been forced to do since going independent, but there seemed little else he *could* do. The police could handle things more efficiently than he and that was the only real consideration.

When he reached the car, he found a parking ticket clipped to his windshield wiper. Cursing, he ripped it out and looked vengefully about for the traffic cop, grateful at finding an outlet for the frustration that had been building up inside him.

It was then that he noticed the car parked about twenty yards farther back on the opposite side of the road.

It was an odd, tingling, constricting sensation, as if candlewax had been dropped onto her palms. Emily brought her hands up close to her face in order to examine them in the light from the street lamp. They appeared shrunken in its glow. The tingling increased to the point where it became painful. She could make out nothing properly in the light. It was playing tricks on her, making everything contract. She winced and lifted one foot from the floor, feeling a sudden stabbing pain in her toes. The action unbalanced her and she fell heavily onto the carpet.

She lay there for a moment, stunned. The tingle began spreading up her arms and legs. Lying face down, she tried to haul herself across the room to the light switch, but it seemed impossible to get a proper grip on the carpet. Moaning, she struggled to her knees—something was happening to her, something awful. She had to get to the light.

Emily tottered forward on her knees, inching over the carpet, each jerky movement sending tremors of pain through her body. Twice she fell forward onto her face, and she shrieked as her cheek hit the floor. Getting up was proving more difficult each time.

Finally she was at the door. She reached for the handle, but her fingers refused to obey. The pain had moved on, deeper into her body, leaving her hands totally numb. She scrambled at the door handle, but it was no use. She couldn't feel it at all.

With a despairing effort she reached up for the light switch above her head and swung her arm in an arc against the wallpaper.

She made contact. The overhead light came on. Emily closed her eyes and slumped down by the wall, weeping. The pain was lessening throughout her body. It flickered like an afterglow in the midst of a general numbness. Hardly any sensation was left to her. It had to be the alcohol. A thousand gin bottles were hitting her nervous system at the same time.

She found it difficult to open her eyes. The lids seemed incredibly heavy. To bed. She would climb up to bed, crawl between the sheets and have a good night's rest. She would forsake drink for a while until she felt better. Her doctor had warned her . . .

Emily managed to get one eye open part way. Everything was blurred. Her breathing was labored as if someone had placed a pillow against her face. She had to work hard to drag air into her lungs. She was lying in such a way that her one open eye was at floor level. She made an attempt to get to her feet but knew at once that it would be impossible. There was nothing left for her but to cry out for help. She strained her vocal chords but nothing came out except a muffled, wheezing sound from somewhere deep in her throat. She could not tell whether her mouth was open. It was as if her nerves were refusing to carry messages back to the brain. Contact between mind and body had almost been severed.

Summoning what was left of her strength, she tried to move one arm across the floor. Through her half-shut eye she saw it coming into view, heard it scraping against the carpet. She blinked several times. Another trick of the light. The arm seemed to stop just above the wrist. She brought the limb up close to her face. Something moved through her mind—a dim, distant memory. Then she realized that it was no memory. Where her hand had once been, there was nothing.

She was staring at a stump of rotting flesh.

The mirror! She had to get to the mirror! She looked back across the room. The task seemed impossible. She knew she was crying but couldn't feel the tears against her cheek. She began to wriggle, head first, using the one arm over which she still had control to drag herself across the carpet. Her whole body was shaking with the effort. She felt that her breath would halt with each movement.

She lost track of time, but finally her arm brushed against the radiator under the window. A red welt appeared on the skin where it had stayed in contact with the metal, but she could feel nothing. Flinging the stump over the top of the radiator she began to haul herself up. Somehow she managed to get to her knees. The bottom of the mirror was edging into her field of vision. The top of her head was just visible. One last shove and she would be able to see herself . . .

For several seconds she did not comprehend. Her most

hideous fears had been realized, the lifelong nightmare had become a reality.

Staring back out at her from the mirror was a pathetic mockery of a human face. All that was recognizable in those muddy, melted features was the glimmer of one eye and a tiny hole where the mouth had been. At first, for one split instant, she imagined it was the leper she had met on that first day at the colony, but then she realized with a crescendo of repulsion that she was gazing at her own face. Her mouth, her eye.

From the small aperture came a pathetic hooting noise that was as close to a scream as Emily could manage before she fell forward onto the carpet for the last time.

The child clambered surreptitiously over the fence. He pulled the hood of his parka farther over his head and loped across the muddy front garden with catlike strides.

When he got to the window he peered hurriedly into the unlit front room. It was empty. He turned to wink at his mates hiding on the other side of the fence. They giggled. Putting a finger to his lips, he turned, took a can from his pocket and shook the plastic cylinder fiercely. Pressing the top button, he slowly began to spray backward letters onto the windowpane, his expression a study in concentration. L . . . O . . . O . . . N . . . His friends' laughter was infectious. He stifled a giggle with great difficulty.

The others, emboldened by his success, were standing by the gate now, mouths ajar, ready to scream in unison and bring the mad old lady to the window.

The child traced the V-top, then started on the long, downward stroke of the "Y," his eyes intent on his work. Just short of the end, he halted, his finger still pressed down on the nozzle. White paint collected in a little heap on the glass and began to run down to the sill. With an odd, lurching motion, the child pressed his face close to the glass, then screamed.

The others started shrieking excitedly but suddenly stopped, sensing that something was wrong. This was not part of the game.

The child by the window was still rooted there, screaming, long after the others had run away.

Chapter Six

The headlights of the black BMW flashed on. Kiley slipped into the driver's seat of his car and peered in the rear-view mirror. The BMW driver was merely a dark shadow above his glaring lights. Kiley was annoyed with himself for not spotting his pursuer earlier. He wondered briefly when he had first been picked up. Either outside The Dug-Out or at Mary Blake's house, he concluded.

He lit a cigarette and smoked it slowly, giving the BMW driver a chance to make nonsense of his suspicions. The car stayed put for ten long minutes.

There was one question that needed answering—did the tail have something to do with Anne Warren's death, or had Willie the barman put one of Bronson's gang onto Kiley? There was only one way of finding out.

He studied Harley Street, then stubbed out his cigarette and opened the car door. There was an intersection some forty yards farther down on his side of the road. Kiley headed for it at a brisk pace, mingling with the early evening commuters, not looking back. Behind him, a car engine started up with a roar. He guessed it was the tail. He turned the corner into New Cavendish Street, and surreptitiously tried a few car doors. The door on the third one, a red Toyota, gave easily. Kiley slid in. The keys were in the ignition and the seat was still warm. He shook his head sadly at such carelessness. He hunched low in the passenger seat, then poked his head up a few inches to look in the wing mirror. The BMW had turned into New Cavendish Street and had paused there, blocking the road. Blaring car horns forced the driver to move on. Kiley waited until the car was about twenty yards away, then lay down across the Toyota's front seats and did an impersonation of a discarded coat. He heard the BMW tooling by, then sat up.

The BMW was at the other end of the street, engine idling. Kiley could make out the driver's head twisting from side to side. He switched on the Toyota's engine, waited until the BMW had turned right, then eased out into the traffic. He was not unduly worried about borrowing a car. A lifetime's work in the interests of the law had left him with a healthy respect for it, allied to a certain lack of conscience about breaking it.

Keeping track of the BMW was relatively simple. Tailing a tail, Kiley had found, was child's play. The hunter, upon losing sight of his quarry, rarely suspects that he is being hunted in turn. The driver of the BMW was making it even easier by committing silly errors, driving like a man with something else on his mind.

The BMW was headed west across town. The rush hour traffic had just started, so neither of them was going anywhere fast. It took the best part of half an hour to reach St. John's Wood Road. There were a couple of cars between them as they motored slowly between the rows of elegant apartment houses, rearing out of the evening gloom like ghostly monoliths.

The BMW turned into one of the driveways, taking Kiley by surprise. He was in the wrong lane to turn in after it. He caught sight of a sign reading "Waterbury Towers" above the glass-fronted entranceway and followed the traffic until he had reached the next set of lights where he executed a U-turn and backtracked.

Several cars were parked in front of the gray stone building, but none of them was the BMW. A sign with an arrow pointing to the side of the building read "Residents' Car Park." A fat little doorman dressed in a chocolate-soldier uniform with a goldbraided cap set at a jaunty angle over his puffy face was blowing heat into his hands and stamping his feet outside the glass entrance. Kiley stopped the car in front of him and rolled down the window. The doorman gave the Toyota a disparaging sneer and inclined his head slightly.

"Yes, sir, can I help you?"

Kiley grinned up at him. "Strangest thing just happened. I saw an old friend of mine driving along the road a way back. I followed him but couldn't catch up. I think he turned in here. Black BMW?"

The doorman narrowed his eyes suspiciously. "I'm not allowed to hand out that kind of information, sir."

Kiley waved a five-pound note. The fat man snatched it from him like an alcoholic going for his first gulp of the day, then touched his cap with his index finger. "That might be Mr. Benson, sir."

"That's the one," Kiley confirmed with a chuckle. "What's he doing these days? We sort of lost touch."

The fat man studied the five-pound note for a few seconds with an ingenuous air, as if admiring the design. This was the second time Kiley had seen this act in two days. He was getting tired of it. If Willie the barman, who had lived with insecurity all his life, respected money, this tub of lard, who spent his days groveling at the feet of those who possessed it, obviously worshipped the stuff.

"Listen, fat boy," Kiley said convivially, "you've accepted a bribe, right? If I let the owners of this building know that, you'd lose your job, right? So stop screwing around and give me the information I want, right?" He spat out the last sentence.

The fear that flashed momentarily across the doorman's face was replaced by a sly look.

"You're *not* a friend of Mr. Benson's, are you?"

Kiley sighed. "Give me the fiver back and I'll tell you."

The fat man shrugged. "No skin off my nose. Benson's an old American geezer, lives in the penthouse apartment. Owns a big drug company. He's the chairman of it. Lives on his own. That's all I know—that's all I want to know. Why, is he in any trouble?"

A gleaming Rolls Royce glided up behind Kiley. The horn blared disdainfully. Kiley managed to control an urge to back up with fender-crushing suddenness.

"Keep this to yourself, and thanks." He heard the doorman mutter something unpleasant as he drove off.

Kiley parked the Toyota in Queen Anne Street, near where he had found it, got back into his car and drove back to his office. Trying to fit the owner of a drug company into the bizarre scheme of things was giving him a headache. By the time he pulled up in front of his office he felt as if he was suffering from brain damage. Things were happening too fast. It was like being on speed.

Outside the massage parlor, a toothless biddy dressed in an army coat was standing baying out a song whose every note was replete with misery and failure. One of the girls in the shop was peering through the Moroccan-beaded curtain, signaling the old hag to move along. A small gang of blacks munching barbecued ribs outside the Chinese take-out were eyeing the scene with mild interest.

Limp with exhaustion, Kiley had decided to phone Withers rather than submit to a personal interview. It would be nice to get the whole thing off his chest. Besides, he couldn't afford to go on indefinitely paying out bribes for information. After all, his client was a dead woman.

He crossed quickly to his doorway, managing to dodge the derelict's eye. She was waggling a half-empty bottle of cheap sherry in one hand, the other was keeping the beat for her rendition of what sounded like "Jealousy." He could hear the blacks chuckling as he shut the downstairs door behind him and leaned his back against it. He closed his eyes and wondered just what the hell was keeping him going.

Three faces were imprinted on his mind's eye, the first two distinct, the third hazy: Anne Warren, Max Bronson, and Alan Brown. He shrugged. Someone else could look out for their interests.

He climbed the stairs wearily, sliding his shoulder against the paint-flaked wall, trying to get clear in his own head how he was going to explain it all to Withers. The old tramp's voice sounded almost melodic behind him. He reached out a key toward his office door and grunted in surprise as it swung open at his touch.

Out of the darkness, a massive fist came racing at him and caught him flush in the face. He felt the shock of the blow run through his whole frame till it reached his knees. He staggered and began to drop, his mind a whirlpool. Hands caught at his armpits and dragged him into his office. He felt a sharp slap against his cheek. A light clicked on and he opened his eyes. The room was weaving in front of him. Someone had propped him up in his desk chair. In front of him, a huge shape was hovering, partially obscuring the light from the desk lamp. He made an effort at focusing.

Withers's impassive, slablike face moved in closer. For once there was some emotion in the inspector's eyes. Kiley registered the big cop's barely suppressed rage and felt distinctly afraid. Withers's hand came up slowly toward Kiley's face as if to caress his cheek. The cop flicked his wrist at the last moment and the crack of his palm echoed in the room. Kiley groaned.

"You're awake. Good! Now, I want you to listen to me, Kiley. I gave you a warning back at the hospital on Saturday. I told you to mind your own bloody business. You've been a very naughty lad." The bland softness of the cop's voice combined with the blazing anger in his eyes to produce a chilling effect. "Now, you've been bothering Dr. Blake," Withers continued, his breath whistling through his nostrils, his teeth clamped together, "sticking your nose in where it isn't wanted and generally making my investigations a lot more difficult than they need to be. Agreed?" The cop paused. Kiley made no movement. "Agreed?" Withers asked louder, bringing his hand up again.

Kiley nodded.

"Good, we seem to be communicating. That's what I call progress. As far as I'm concerned, you're a cowboy, a grubby little sod who lives off the weaknesses of people. I *protect* 'em. You make me sick, but as long as what you do doesn't affect what I do, I don't give a damn. But when you interfere, that makes me very, very angry." One stubby finger appeared in front of Kiley's eyes. He guessed it was a much longer speech than Withers was used to giving. "If I hear that you've been bothering Dr. Blake or any of Anne Warren's friends again, I'll have your license, and *then* I'll get you put away for obstructing justice. Any idea how an ex-cop gets treated in prison?"

Kiley knew only too well. He nodded again. It seemed the wisest course of action. One of his eyes was beginning to swell.

"So just stick to divorce cases, old son. More on your level," Withers sneered.

Kiley had opened his mouth to say something, but the last remark did it. Withers could go on barging around in the dark as far as he was concerned. The big cop had been on the verge of receiving the lead to a juicy case and he'd blown it.

Withers walked to the door of the office and turned. For a split instant there seemed to be some compassion in his gaze, a need to explain himself. "You used to be one of us. You should understand." Then, as if thinking better of this momentary lapse, Withers barreled out, almost taking the door off its hinges as he exited.

Chapter Seven

With adrenaline supplying the energy drained from him by sleeplessness, Kiley returned to his apartment under a sullen dawn sky that matched his mood; he showered, shaved, and changed into his only decent set of clothes—a black crew-neck sweater, tan sports jacket, gray slacks, and brown leather boots.

He checked Portobello Road to make sure there were no black BMWs around and drove to the Paddington Public Library in Porchester Terrace a few blocks away. He could see his own face scowling back in the dusty windshield. He checked in the mirror; his left eye was ringed by a puffy, blue-black swelling. The other was red from lack of sleep.

He had spent the night in his office, figuring things out. He could understand why Withers had acted as he had; a cop's activities were bound by a set of frustrating rules and conventions that precluded the use of force on suspects. Every now and then the frustration of maintaining the law while working within its framework got too much and it exited in drunkenness or physical violence. Kiley guessed that Withers was confused by the Anne Warren case because, although his cop's instinct told him that something wasn't right about her death, he had been unable to come up with anything concrete. Kiley had proved the ideal whipping boy.

So he understood, but he did not forgive. The case was personal once more, and he had an important lead. A name. Benson. On the other hand, another obstacle had been placed in his path—time. Given half a chance, Withers would see that his license was taken away. The mystery of the three deaths had to be resolved before Withers got a chance to carry out his threats.

Kiley's smart clothes made him feel rather conspicuous in the shabby surroundings of the library. He found Benson's name soon enough in the first volume of the 1979 edition of *Who's Who*, jammed between Arthur Byron Benson and the Reverend Edward McNeil Benson.

Kiley studied the entry for a long time, aware of the snores of the old-age pensioners who had wandered into the reference room for its heat. The pleasant, dusty fragrance of old books mingled with the odor of methylated spirits and mothballs.

David Sherman Benson was the chairman of Benson Pharmaceuticals. He had been born in New York City, Jan. 8th, 1925. Education: Harvard. Served 1942-45, U.S. Marines. Decorated twice for gallantry. Married 1964. One son, died 1974. Wife died 1975. Lived in London since 1946. Address: Waterbury Towers, St. John's Wood. No telephone number given. No mention of club membership. Recreations listed as reading and overseas travel.

When he was positive he had the facts memorized, Kiley returned the squat volume to its shelf, left the library, and drove over to Mary Blake's office. She was with a patient and he had to sit twiddling his thumbs in the outer office while her secretary, a correct middle-aged spinster, clacked savagely at her typewriter.

When Mary emerged, she seemed surprised to see Kiley, but invited him in cordially enough. Her hair was slightly mussed, as if she had been running. It suited her. "I was expecting to see Withers," she said, then added, "How did your interview go?"

With a rueful smile Kiley pointed at his battered eye.

"Withers did that?"

Kiley nodded. "Aren't our policemen wonderful? I never got a chance to explain things to him." He recounted everything that had happened since he left her office on the previous afternoon. "I intend to carry on," he said quietly, after a pause. He waited for her to show some of the nervousness she had displayed at their last meeting, but she remained impassive.

"It's personal again," she said softly.

"Yes. Now you have a choice. Either you agree to help me by keeping quiet, or you can go straight to the police and tell them everything. I wouldn't blame you if you wanted to."

He saw some of his own determination reflected in her face. "There isn't any choice," she said. "I'll stick by you, just to prove I'm a foul-weather friend. Besides, the police don't exactly seem to be blazing a trail with this case."

Kiley couldn't help smiling. The serious frown on her catlike face made her more attractive than ever. "And now for the inevitable question . . ."

She was ready for it. "Benson and my sister? No connection that I know of, but I have heard of him."

"In what connection?"

"Professional. Although Benson Pharmaceuticals might not be the biggest drug company in the country, they are the leaders in my particular field. Psychopharmacology is—"

"Could we try that again in words of one syllable? Remember the backward child approach?"

Mary drummed her long fingernails impatiently on the desk top. "Drugs that alleviate mental conditions. At least a third of the drugs I prescribe for my patients are produced by Benson Pharmaceuticals. The company specializes in antidepressants; both tricyclic antidepressants and monoamine oxidase inhibitors."

"Are we talking about tranquilizers or what?" Kiley interrupted curtly.

"I'm sorry. I'm probably going a little fast for you. No, antidepressants aren't tranquilizers. They're far more powerful and the effect is quite different." Kiley began to look interested. Mary shook her head. "I'm going to dispel your suspicions at once. There's nothing the least bit sinister about them—they've been in general clinical use for over twenty years and their use is widespread."

"Was Anne on anything like that?"

"No, she hated pills of any kind—she wouldn't even take an aspirin. Besides, she had no reason to take antidepressants."

Kiley put his chin in his right hand and began to tap reflectively at the side of his nose with his index finger. "I know I'm probably heading down a blind alley, but just let's suppose that Anne was taking these tablets, unknown to you. Do they have any particular side effects?"

"Dizziness, sweating, blurred vision, palpitations, dryness of the mouth—nothing that would account for Anne's death. Besides the tablets take at least five days to work, and even then the effect is gradual. *If* Benson had anything to do with Anne's death, then it wasn't through the use of any of his products, I can assure you."

Kiley made a face. "Pity, I thought we were on to something that might explain the missing hours. You know, they could have been pumped full of something or other . . ."

"Forget it. It's simply not possible. In any case, you're making an inductive leap. We know that Anne and Max Bronson were missing for short periods of time before their deaths, but we don't know that about Alan Brown."

Kiley frowned. "Inductive leap, eh? Perhaps you could write these phrases down and I'll spring them on my next client," he said testily.

Mary raised her eyebrows, surprised at his reaction. "I'm sorry, it's just my academic training. I wasn't trying to bruise your male ego."

Kiley grinned. "Okay, it's not important. Unfortunately I can't contact Brown's widow. Withers would be down on me like a ton of bricks. For the time being I'm willing to work on the assumption that the events leading up to Alan Brown's death match those of Anne and Max Bronson." He paused. "My work's a little more urgent than academic research."

"I stand corrected."

Kiley ignored the sarcasm. "What do you know about Benson?"

"Not very much. He's not a scientist, just a shrewd businessman. He employs the best researchers available and his products are top quality. He's a powerful, highly respected man . . ." She halted as if she had something else to say, but was unwilling to.

"Go on," Kiley prompted.

She shrugged. "It's just that . . . are you sure the doorman at Waterbury Towers told you the truth? Maybe he fobbed off the first name that came into his head in order to pocket the bribe. The very idea of someone like Benson being mixed up in all this is just so bizarre . . ."

"Would you like me to recount to you the parable of a man named Richard Milhouse Nixon. Respectability isn't all it's cracked up to be."

"You've made your point. What's the next step?"

Kiley stood up abruptly and walked to the window. He stood for a while with his hands behind his back, staring down at the cars crawling in both directions along Harley Street.

"If this were a normal investigation and I didn't have the fuzz breathing down my neck, I'd do some thorough checking on Benson, but I just don't have the time. I'm going to go and meet him at his apartment. If he's around, fine; if not, I'll search the place."

"What in God's name do you hope to find?"

"I have no idea."

"Aren't you rather handing your head to Withers on a platter?"

Kiley turned from the window to look at her. He shoved his hands in the pockets of his gray slacks. "Three seemingly connected deaths occurred within a seventy-two-hour period—one on Friday, one on Saturday, and the last on Monday. That strikes me as the beginning of a pattern. If it's the whole pattern, well and good. We could flush out whoever or whatever was responsible at our leisure, but if the pattern doesn't end there, if it's still going on . . . Someone may have died yesterday and we just don't know about it yet. We would never have connected Alan Brown with the others unless you'd known about his relationship with your sister. Someone could be dying right this minute . . ."

"I see," Mary said softly. "I see why you have to take risks." She looked up at him suddenly. "You know you can count on me for any support." A mischievous look came into her wide green eyes. "I'd love to know what you're going to say to Benson: 'Excuse me, sir, I believe you're involved in the deaths of these three people. Would you care to discuss it?' "

"It'll go something like that." He glanced at his watch. "It's almost eleven o'clock. Give me two hours. If I haven't contacted you by then, phone Withers and tell him everything . . . especially where I am. If this guy Benson had anything to do with abducting Max Bronson, who, by the way, was built like the side of a barn, then I don't fancy my chances against him. Besides, I'm getting tired of being hit."

Mary snapped her fingers suddenly. "Maybe you can't

speak to Alan Brown's wife, but there's absolutely nothing to stop me from doing it. After all, Withers is hardly likely to come around here and start beating me up." A vague look of dismay flitted over Kiley's face. "Don't worry, I'll be discreet," she added.

Kiley shrugged. "Okay, it can't do any harm, I suppose. Do you know what to ask her?"

Mary frowned. "Don't be so bloody patronizing. I spend several hours a day doing nothing but asking questions . . . and with a damn sight more subtlety than I've seen you employ."

"My, but you're gorgeous when you're angry." Kiley grinned and walked to the door. "Remember what I said, two hours and no more."

Mary gave him a wry smile. "I'll think about!"

"C'mon, Clem, good buddy, time to rise and shine!"

Buckeye moved his paunchy, stubby body across the fadedly elegant hotel bedroom and drew open the curtains. Gray daylight dispersed a few shadows but did nothing much to brighten the room. He turned, rubbing his hands eagerly. By the side of a double bed stood a cart loaded with a massive, untouched breakfast. Buckeye walked over to it, tilted his snap-brim hat farther back on his squarish head, and perched on the edge of the bed. He removed one of the silver platter covers, extracted a sliver of cold bacon and popped it in his mouth.

As he munched, the heaped bedclothes beside him stirred and a fuzzy groan came from their depths. A mass of hair appeared, followed by two screwed-closed eyes.

"Get the hell outta here, Buckeye!" The covers were pulled back over the occupant's head. Buckeye leaned forward with a good-natured grunt and pulled them back. The sleeper sat up abruptly.

"You bastard, get the fuck outta here!"

Buckeye grinned and reached out for another piece of bacon. "Hey, Clem, is that any way to speak to your guardian angel, the Svengali who's guided you through thick and thin?"

Clem Danaher lay back on the sheets. "Times are thin, Sven. When did I last have a hit record? Jesus, must have been a '78.' Maybe even a wax cylinder."

Buckeye shrugged. "It'll come, just give it time." He

adopted a smooth, placating tone. "I told you, we just keep plugging away. You used to be sitting up there on top of the world. We'll get you back up there. The fairy on the Christmas tree."

Clem sighed. "You're fulla shit."

"You may have a point there, good buddy," the older man laughed. "All we need is time."

Clem groaned. "I'm sick of you and your lousy time. And I'm sick of this asshole country." The young man propped himself up on one elbow. "Can't we go back to the States. I'm ready for it now, I can feel it."

Buckeye began licking his fingers clean. "Maybe, Clem, maybe. But first we gotta break back here, bury the past. Get the U.K. back under our belts and we'll return in triumph. Bookings at the MGM Grand in Vegas, film contracts"—he poked him with one fat finger—"you name it, you can have it."

Clem sank back on his pillows. "You're fulla shit."

Buckeye gave a less convincing laugh and strolled over to the window. "Jeez, that river looks nice," he mumbled to himself. A wave of hopelessness hit him. London was pretty fair as cities went, but he would have given an arm and a leg to be back home in New York. Any part of it—even the South Bronx. He missed it badly. Instead of dining at the Four Seasons and dancing the night away at Studio 54 he was stuck in exile in England, plodding around the sticks on a series of on-off gigs in small-time clubs with a twenty-eight-year-old no-talent pretty-boy who couldn't tell a musical key from a Yale lock.

And what for?

He reached into his pocket for a cigarette, lit it and puffed reflectively. Even English cigarettes tasted wrong. A few stories below him a barge chugged along the river behind the hotel, a remnant of a bygone age. It reminded him of Clem Danaher.

And yet there had been good times, like the early Sixties. Back then every pop singer was an Italian called "Bobby" and he'd had just about every one of them on his artiste's roster. One crappy prefabricated teen-beat ballad after another, replacing each other at the top of the Billboard 100 with the inevitability of night following day. Buckeye grinned at the memory. Riding high. Fat City.

And then the Beatles had blown that scene wide open.

Suddenly you had to have English name acts to make it. For years he'd trailed his tired old "Bobbys" around the States playing every seedy cabaret in the Deep South and Midwest. Flower power and psychedelia had been like an eviction order on Tin Pan Alley.

Then, in 1970, a miracle. Clem Danaher had appeared out of nowhere. A sweet-faced kid with bad acne and a voice that only the best recording engineers could do anything with. Buckeye had taken one look at Clem and had known instantly that here was his passport back to the top of his profession. The timing had been perfect for a return to mindless teen-fodder. Clem had scored nine number-one hits on both sides of the Atlantic. Danahermania. Buckeye had taken immense delight in the fact that at one stage they had even outsold the Beatles.

Buckeye turned from the window and took in the room. Clem had the sheet back over his head. Buckeye decided to let him have a few more minutes' rest. He had a big day ahead of him.

For five years they had been the hottest property around: lunch at the White House, weekend parties at Hugh Hefner's mansion. And during all that time Clem was washing down uppers and downers with neat bourbon. His voice had gotten even worse. The recording producers had torn their hair out trying to make him sound even average. The makeup experts had been forced to smear on so much pancake that you could have stubbed out a cigarette on Clem's face and he wouldn't have felt a thing.

And then the nervous breakdowns, three of them, all with maximum press coverage. Buckeye had worried about adverse publicity at the time, but all it had done was bring the teenyboppers closer to their idol. The poor misunderstood little rich boy. Marilyn Monroe in drag. Nothing, it seemed, could go wrong . . .

Standing by the window, Buckeye shut his eyes. He could remember the tragedy as if it had happened the day before. Twelve eight-by-ten glossy photographs had landed on his Madison Avenue office desk one day; grainy black-and-whites, but as clear as day. There was no mistaking Clem's drink-bloated visage—and no mistaking what was in bed with him, clutched lovingly in his arms. A mere child, about twelve years old. That wouldn't have been so bad in itself—pedophilia was an accepted Hollywood disease—only in this case Clem had been photographed in bed with a boy.

Of course, Buckeye had known about Clem's proclivities all along. His great star was a twenty-four-carat fruit, a fairy, faggot, flit, queen . . . whatever. It had been the only area of Clem's life in which Buckeye had not interfered; he preferred not to think about it at all. He had simply hired people to insure that Clem's sexual desires were satisfied with the maximum discretion, and then the people he had hired had screwed up, or else one of them had decided to bite the hand that signed his salary check. The massive blackmail demand had been met. Clem had undergone another breakdown and Buckeye had sent him on an extended vacation around the world until Clem felt he could face the crowds once more. For the moment, they terrified him.

The hiatus in his career had proved to be commercial suicide. Six months is a lifetime in pop music. By the time Clem was well enough to resume his career, the fans had deserted for some other bland nonentity. The young man had raised his arms high to receive the accolades of an adoring public and had received a chorus of raspberries instead. A year spent slogging around the States had convinced Buckeye that resurrection would have to be achieved on foreign soil. England, where pockets of Clem Danaher fans clung on like resistance fighters, had seemed an ideal choice. They had been at it solidly now for two years. Progress had been slow, as Clem constantly pointed out, whenever he was sober enough to think about it.

And why did Buckeye do it? It was never going to work. No one rises from the dead twice. Christ managed it once and look at the fuss they made over him. If anyone deserved a rest it was Buckeye, but no, he had to do it for Clem's sake. The poor little bastard had never been allowed to develop into a real human being. At twenty-eight, he had the stunted mind of a delinquent seventeen-year-old. His moral values were nonexistent. His only pursuits were sensual gratification and, when the real world impinged on his consciousness, mental oblivion. Remove the money and the fame and he was a dead man. In the final analysis, Buckeye held himself responsible for the human wreckage stranded in the big bed behind him.

"Okay, Clem, time to get up. Your public awaits."

Clem groaned. "Couldn't we skip it just this once, Buckeye? I don't feel so good. If you could get me a hit record, I wouldn't have to do all this shit," he added accusingly.

The smile froze on Buckeye's lips. Kindness was one thing, but no one said he had to be a masochist. "If you could sing a frigging note without cracking on it, maybe some sucker could be persuaded to write you a good song. No one likes their material to be murdered." Clem eyed him like a wounded animal. Buckeye smiled guiltily. "Look, the reason you don't feel good is because downers and Jim Beam were never meant to mix, for Christ's sake! Just ease up on all that stuff and you'd feel brand-new."

Clem grunted noncommittally. Buckeye noted with sadness the deep lines of despair that had begun to crack the skin around the mouth and eyes of Clem's once-youthful face. His cheeks had begun to puff out once more and there were broken blood vessels on his nose. Buckeye's teen-idol was just about ready for a face-lift.

Buckeye walked over to the bed and put his hand encouragingly on the singer's arm. "Listen, Clem. This is just a little photo session down in the lobby. We got some fans together to mob you. They're all paid for. It's all arranged. All the newspapers are going to be there. There's no sweat and it cost a lot of dough." He paused, waiting for a reaction. "C'mon, Clem, we really screwed up when we missed that gig last week. You let me down already. Hey, don't do it again."

"I didn't walk out on it, I keep telling you." Clem frowned. "I don't know what happened to me."

"Do it for daddy, huh?" Buckeye cajoled.

Clem's lips began to quiver. "I get so scared, Buckeye, real frightened sometimes." Two tears rolled down his hamsterlike cheeks and he began to sob openly. Buckeye felt the man's body shiver under his grasp and he drew Clem's head down against his chest.

"I see 'em all there in a big bunch and I get real scared, y'know, like they've all turned against me, like they *found out*, y'know . . ." He sobbed.

Buckeye nodded sympathetically and stroked his star's carefully coiffured hair. "Yeah, kid, I know, but they won't harm you. They're paid for, I told you. Look, just do this one for me, huh? We've got two gigs left before we release a single, then maybe we can see about getting back to the States."

Clem brought his head up off Buckeye's chest. His tear-filled eyes sparkled with pain and hope. "You mean it, Buckeye?"

Buckeye nodded. "Sure do. Look, it's already November twenty-second . . . We'll be all through in a couple of days."

Clem's expression seemed to change all of a sudden, and Buckeye felt the singer's body stiffen.

The doorman looked distinctly nervous when Kiley pushed open the frosted-glass entrance doors of Waterbury Towers and headed across the spacious hallway toward the reception desk. The fat man folded the paper he had been reading and rose from his seat.

"What do *you* want?" he growled.

Kiley smiled broadly. "Terrible the way you can't get decent servants these days. Less impertinence, my man." He leaned across the desk. The doorman took a protective step backward and plopped down into his seat. His jowels wobbled. "Is Benson in?" Kiley asked. "And don't give me any crap about not being allowed to hand out that sort of information." Kiley produced another five-pound note and waved it under the fat man's nose.

The doorman eyed it greedily. "He might be."

"Good. Now, how many entrances are there to Benson's apartment. Think carefully."

"Two. One front door and an elevator that goes direct from the car park into his apartment." The fat man reached out for the note. Kiley jerked it back.

"Tut, tut, not so fast. This is a three-part question. Now, phone Benson and tell him there's a policeman in reception who would like to come up and interview him over a little matter of murder."

The fat man's eyes bulged and he gulped audibly. "I can't do that!"

"A fiver says you can," Kiley said, wafting the note back and forth in front of him.

The doorman reached for the phone, dialed, and spoke briefly. "He says it's okay for you to go up. Take the elevator, press fifteen."

Kiley crumpled the fiver into a ball and flicked it at the

fat man with his thumb. It bounced off his shiny forehead.
Kiley heard him scrambling around for it on the floor as
he stepped into the elevator. The stomach-heaving ascent
took a few seconds. The elevator gave onto a long, narrow
corridor that ran the length of the top floor. A door stood
slightly ajar in front of him.

Kiley walked across a thick pile carpet and stepped into
a small, square entrance hall with three doors leading off
it. The place smelled of money as soon as you entered. He
knocked at the door in front.

"Please come in," called a mellifluous voice.

The living room was the size of a small aircraft hangar.
Chandeliers hung from a high ceiling. A vast picture window took up most of the opposite wall, revealing the bleak
midday sky. The room was sparsely furnished with exqui-
site leather and mahogany furniture. The walls were fes-
tooned with watercolors and nineteenth-century "Spy"
political cartoons. Stainless-steel sculptures gleamed in the
light from the chandeliers. It was like something out of
Ideal Home.

Kiley didn't see Benson at first. The American, who was
seated in one of a circle of low-slung chairs near the center of the room, rose slowly, laying aside a glossy maga-
zine. He motioned for Kiley to sit in a studded red-leather
chair facing him. They shook hands briefly—Benson's grip
was dry and firm, Kiley noticed.

"So you're a policeman," Benson remarked after a
pause, with a faintly amused smile. His head was cocked
to one side, cradled by his hand. His index finger extended
along his temple, creating folds in the skin. There was
something in Benson's tone that suggested he already knew
that Kiley was lying.

Kiley had been expecting an unathletic businessman.
Benson came as a surprise—a short, stocky man with powerful shoulders and a head that was a bit too large for his
body. His face was dominated by a full salt-and-pepper
beard and a severely broken nose, above which were two
lugubrious brown eyes. His smile was knowing, worldly.
As if to enhance his nonexecutive appearance, he was
clothed in a tight-fitting blue safari suit that showed off
bulging muscles. The backs of his large hands were covered in a mat of black hair. Benson was certainly the right
build for abducting people.

"I'm not a policeman," Kiley admitted. "I'm a private detective."

Benson raised thick eyebrows. "Why did you lie to the doorman?" Kiley noticed that, although Benson's gray hair was thinning, he had avoided the temptation of brushing it forward into a fringe. That fact put Kiley slightly off guard—he tended to trust people who had the good grace to admit they were going bald.

"I just wanted to make absolutely sure of seeing you. I've something very important to discuss."

"The hint that I was to be involved in a murder investigation would have assured you of that privilege." Benson's voice matched the color and texture of the living room walls—smooth and creamy. It reminded Kiley of Hal the Computer in *2001*. "May I see some identification?" Benson asked without apparent aggression.

Kiley slipped a card out of the back pocket of his slacks. Benson perused it. "May I keep this?"

Kiley nodded. If he had been hoping to shock Benson into revealing anything, he was in for a disappointment. The American appeared to be imperturbably relaxed and self-confident. Kiley decided to try it anyway, now that he was here. "I'd just like to ask you a few questions."

Benson interlocked his fingers over his muscular chest. "Go ahead, Mr. Kiley, I'm intrigued."

No outside sound penetrated through the double-glazed picture window. Kiley spoke quietly so as not to disturb the tranquil atmosphere. "Have you heard of a lady named Anne Warren?"

Benson paused and then gave a slight shake of his massive head.

"She used to appear regularly on television," Kiley added.

Benson shrugged. "I do seem to recall the name from somewhere."

"She died in a car accident last Friday morning. I expect you read about it in the papers."

Benson shrugged again. He looked about as discomforted as if Kiley had just informed him of the sinking of the *Titanic*.

"Let me try another few names on you," Kiley continued. If Benson was going to show any sign of guilt, this would be the moment. If someone were responsible for the death of Anne Warren and the others, they would probably have counted on no one making a connection between the happenings. "Max Bronson, a big-time crook, and Alan Brown, the head of an advertising agency."

Benson squinted up at the ceiling as if searching there for inspiration, but otherwise his manner remained unchanged. He looked at Kiley. "I'm afraid I can't help you with either of those gentlemen." If he was lying, Kiley had to admit it was a fine performance.

The detective reached into his jacket pocket for a cigarette, playing for time.

"I'd rather you didn't smoke, Mr. Kiley," Benson said easily. "Please don't think me rude, but I find that tobacco smoke irritates my sinuses." He gave a small snort as if to emphasize the point.

Kiley mumbled an apology and put the packet away. "I find it hard to believe that you've never heard of these people. Max Bronson died in an underground accident last Saturday and Alan Brown drowned in his bath the day after. It was all covered by the press."

Benson paused before answering, almost as if he had been expecting another name. He gave a faint smile. "I relinquished absolute control of the day-to-day running of my company last year, Mr. Kiley. Since then I've led a quiet, reclusive sort of life. I've let the outside world retreat further and further into a sort of mist of indifference. I don't bother the world and it usually doesn't bother me—except for the tax man. I read only the business sections of newspapers and refuse to subject myself to the drivel that passes for entertainment on television. I prefer to relax with the novels of Henry James or go to the theater." He unlocked his fingers and his hands made a tiny, almost apologetic gesture. "I feel I have earned the right, by dint of hard work and longevity, to concern myself with life's more pleasing aspects."

"I wouldn't argue with that." Kiley wondered whether Benson's loquacity was a sign of nerves.

There was a slight pause. Benson broke the silence: "So you are investigating these deaths, these suicides . . ."

"I didn't mention anything about suicides," Kiley said softly.

Benson shrugged. "I naturally assumed from the circumstances, subway trains, bath drownings . . ." He let the statement peter out. Kiley wondered if the American had made his first mistake. Had the deaths been planned to look like suicides?

Benson's drooping eyes narrowed suddenly and he frowned. "So at least there was one element of truth in what you told the doorman. We *are* discussing murder."

"Not necessarily. We're talking about a series of deaths whose real causes have yet to be explained."

"And what exactly is your interest in all this? Are you working for someone?" Kiley was aware of small, troubled currents eddying under the placid surface of their conversation.

"I was in the car with Anne Warren a few moments before she died."

Benson's stare was fixed. It was the gaze of a man with a sense of purpose, and Kiley found it disconcerting. He had yet to see Benson blink.

"Does this concern me in some way?" the American asked.

"Perhaps."

"Is my company supposed to be involved, by any chance?"

"Maybe."

Benson sat upright suddenly, as if stung. A nerve had been touched. The action was in such contrast to his previous manner that it made Kiley nervous.

"I think I see what you're up to, Mr. Kiley. I think I know what your game is."

"Game, Mr. Benson? I'm not playing games," he said quietly, determined to underplay the scene. He was beginning to wish that Benson had allowed him a cigarette.

Benson's frown turned back to a knowing smile and he visibly relaxed. Kiley wondered if it was all an act.

"Let me see if I can guess what you want. One of the dead people was on a course of medication from Benson Pharmaceuticals. You're attempting to prove a connection between my company's products and the events under discussion." He rose abruptly from his seat. "I think I'd better call a lawyer before you begin making any blackmail demands." Benson walked behind his chair to a phone perched on a table by the window. He moved with surprising speed for such a heavyset man.

"I didn't know I looked like a blackmailer, Mr. Benson.

I'm just a hard-working, underpaid detective trying to get at the truth. You seem to be jumping to a lot of conclusions."

Benson halted by the table, looked briefly out of the window, then turned back to face Kiley. When he spoke, a harsh note had crept into his voice. "You come in here under false pretenses and start spouting about the deaths of three people with whom I have absolutely no connection. As you seem to be unwilling to come to the point, I have to draw my own conclusions. This isn't the first time this sort of thing's been tried on us. I warn you. It has never worked."

"I see your point, Mr. Benson, but it isn't that way at all. I know all about the fine reputation of your company. Besides, if your products were involved, I'm sure the police would have paid you a visit by now."

Benson moved back to his seat and sat down gingerly. He was smiling again, but it was a little forced. Kiley noticed that there was a sheen of sweat on his forehead which could not be accounted for by the temperature in the room, which was chilly. "Please, Mr. Kiley, forgive me. I've always had a rather short temper. If you could come to the point I'd be most grateful."

Kiley couldn't shake off the suspicion that he was taking part in a contest that he was losing badly. "Yesterday, while I was investigating these deaths, I spotted a car tailing me—I turned the tables on it." He paused. In the silence he could hear the breath whistling through Benson's nostrils. "I followed the car back here."

"To this address?"

"Correct. It was a black BMW." Kiley smiled. "Ring any bells?"

Benson chuckled easily. "As you obviously know, I drive a black BMW. Just where did this car *apparently* start following you?"

"I can't be sure, but I became aware of it yesterday afternoon in Harley Street."

Benson shook his head sadly, as if he were sorry for Kiley. "That's hardly surprising. I was paying a visit to my doctor, man called Dalziel. Heart specialist." He patted his chest. "Heart condition, you know. One of the reasons for my retirement."

"I'll check that with him."

"By all means do so. I admire professionalism."

Kiley had to concede game, set, and match.

"You can at least appreciate why I felt it necessary to come and see you."

Benson made a magnanimous gesture with his hands. "Of course, dear boy, of course. But you've obviously made a mistake. I wasn't, I assure you, tailing your car. I'm a rather hesitant driver. Besides, I'm not physically well enough to involve myself in murder. I should imagine it requires quite a lot of effort . . ."

He was laughing at Kiley now. The interview had become pointless. Any advantage that might have been gained by surprise was gone. The sky had opened and rain was beating against the windowpane with a strange, muffled violence.

Kiley rose and strolled to the window. The town lay neat and ordered below. There was a plan to the city that wasn't apparent amid the noise and confusion of its streets. The world of murder seemed far away.

Benson appeared at his shoulder. "I didn't mean to be sarcastic."

Kiley nodded. "It's me who should be apologizing." He looked down at the table in front of him. The phone was a gold 1930s model. Beside it was a pad on which was scrawled "Mj Badel." Benson placed his hand over the page.

Kiley smiled at him. "I've taken up enough of your time, Mr. Benson. You've been most kind."

"Nonsense. You've provided a nice break in an otherwise tedious day. I'm sure you'll find a simple, rational explanation for these deaths," he said in an urbane, conciliatory manner as he accompanied Kiley to the door.

They shook hands briefly. Kiley stared hard into Benson's eyes for a few moments. The American's gaze was disconcertingly open.

Clem Danaher checked himself over one last time in the elevator mirror, patted the hair down over his ears on both sides, adjusted his open-necked Italian silk shirt, and centered the Zodiac-sign silver medallion on his hairless chest. As the elevator door started to open, he shot Buckeye an accusing glance. The older man gave him an encouraging smile.

The squeals started on cue, as soon as the elevator doors had opened to reveal the occupants. Clem pasted a big grin on his face and stepped out into the lobby. Thirty teen-agers were grouped in a semicircle some twenty yards away near the hotel's twin revolving entrance doors; the group was being held back by six security men. In front of the cordon stood a bevy of Fleet Street's finest, looking bored and sneering at what they knew to be a phony setup. Drinks had been served to them in the bar to take the edge off their viciousness.

Buckeye gave them a cheerful little wave that wasn't returned and led Clem to a small table with a microphone, which had been set up to the left of the elevator. Clem sat down as Buckeye began his patter to the press. He placed his elbows on the table and let his head sink into his hands for a moment. The excited squeals of the spurious fans shredded his nerves. Knowing they were all paid for and carefully orchestrated didn't make it any easier. If anything, it made it a whole lot worse. Sometimes when he woke up in bed at night and the booze and the pills had worn off, he wondered whether he had a single genuine fan left. Most of the halls he now played to were less than half-filled. He often suspected Buckeye of handing the tickets out free.

When Clem looked up, the reporters and photographers were moving in on him. He gave them an endearing, adolescent grin. First a few questions, then some staged mobbing by the fans for photographs, then back to bed for the rest of the afternoon. His stomach was quaking, and for a moment he was afraid he would vomit right then and there.

Buckeye walked back behind the desk and stood beside him as the photographers came up close, flashbulbs popping. Clem winced at the lights. Buckeye pointed to the first of the reporters. Initially Clem's microphone produced nothing but high-pitched feedback, then it caught his quietly muttered curse and echoed it superloud around the lobby.

"Clem, would you say that you'd really missed the boat . . ."

"Not at all. I think the kids still have faith in me (*squeals*). I have a great many fans who, with all their hearts, wish me to carry on (*cheers*). I'd feel I was really letting them down if I, y'know, didn't try . . ."

"Why did you leave the States? That matter was never really cleared up, was it?"

" . . . (*grin*) Well, it was for me (*laughter*). Naw, it was just a . . . we felt we needed a change of scene, y'know, and I'd been doing so well in this wonderful country we thought it was time we gave the fans a break here . . ."

"When's the next single coming out. It's been a while."

" . . . better ask Buckeye here. He takes care of all that stuff (*groans*) . . ." and on and on until he had a blinding headache. As he answered the questions mechanically, his eyes wandered over the youngsters who could be glimpsed in between the shoulders of the security guards. They all looked about fourteen, half his age. He noticed a pretty boy with long blond hair and a cherubic face. Clem smiled at him. The child smiled back. Clem wondered if, just this once . . . but, no, Buckeye would kill him if he ever got into that kind of trouble again, and this time there would be no money to take care of blackmail.

Clem was sweating badly as they neared the end of the question session; beads of perspiration were beginning to run down his face, forming deep grooves in his pink pancake makeup and dripping onto his shirt. He thought about wiping his forehead but knew that the whole carefully constructed cosmetic edifice would crumble at a single touch, revealing him to be just an average-looking twenty-eight-year-old man with bad skin and a chronic hangover.

He suddenly thought about the mobbing he was going to have to endure and he began to sweat. He started spinning out his answers. Goddam fans all crushed around him, choking him, yelling in his ear, tearing his clothes. One of these days, he felt sure, it would end badly . . . but, what the hell, he had to do it for Buckeye. The poor old bastard had nothing else left in the world. Without Clem he was washed up.

When the last question had been put and Clem's final answer tapered out, Buckeye began hustling the reporters out of the way. The noise from the fans increased. Buckeye grinned. He was getting his money's worth from the kids. The security men stepped forward a few paces, arms linked.

Clem got up from his seat and walked around to the front of the table, rubbing his hands together nervously. The crowd was about twenty yards away. He walked ten yards, then halted. The corners of his mouth twitched as his tired smile faltered. When Buckeye, who was clearing a path for him, turned, he could see fear in his star's eyes. He walked back to Clem, smiling ferociously, and caught him by the arm. The crowd began to grow restless at the unexpected delay. Buckeye hissed in his ear: "Go on, Clem. You're screwing it up. What the fuck's the matter with ya?" The boy's body was taut, shaking like a steel cable in a high wind.

"C . . . can't do it, Buckeye," he stammered.

"You're finished, you bastard, you hear me? Finished!" Buckeye snarled savagely through clenched teeth. Clem let out a vast sigh. The crowd was almost silent now; perhaps it would be all right. He shrugged and moved forward again. The cheering began at once.

The fans were straining against the human cordon, hands stretching over security guards' brawny shoulders, clutching free copies of an old Clem Danaher album. Their noise increased at his approach. They were baying by the time he reached out for the first album. He scrawled his autograph over the cover, careful not to disfigure his own face staring soulfully out at him. He handed it back, not knowing whether it had gone to the rightful owner, and not caring.

"Glad to see you . . . Pleased you could make it . . . Hey, you're looking swell . . . Gee, I'm really delighted . . ." The phrases came tumbling from his lips like an old actor's stock of Shakespearean quotations. He grasped a few wet paws, hurriedly withdrawing his fingers before a proper handshake could be established, and signed some more albums. He was about to walk away, relieved, when he saw the boy again, between the bodies of two security guards. The kid was even more attractive up close. The boy held out his hand. For a moment it was as if he and Clem were the only two people in the room. Clem clasped the boy's hand firmly as their eyes locked. His fingers lingered for a few moments.

"C'mon, Clem, let's beat it. That's enough," Buckeye whispered into his ear. "You done okay."

Clem disengaged his hand with a sigh, regretting a missed opportunity.

The boy's grip held firm.

Clem tugged, but the child's fingers held tight. Clem looked up, startled. The boy's expression had changed—the sweet smile had metamorphosed into a malevolent grin. Clem gave a squeal of fear. Another hand locked around his forearm. The boy's mouth opened. Light from the lobby's main chandelier flashed off sharp teeth. The boy's head stooped toward his captive's arm.

"Buckeye!" Clem screamed. He tried to pull his arm back with all his might but the grip was too firm. The boy's teeth sank into the flesh of Clem's hand. The singer shrieked. The teeth went deep enough to puncture the skin. Blood spurted out over the boy's face. His eyes were glazed in ecstasy. He didn't seem to notice. The jaws gave a final, convulsive clamp. Clem could feel the teeth meshing together somewhere amid the raging agony of his mutilated hand.

The security men seemed to melt away. Clem was dragged forward. He struggled and bucked, but it was no use. He toppled to the floor. There was a sharp pain at the base of his spine as a foot caught him. He yelled and twisted over onto his back.

"BUCKEYE!" he screamed again.

His eyes were blinded by the lobby lights, then a sea of swimming faces appeared on the periphery of his vision. They descended in one swift motion, like a wave. His arms were pinned to his sides. Fingernails rasped against his skin, scraping it away, tearing his clothes. Teeth nibbled almost gently at his arms and legs, then sank into his flesh. He thrashed about helplessly.

Through the strands of hair which had fallen over his eyes he saw an open mouth descending toward his chest. He felt hot breath against his skin. There was a moment of indescribable pain and then the head came up again. Hanging from the closed teeth of his attacker's mouth was a chunk of flesh, dripping blood.

The boy who had first grabbed his arm appeared directly overhead. He smiled sweetly at Clem. His head descended nearer and nearer, his mouth opening invitingly. Slowly, lovingly, he placed his lips over Clem's mouth. A searching tongue poked between the singer's lips. Even amid the pain and terror, Clem could feel a familiar sensation in his groin. His mouth opened wide to receive the boy and their tongues mingled for an instant.

The boy's teeth bit savagely, severing Clem's tongue. The singer's eyes clouded over as warm blood began flooding his throat. From far away he was aware of a hand wriggling inside his trouser belt, reaching for his stiffening penis. Fingernails touched the soft skin tentatively and traveled down the shaft to cradle his testicles. For one tantalizing second nothing happened, then the hand squeezed inward with crushing force.

Clem tried to scream again, but the only sound that reached his ears was that of the blood gurgling in his throat.

Chapter Eight

Kiley balled his fist and smashed it against the dashboard of his car. The interview with Benson had revealed absolutely nothing. He was back where he started—confused, in the dark. What had he been hoping for, anyway? A confession?

Kiley was used to interrogating people who spoke his language. After a few years, villain and policeman ended up talking in the same way. Benson, a refined, cultivated, urbane man, was a different proposition. His conversation was a series of nuances and innuendoes; his behavior was designed to act as a smokescreen. Kiley had played his ace. Benson had trumped it.

He lit a cigarette. Benson's performance had been cool, calm; no hint of fear or worry. Was he lying? Had it all been an act? Kiley was prepared to give him the benefit of the doubt.

He drove away from Waterbury Towers in a distinctly gloomy frame of mind. Anne Warren had died during a fit of temporary insanity. Max Bronson had been genuinely attempting to escape killers. Alan Brown had perished in a simple domestic accident. Benson really *had* been visiting his doctor.

Kiley glanced at his watch. It had been over an hour and a half since he had spoken to Mary. He remembered the promise he had extracted from her about contacting Withers after a two-hour delay. He went into the nearest pay phone. Rain pattered against the glass panels.

"I think I just blew everything," he told her despondently after her secretary had put her on the line.

"You don't think Benson is involved?"

"I have my doubts. It was his car all right, but he was

91

apparently just visiting his doctor. Also, he genuinely didn't seem to have heard of any of the dead people. If he was acting, Laurence Olivier could take lessons from him. I think maybe you were right when you said I was jumping the gun."

"Ready to give up?" There was a mischievous lilt to Mary's voice.

"I suppose I am. Would you be very disappointed?"

"No, not really. Only did Benson say he had actually never heard of Alan Brown?"

"That's right. He doesn't take much interest in the outside world."

"Mmm." She sounded pensive. "I find that very strange."

"Look, there's no law that says people have to read newspapers—" Three beeps sounded on the line. Kiley slotted in another tenpence. A chubby little woman was clinking the edge of a coin against the glass door of the phone booth. He turned and gave her a thumbs-up sign. Her efforts at breaking the glass increased.

" . . . knew Alan Brown," he heard Mary saying.

"What was that? I didn't hear you."

"I said, it's rather strange that he claims not to know Alan Brown. According to Erika Brown, her husband handled the Benson Pharmaceuticals advertising account for three years between '71 and '74."

Kiley frowned. "You mean his company handled it?"

Mary sighed. "No! Alan Brown did, personally. It was before he set up his own agency. He was working for J. Walter Thompson at the time. It was his first big account. I happened to mention Benson's name to Erika Brown, you know, just on the off chance, and she remembered seeing the name on her husband's résumé. She was positive that Alan dealt with Benson personally. Did you tell Benson that Brown was in advertising?"

A surge of excitement pulsed through Kiley like an electric current. "Yes, I mentioned it—Mary, you're a genius!"

"I have my moments. I've also got some news for you about something strange that happened at Benson Pharmaceuticals recently. It concerns Benson's chief researcher . . . Hang on. My next patient has arrived. I can't talk any more now. Come round and see me at three o'clock. I'll be free then." The phone clicked in his ear.

Kiley flicked through the Yellow Pages and put in a call to Dr. Dalziel. The receptionist would not let him speak to the doctor, nor would she divulge his patients' visiting times. Kiley shrugged. It didn't matter for the moment. He had enough to go on.

He opened the door of the phone booth. The chubby woman shot him a look of pure hatred and bustled past him. Kiley winked at her. He stood by his car for a few moments, ignoring the rain, and chuckled. If Benson were somehow mixed up in the deaths, then it would be a fitting irony if Anne Warren's sister led Kiley to him.

The phone was ringing when he arrived at his office. Kiley, hoping that Mary had decided to put him out of his misery by telling him more about the chief researcher at Benson's company, was faintly disappointed to hear Prince's voice on the line.

"Hallo, Prince, what can I do for you?" Kiley asked, twisting the cap off a celebratory bottle of Teacher's he had just purchased.

"Ask not, old son, what you can do for me, but rather ask what I can do for you," the reporter responded pompously.

"Okay, Prince, fire away." It always surprised Kiley that someone whose journalistic style was a model of brevity enjoyed such flowery verbal exchanges.

"You recently phoned me about an advertising executive who came to a sticky end in his jolly old bathtub."

"Alan Brown, that's right. You gave me some useful information about him. I'll buy you a drink sometime." And, as if reminded, Kiley took a sip from the bottle in his hand.

"A magnum of Dom Perignon would be more to the point, old son. However, I didn't ring you up to remind you of past favors, numerous though they are and unreciprocated though they remain, but to do you yet another good turn. Are you excited? Burning with anticipation? Gripping the telephone? Biting the desk top?"

"Unless you come to the point, Prince, you know where you'll be receiving the champagne bottle," Kiley cut in.

The reporter laughed. "Others, I warn you, have tried it and found it physically impossible. That's why I walk in this strange fashion. However, during our conversation relating to the aforementioned Brown, you asked to be kept informed of any other mysterious departures from this earth. Of course, if you're not interested, I could—"

"Okay, Prince, cut it out! What's happened?"

"Have you heard of Clem Danaher, an American pop singer totally devoid of talent?"

"I know him well enough to switch the radio off whenever he comes on."

"Excellent. I have just come from his hotel where I attempted to interview him—with very little success, I might add."

Kiley sighed. The only way to extract information out of the Prince was to play his little game. "Was the little queen acting coy, or what?"

"The interview was rather one-sided. Clem Danaher is very dead. Our show-business editor asked me how I was able to tell, which I thought a rather cruel remark under the circumstances."

"Don't tell me—he was killed by a convention of music lovers."

"No, although I'm sure any such organization would have been acquitted on the ground of justifiable homicide. The point is, old son, that no one killed him. He just died."

"I don't catch your drift. If there is any."

"Mr. Danaher was attending a press conference which, naturally, was a total non-event—until just before the end. Some pre-rehearsed fans broke through a thin cordon of security guards in order to smother their supposed hero with kisses."

"Don't tell me he was killed in the stampede." Kiley's mind was beginning to wander. He had more important things to think about.

"Hardly! Danaher reacted well at first, then suddenly began yelling his head off. The fans backed off, somewhat mystified, to reveal him thrashing about on the ground, bellowing with terror, quite convinced that someone was attacking him."

"And was anyone?"

"No. Apart from a few smears of lipstick on his cheeks planted by girl fans, he was totally untouched. His yells became choking noises, which became silence. He has gone to a better world."

"What was it? Poison?"

"Not at all. He apparently died of a heart attack. The general consensus of those lucky enough to witness this great step forward for popular music was that he had been suffering from hallucinations."

"Oh my God!" was all Kiley could manage for a moment.

Pleased with the effect of his information, Prince added: "I thought that might quicken the blood, Kiley. As a reward for my labors, how about letting me in on whatever you're involved in? Your old pal the Prince would like to know what connection there is between Anne Warren, Alan Brown, and Clem Danaher. From your reaction, I take it there is one."

"I can't tell you, not yet. Besides, I don't really know myself."

"Don't be a shit, Kiley!" The reporter paused. "If you are seeking some pecuniary advantage, then I'm sure I could get the paper to cough up some green stuff for you. You're probably a little short of the old happy lettuce, *n'est-ce pas?*"

"I mean it, Prince, I can't tell you anything. Soon, but not yet. Thanks for the info. You'll be the first to hear about it when I've cracked this case . . . and it'll be an exclusive. I'll leave you with a hint. I think Max Bronson might be involved as well."

Kiley registered the sharp intake of breath on the line before he hung up. He checked his watch. An hour and a half to go before meeting Mary Blake. He took another slug of whiskey and sat staring at the hat-stand for five minutes. He got a note pad out of his desk, found a pen, and began writing the names of the four victims in a line down the page. Alan Brown had handled the Benson Pharmaceuticals account between '71 and '74, so he and Benson had obviously met during that period. Kiley inserted the dates after the ad-man's name.

According to Mary Blake, Alan Brown had known Anne Warren since before his marriage. A phone call to Brown, White, and Holgate revealed that he had been married in 1975. Kiley wrote "Knew Alan Brown '74 onwards" next to her name.

Clem Danaher proved to be a stumbling block at first. Kiley's interest in pop music had waned after the Sixties.

On a hunch, he phoned Anne Warren's old television company, Thames and asked the press officer whether Anne had ever interviewed Clem Danaher. She had. Kiley wrote "Met Anne Warren July '74" next to the singer's name.

Bronson came last. The only significant event Kiley could recall about the gangster involved his one week of surveillance duty on The Dug-Out. Bronson had been forced to flee the country temporarily during a period of gang warfare. He had been incorrectly informed that the Chinese had brought in an assassin to take care of him, so that the Brewer Street Tong faction could extend their Soho operations. Kiley thought long and hard about the date, then wrote "November '74" next to Bronson's name.

He added "Mj Badel" to the list and followed it with a question mark. It was a very long shot. Probably the name of Benson's laundry company.

Kiley sat back and studied the page. His eyes wandered down the date column. The year 1974 ran through the entries like a scratch across a record. Kiley knew he had seen that date before, and recently.

He checked his watch. Another hour to go before he was due to see Mary Blake. He took another slug of whiskey and waited until the fire in his throat had lessened before dialing her number. Her patient could wait. He had to know whether 1974 was a significant year in Anne Warren's life.

The secretary came on the line. "This is Kiley again. I'd like to speak to Dr. Blake at once."

There was a momentary pause. "I have already passed your message on to Dr. Blake as you requested."

Kiley sighed. "Look, I don't know what you're talking about. Could you just get Dr. Blake on the line. I don't care if she's with a patient. She'll want to speak to me."

"Young man," the secretary responded primly, "I have passed your message on to the doctor and she has responded to it."

Kiley groaned. "Listen, you're obviously confusing me with one of Dr. Blake's patients. I was on the phone to her about an hour ago. I was in the office this morning. I have something important to tell her, so just get her on the bloody line!" His voice had risen to a shout.

"There is no need to adopt that tone with me, Mr. Kiley," she responded huffily. "I am *not* confusing you with one of Dr. Blake's patients." She managed to make the observation sound like an insult. "You phoned me less than half an hour ago and asked me to interrupt Dr. Blake's session to give her a message. I did so. I don't know what you're shouting about."

"I didn't phone half an hour ago," Kiley said quietly. "Are you sure the message was from a Mr. Kiley?"

"Oh yes, quite sure. I naturally assumed it was you. You *are* the tall gentleman with a black eye?"

"I am indeed."

"Oh, dear, I didn't realize that Dr. Blake knew two Mr. Kileys."

"She doesn't. What was the message?"

There was a rustling sound on the wire. Kiley's jaw muscles were working overtime.

"Ah, yes, here it is. You . . . that is, the other Mr. Kiley, asked Dr. Blake to meet him at her house as soon as possible. *Very* urgent. He kept repeating the phrase. Dr. Blake cut one of her sessions short. The patient was not pleased, I can assure you . . ."

"Did the caller sound like me?"

"Now that you mention it, I don't suppose he did. He was *extremely* authoritative."

"When did Dr. Blake leave the office?"

The secretary paused. "I should say about twenty minutes ago. Why, is something wrong?"

Kiley slammed the phone down hard and took off.

Marylebone Road was badly congested. There was nothing much he could do except skip a few red lights, and even then it was only a question of gaining a few miserable yards.

He kept glancing at his watch and slamming his fist on the steering wheel. It seemed hopeless. Mary would have been home for at least a quarter of an hour. He muttered violent curses between clenched teeth and wriggled in his seat as if attempting to shift the traffic ahead through sheer willpower. His mind was filled with violent images of what he would do to Benson if Mary had been harmed. It had to be the American.

The road running along the side of Regent's Park was a distinct improvement. He shifted the Jag to the crown of the road and kept up a steady seventy the whole way down, his hand clamped to the horn, headlights on. The asphalt surface was slippery. Whenever he had to alter course slightly, it took all his strength to keep the powerful car from skidding.

At the entrance to Marlin Crescent he slewed the Jag across two lines of traffic. Squealing tires sounded behind him. He slammed on his brakes as he approached the middle of the crescent and brought the car to a skidding halt in front of the house. Out of the corner of his eye he saw the black BMW parked some thirty yards along the road. Anger surged through him. He knew he was approaching this in the wrong way, but years of training were swept aside in an instant by his concern for Mary's safety.

He tried to calm himself, but it was as if his body had taken over. He pushed the car door open and, half-running, half-stumbling, headed for the house. He took the waist-high gate in a hurdling stride and he leaped up the four steps leading up to the front door. The door began to open a split second before impact, and Kiley found himself racing helplessly along the hallway. He tripped and went sprawling over the first few steps of the staircase leading up to the first floor.

He struggled to his feet, ignoring the pain in his skull. The front door closed. A figure was discernible against it. As Kiley, weaving badly, started to lunge at the intruder, he heard his own name being called. The hall light came on overhead.

Benson was standing by the front door with his hand on the light switch and a genial smile on his face. In his hand was a .32 caliber automatic, pointed at Kiley's stomach.

Chapter Nine

"A spectacular, if rather clumsy entrance, Mr. Kiley. I should have thought you'd have been better taught at the police academy." Benson motioned with his gun toward the open living room door.

Kiley brought up his hand to rub at the back of his head. He could think of nothing to say. With a shrug he moved into the living room.

The lights were off and only a dim glow of daylight came from the tall windows at either end of the room. The place was a mess. Furniture was everywhere, paintings had fallen or been knocked off the walls, and a pile of shattered glass lay next to the upended drink cart.

Kiley walked to the coffee table, miraculously untouched in the center of the room, and waited for his eyes to adjust to the light. The door closed softly behind him and, as he turned toward Benson, he caught sight of Mary lying face down on the couch. At first sight she looked as though she was merely resting. Her head was turned to the wall; one arm hung down from the couch, the hand lying limp on the carpet.

Kiley moved quickly to her side. He knelt down, lifted her arm, and fumbled for the pulse in her wrist, then heaved a sigh as his fingertips located the steady throb.

"Okay, Kiley, she's still alive. Now please move to the chair by the window."

Kiley turned his head and stared at Benson with hatred. The American, still dressed in his blue safari suit, was standing at one end of the couch. There was something about his smile of amused indifference that convinced Kiley it would be wise to obey. The hand holding the .32 was too steady and Benson appeared too relaxed and confident for the detective to even consider a sudden attack.

"Please be assured that I'll kill you if I have to, Kiley. I visit a shooting range at least once a week. I'm officially classified as a marksman."

Kiley rose and examined the exposed side of Mary's face. He reached out to touch her cheek where an ugly blue-black swelling was clearly visible.

"Get your kicks beating up women, Benson?" he sneered.

"Kiley, schoolboy sarcasm will have no effect. Just move to the chair as I requested."

Kiley obeyed. The pale light trickling through the front window illuminated patches of sweat on Benson's forehead. Otherwise, the American showed no signs of exertion. His hair was neatly in place, his beard immaculate, his suit uncreased.

Benson perched on the edge of the sofa, keeping his gun trained on Kiley. From the angle at which it was pointed, the detective guessed that a bullet fired at that moment would have shattered the major arteries of his heart. Benson chuckled softly. Kiley's stomach felt gnawingly empty. There was a crawling sensation in his testicles, and the palms of his hands were sweaty against the arms of the leather chair.

"If she dies, Benson . . ." he began with false bravado.

Benson raised his eyebrows in mock-surprise. "Tut, tut, Kiley. You're hardly in a position to be making grandiose threats." His voice had the same soft, caressing quality that Kiley had noticed back at his apartment, but now he thought he could detect an edge of suppressed excitement in it as well.

"You don't honestly think you can fool the police for much longer, Benson. They'll realize soon enough that someone's slaughtering these people . . ."

In lieu of response, Benson walked to the coffee table, picked up the receiver and placed it on the table, the gun in his other hand. As he dialed, his eyes flickered constantly back to Kiley. "Fool the police?" he said as the dial whirred back from the last number and he picked up the receiver again. "What can you mean?" He paused. "Hallo, Scotland Yard. Put me through to Detective Inspector Withers, Murder Squad. It's very urgent. Hallo, Inspector. My name is Benson. You don't know me. I'm a friend of Mary Blake—Anne Warren's sister. That's correct. I'm at her house at the moment—Fifty-three Marlin Cresent. She's been severely beaten, but she's in no immediate danger. I'm holding a gun on a Mr. Kiley, who claims to be a private detective and who I believe you *do* know. Ah, good, I thought so. Yes, I'll be able to hold him until you arrive." Benson replaced the receiver.

Kiley's mouth opened in astonishment. "You must really be out of your bloody mind!"

Benson moved back to the couch. "Madmen often impute their insanity to others, Kiley. It's a classic symptom, as I'm sure Dr. Blake will confirm when she regains consciousness."

"You're going to let her live?"

"Oh, but of course."

"Just what the hell are you up to, Benson?"

"Ah, another symptom. Paranoid delusions, I believe they're called; imagining vast plots, with yourself at the center . . ."

Benson jerked the gun up tensely as Kiley shifted in his seat. "Kiley, it makes no difference to me whether the police catch up with you dead or alive. Remain perfectly still, please."

"Okay," Kiley whispered. His throat was sandpaper dry.

Benson relaxed again and smiled. "You've been under a tremendous psychological strain, Kiley. The accident with Anne Warren obviously affected you more than was at first realized. You should really still be in the hospital. You're in no fit condition to be running around the streets . . ."

"Do you seriously think the cops are going to believe you? There's a trail of dead bodies . . ."

"The most disturbing aspect of your condition is this appalling obsession with death. Some mysterious agent is supposed to have been responsible for the death of five totally unconnected people—"*Five! Benson was giving information away for free*"—which is melodramatic claptrap. The Murder Squad is, I suspect, a little too busy dealing with planned violent death to worry overmuch about road accident casualties, heart attack victims, and people who manage to drown themselves in their baths. You need a rest, Kiley." He paused and added in a slightly harsher tone: "A long one!"

"It won't wash, Benson."

"Oh, I think it will, you know." He motioned toward Mary with his free hand. "Especially after this distressing incident."

"You'll have to kill both of us."

Benson shook his head with a sad, resigned air. "Poor boy, completely gone. You burst in here and make a brutal attack on a defenseless woman. The hospital authorities should really have kept an eye on you. It's them I blame."

Kiley frowned. Benson couldn't possibly make this fairy story stick unless he killed both of them. "You can shoot me easily enough, Benson, but you'd have to kill Mary Blake with your own hands. Could you do that? Are you that crazy?"

"You're a very sick man, Kiley. My heart goes out to you." Benson stroked his beard meditatively.

"Look, when Mary comes round . . ." Kiley let the statement peter out. There was no point in goading Benson into drilling them both full of holes. If the American wanted to hand himself over to the police, Kiley wasn't going to dissuade him. "Bad for your heart condition, all this?" he ventured instead.

Benson looked surprised. "Heart condition? I'm in the very pink of health, as Dr. Dalziel will confirm."

Kiley's instincts told him to keep quiet, but he wanted to clear up the mystery before the police arrived. "The year 1974, Benson. This is all connected to something that happened in 1974."

Kiley thought he discerned a glimmer of surprise in the American's steady gaze, but it was quickly extinguished.

"Ah, '74. Good year for Claret, even better for Burgundy. I can't think of any other significance it might have." Still, Benson's genial smile was a little forced, as if Kiley had hit a nerve.

"This time I'm not fooled, Benson—1974 was a bad year for you, wasn't it? Tell me what happened."

The American's hand trembled. The gun shook slightly. Kiley had drilled clean through the nerve.

"I suggest silence until the police arrive, although I could always ring for an ambulance if you'd prefer to be carried out with a blanket over your head!"

The two men eyed each other sullenly for a full minute. The room grew steadily darker as storm clouds gathered outside, emphasizing the charged silence in the room. Benson was sweating badly now despite the definite chill in the air.

On the sofa, Mary moaned, as if dreaming. A slight tremor passed over her body. Both men looked at her. Kiley wanted badly to go to her side, but he knew that another unannounced movement would mean certain death.

In the distance, a mournful police siren cut through the sound of the now torrential rain. Kiley sensed Benson relaxing. His own body stiffened involuntarily. Nausea fluttered in the pit of his stomach and his breathing had almost stopped. If Benson intended murdering him, then this would be the moment to do it. Kiley fixed his gaze on Benson's trigger finger, just discernible in the gloom. He had made up his mind that he would be out of his chair and charging across the room at the first indication of extra pressure on the trigger.

The siren came closer and closer until it sounded to Kiley as though the police car would drive straight through the front door.

Benson smiled. "I'm about to prove to you just how useless opposition is, Kiley."

"Why don't you just kill me?" It was a gamble, but he wanted to keep Benson talking.

"I'm sure you won't accuse me of being a sentimentalist, but I just need you out of the way for forty-eight hours. That should do nicely. Besides, I hate *unnecessary* suffering."

Heavy, authoritative footsteps sounded on the path. Kiley closed his eyes and let out his breath in relief. Now the mystery would be revealed and he might be alive to hear it.

Benson must have left the front door on latch because it opened without a key being turned. The American left his perch on the couch to move over to the center of the room. He adjusted his features to give an impression of fearful anxiety as Withers appeared in the doorway. The inspector's huge hand moved over the wall until it hit the light switch. He scanned the room swiftly without displaying any emotion. Two policeman entered the room after him. Kiley squinted against the light, realizing what a strange tableau they presented. As he opened his mouth to speak, Benson cut in.

"Thank God you're here, Inspector! I don't know how much longer I could have kept this up."

Kiley butted in. "He's bullshitting, Withers. Mary'll tell you all about it. Benson was res——"

Withers gave Kiley a warning glance, which silenced him, then went over to the couch and looked down at Mary. He turned to Benson. One of the uniformed constables moved swiftly to Kiley's side, and when the detective tried to rise, the cop pushed him back down. Withers motioned the other constable to look after Mary, then walked over to Benson.

"The gun." He held out his huge hand and Benson slipped the weapon into it, where it seemed to disappear. "Jesus, Inspector, I've never been as frightened in my life." He drew one shaky hand over his sweating forehead.

Withers turned toward the couch. "How is she, constable?"

"Unconscious, sir, but I think she'll be all right."

Withers turned back to Benson. "Just tell me what happened."

"I'm an old friend of Dr. Blake's from way back . . ." he began.

"You're a bloody liar!" Kiley growled.

Withers turned to Kiley and held out a warning finger. "Remember what happened the last time we met? Just keep quiet. You'll have your say. Carry on, Mr. Benson."

"I got a phone call from Dr. Blake about an hour ago—I live in St. John's Wood, not too far away—and she told me she was worried about this private detective who had been hanging around for the last few days. Apparently he was involved in a crash in which her sister was killed. He'd phoned the office to ask her to see him back here as soon as possible. She felt sorry for him, so she agreed to come, but then, just before she left the office, she got nervous. She phoned me and asked me to come over in case she needed protection. We're old friends, and she knows I carry a gun."

"Why was she worried about him?"

Benson shrugged. "She didn't say exactly, but she led me to believe that this man had been acting rather strangely. She wasn't sure she could handle him on her own. Being a psychiatrist and all, I guess she knew what she was talking about. I told her to call you, the cops, but she felt sorry for him and didn't want to see him in any more trouble. I started over at once, but I had some trouble with the car and was held up. I almost called you. I knew this Kiley was a pretty strange guy because I'd already met him . . ."

"Met him? Where?"

"He came to visit me at my apartment earlier this morning. Mary must have mentioned my name to him or something. He barged in and started making wild accusations—apparently I'm a mass murderer. He even claimed I'd been tailing his car." Benson gave Withers an exasperated look. "I was genuinely scared, even though I had my gun on me at the time—I always carry it, what with all these businessmen being kidnapped, and I've got a police license for it. He seemed in a very agitated mental state. I suggested he visit a psychiatrist, and he got very abusive and stormed out. When I got Mary's call, I could understand her fears only too well."

"What happened when you arrived here?" Withers asked.

"I saw his car parked across the road. The front door was ajar. I heard Mary's screams from outside. I ran in here and found him"—Benson gulped as if he was finding it painful to continue—"found him attacking Mary. He was completely deranged. He was following her around the room, just hitting and kicking her, knocking over the furniture. He was like an animal. She was almost unconscious, just stumbling about, trying to get out of his reach, pleading with him to stop."

"How did you manage to control him?"

"I shouted for him to stop. I had my gun out. The sight of it seemed to bring him to his senses. I ordered him to sit down. I somehow got Mary onto the couch—she'd passed out by that time—then I phoned you." Benson shook his head and his eyes seemed to turn glassy with fear. "I feel so damn guilty. If only I'd been on time."

Kiley barked out a laugh. "Great performance, Benson. Definitely Oscar class."

"Shut up, Kiley!" Withers growled.

From the sofa came the sound of a groan. The constable bent down over Mary and helped her onto her back. She shook her head a little and raised her hand to her forehead. Her dress was torn in several places and her legs were bruised. Her hair lay across her face in sweaty strands.

"Now we'll get the truth," Kiley muttered.

Withers went to Mary's side and leaned over. "Dr. Blake, this is Inspector Withers," he said, with an approach at tenderness.

There was movement beneath her eyelids. Her eyes fluttered open. Mascara had run down both cheeks. She stared at the policeman for a moment. Then her whole body went rigid and she started shaking violently as if she were still being attacked.

Withers reached down a hand and stroked her shoulder soothingly. She bleated at the contact. "That's all right, you're fine. That's all right," he cooed softly. Slowly her body began to unstiffen and the jerking ceased.

Kiley strained forward to see her face better. The policeman beside him put a restraining hand on his arm. Mary gulped and began to cry.

"Dr. Blake, are you able to talk? Would you like to go to the hospital first?" Withers asked.

"N . . . no. I'm . . . fine," she stuttered.

Withers made an attempt at a smile, which didn't come off. "Will you just tell me what happened?"

All breathing seemed to have stopped in the room. Mary's voice was tremulous when she spoke, but the stutter had gone. "I was attacked. I got a telephone call to meet him here . . . and he attacked me." She broke off with a sob.

"Take your time, Dr. Blake. When you're ready . . ."

She swallowed hard. "I'm all right. I'd like to go on. He just kept hitting me, kicking me, following me around the room. I couldn't get away. He was berserk."

"Who did this to you, Dr. Blake? Think about it now."

"I don't need to think about it." Kiley leaned forward. This time the cop didn't restrain him. Mary's next words were quite distinct. "The private detective. Kiley. He attacked me."

Kiley was on his feet in an instant, running toward the couch. He pushed Withers aside. "Mary, for Christ's sake! What are you saying?"

She screamed when she saw him. Her legs and arms began moving wildly. "Get away! Get away from me!" she yelled.

As Kiley reached out his arms toward her, Mary opened her mouth and let out a shriek. Kiley felt his arms being grabbed and twisted up against his back almost to the breaking point, his head forced down toward Mary by Withers in the classic police hold. In an instant, both her hands were at his face, attempting to tear his flesh.

Kiley was hurled across the room. Withers followed and booted him in the stomach. When Kiley opened his mouth to yell, no sound came; the wind had been knocked out of him. He put his hands over his stomach as protection against Withers's next kick, but it never came. Beyond the policeman, he could see Benson, half out of his seat, his eyes gleaming with excitement.

"Mary!" Kiley gasped. "It was Benson, tell them it was ... Benson."

Withers stepped aside so that Kiley could see his accuser. Mary had struggled into a sitting position, one hand on her bruised cheek. The pupils of her wide, green eyes were pinpricks of hatred.

"You bastard!" she exploded.

Kiley looked up imploringly at Withers. "She doesn't even know Benson."

Withers frowned down at him, then turned toward Mary. "Kiley here says you don't even know Benson. Is that correct, Doctor?"

Mary closed her eyes. All the fight, which the sight of Kiley seemed to have awakened, was drained out of her, and she slumped back, exhausted. "I've known him for years, Inspector. An old, old friend. I . . . called him round to protect me. This man Kiley had been acting so strangely . . ."

"I warned you about him, Doctor," Withers reminded her.

She nodded wearily. "I know, Inspector. I suppose I just felt sorry for him. The accident must have placed a great psychological strain on him. I should have listened to you . . ." She began to cry again.

Benson went to Mary and sat down next to her, placing a protective arm around her shoulders. "Inspector, I think Dr. Blake has been through enough for one afternoon. She needs medical attention. Couldn't you get this wretched man out of her sight? You can see how much he's upsetting her."

Kiley groaned in frustration and closed his eyes. He let his head sink back onto the floor. The whole bloody world had gone crazy. He made an effort to pull himself together. If Withers took him back to Scotland Yard, it might take days for the truth to come out. He knew his only hope of foiling Benson's plans—whatever they were—was to stay in circulation.

He studied the room from half-closed eyes: one cop by the door, another by the window at the front, Benson and Mary on the couch, Withers standing beside them. The only possible escape was through the french windows at the far end of the room. He moved his arms until the palms of both hands were against the floor. He drew his knees up toward his chest, then looked again. Withers was giving orders to his men. Benson was engrossed in the exchange.

Kiley pushed himself onto all fours, paused for a split instant, then surged across the room, fighting to keep his balance. There were shouts of alarm behind him. The french windows loomed ahead. He crossed his arms over his face and launched himself at the glass. Somersaulting through the air, he hit the ground of the small, muddy garden with one shoulder, glass shattering around him. In an instant, he was on his feet running blindly, with no idea where he was heading. The freezing air shocked him into alertness.

Close behind, he heard feet crunching over broken glass. There was an eight-foot-high brick wall directly in front of him. He ran at it with a roar, springing up at the last possible moment. Clutching its top with his hands and straddling it with his legs, he dropped into the garden below, where a child was studiously riding a three-wheeler bike round and round in perfect circles. The kid stopped in mid-circuit to study Kiley reflectively as he belted past, heading for the road beyond.

Chapter Ten

Kiley stood shivering in a shop doorway, staring disconsolately at the flurries of rain whipping along Fleet Street. Around him, commuters huddled waiting for a bus. A shaft of light from a nearby street lamp fell across his legs in a dissecting wedge. He glanced at his watch. Nearly seven o'clock. A gust of wind curled into the shop entrance and left its chill behind in his clothes, which were soaking wet. Kiley shifted from foot to foot and clamped his teeth together.

The front entrance of the Daily Express building on the opposite side of Fleet Street opened. Kiley offered up a silent prayer of thanks as the Prince of Darkness came scuttling down the steps and hurried across the street toward him. Kiley stepped out of the doorway and grabbed the reporter's arm.

"Not here. I've got a car parked in the next street."

"Your Jag? Isn't that rather ostentatious?"

Kiley grinned. "Ford Cortina. I stole it in Camden Town earlier today." He grasped the Prince's arm tightly through his black raincoat and hurried him along the pavement into a dark side street.

When they were inside the borrowed car, the Prince removed his sunglasses to display tired, red-rimmed eyes.

"Did you do what I asked?" Kiley demanded.

Prince nodded and began wiping the lenses of his spectacles on the inside of his raincoat. He studied the result with a disgusted expression. "Yes, I did, dear boy, but, before we talk about that, why didn't you tell me when you phoned earlier that the boys in blue were after you? This places me in a very awkward situation. Some of my best friends are policemen."

Kiley shrugged. "If we get picked up, just tell them I'm holding you by force. When I phoned this afternoon, it was from a public phone. The cops were all over the place. I didn't have time to explain any further."

Prince sighed. "Ah, my dear Kiley. Perdition and damnation beckon you. I've got a report on my desk all about you. The police describe you as 'extremely dangerous.' The public are warned to 'approach with caution.' I admit I had to think twice before keeping this appointment. What in God's name did you do to deserve all this attention?"

"Nothing, Prince, believe me! They claim I attacked a woman. It was a setup job."

"Not exactly your style, I would have thought."

"Of course it isn't! Enough about me. What did you find out?"

"Did this Benson character set you up?"

"Yes, he did. Look, Prince, you'll have the whole story within forty-eight hours—you and nobody else."

"Just one thing—are you sure you haven't gone raving, bloody mad?"

Kiley grasped Prince's arm. "I'm as sane as I ever was. Now, that might not mean much, but just trust me for the time being, eh?"

The Prince eyed him dubiously for several seconds. "My God, you look dreadful, Kiley." He paused. "You say there have been five deaths so far?"

"Murders, I'm convinced of it."

"All carried out by this Benson chap?"

Kiley nodded. "Arranged by him would be nearer the mark. Don't ask me how or why, because I just don't know. That's all I've got to say for now. If you've got something for me, spit it out! If not, then for Christ's sake let me get out of this area of town. We're as conspicuous as a couple of blacks at a National Front meeting."

At that moment Kiley caught sight of a policeman, reflected in the Cortina's wing mirror. He was strolling down the sidewalk toward them. Kiley bent down low and pretended to tie his shoes. The cop paused momentarily by the side of the car before heading on, apparently unsuspicious.

"It's all right," Prince whispered. "He just thinks we're a couple of queers."

Kiley sat up straight and blew air out from his cheeks.

"Prince, if you don't get a move on, there'll be a sixth murder . . . right in this car!"

Prince grinned. "Too late, my friend. It looks as if Benson's beaten you to the punch."

"Jesus!" Kiley hissed, thinking for one dreadful moment that the reporter might be referring to Mary Blake. "Who is it this time?"

The Prince reached one hand inside his raincoat and brought out a note pad. "Can we have the overhead light on?"

"Don't be so bloody silly!" Kiley growled.

Prince put the notes away. "I think I can remember most of it anyway. You asked me to check up on the former head of research at Benson Pharmaceuticals."

"That's right. I heard there was something interesting about him."

"There is." Prince smiled. "He's dead. Does that surprise you?"

"Nothing surprises me about this case. Tell me about it."

"Hiroko, a Japanese gent with a considerable reputation in the field of psychopharmacology, was discovered on the morning of November eighth this year lying dead on the floor of his laboratory."

"Heart attack?"

"Precisely. Like our friend Clem Danaher. There's a connection?"

"Yes, but don't ask me what it is. I don't know yet."

Prince shrugged. "Hiroko's doctors blamed it on overwork. According to rumors, he'd been working nights for a considerable period of time on a special hush-hush project for Benson. The details of the project were not generally known, and now it looks as though we'll never discover them. Hiroko's assistant, who has taken over as chief researcher now that his boss is dead, mentioned something about Project Alpha, but didn't know anything else about it. Does the name mean anything to you?"

"Alpha?" Kiley frowned. "First letter of the Greek alphabet, that's all I know. Why do you think we'll never know what it was about? Surely Hiroko must have left behind some notes on his research. Scientists don't carry things around in their heads."

"Hiroko's personal research files were missing from the

laboratory on the morning of his death. And no papers were discovered at his house."

Kiley whistled softly. "Didn't that make the police suspect that something strange was happening?"

"As we both know, the police need subtle hints like bullet holes or knife wounds in a dead body before they begin to suspect foul play."

A car swooshed close by, sending a spray of water over the car window on Kiley's side. It oozed down the glass like melting ice.

"Listen, Prince, thanks a lot. You'll get your reward. Now, would you mind taking off?"

"What are you going to do?"

"Let me worry about that. One thing's for sure—the cops aren't getting to me before I do it!"

Prince smiled. "Careful, old chum. Your picture will be plastered over the newspapers tomorrow. Luckily the photograph was taken years ago. It makes you resemble a Boy Scout rather than the battered hulk I see before me."

Kily reached across and opened the passenger door. "So long, Prince. Keep up the good work."

"Oh, I see, thank you and fuck off!"

"I'm better at showing gratitude when I'm not under pressure."

The Prince shrugged. "Okay, I'll let you go on your way. Can I arrange anything for you?"

Kiley chuckled. "Yeah, a miracle."

Kiley watched Prince as he shuffled back along the wet pavement toward Fleet Street, then switched on the ignition, pulled out into the road, and headed south for the river.

He reflected on what Prince had told him as he edged through the evening traffic. Benson had been using his own head of research to work on a private project—Project Alpha—up until a few weeks before Anne Warren's death. Hiroko had to be the first link in the chain of death Benson was forging. Whatever the Japanese scientist had come up with had to be lethal. No doubt it was Benson who had removed Hiroko's papers to prevent the results of Project Alpha from being discovered.

As the Cortina crawled over Battersea Bridge, Kiley had to fight hard against exhaustion. He had one more job to perform that night. While he was phoning Prince from a pay phone soon after escaping from Mary Blake's house he had decided, in sheer desperation, to try a long shot. The London Telephone Directory had yielded three M. J. Badels, but it was when he called the first of them that he had spotted a Major Aaron Badel farther up the page and that had seemed a more likely fit for the words he had seen on Benson's telephone pad. A maid had answered, informing him that the Major and his wife had left for the day and would not return until midnight. Kiley had declined to leave a message. Badel might prove to be a close friend of Benson's rather than a potential victim, and Kiley didn't want to tip his hand any further than he had to.

Now he swung the car off the main road and headed for the mean backstreet slums of Battersea. He traveled past rows of dilapidated terraced houses until he came to a bomb site surrounded by wooden fencing with several car-sized gaps in it. He drove through one of them onto the bumpy ground and pulled the Cortina in close to the fence on the other side. He killed the engine and looked around. It was the kind of bleak oasis that still cropped up surprisingly in the overcrowded city.

He sat for a while staring up through the windshield at the rainswept sky. A wave of self-pity washed over him and he felt thoroughly, completely alone. Benson had framed him; Mary—what the hell was *she* playing at—had lied about him; the police were after his hide. On his side were ranged one reporter and six ghosts. Kiley managed a tired grin. The way things were going, he might need supernatural help before this business was explained.

Gradually his exhaustion won over the hyperactivity of his mind. He slumped sideways on the front seat of the car. In the last seconds of consciousness he tried to concentrate on the date 1974. He was convinced that somewhere locked in his head was a significant fact that he had so far overlooked, something connected with Benson . . .

There were no dreams for Kiley that night. As he slept, his mind was as impenetrably blank as the black sky that arced over London.

Major Aaron Badel stood at the top of the wide staircase and ran his fingers down the sides of his bushy mustache. He pulled the sash of his silk dressing gown tighter, filled his barrel chest with air, and padded down the stairs.

He paused for a moment in the spacious hall and smiled. Silence. Peace. Early morning stillness. The golden hours that were his own.

In addition to leaving Badel with a preference for cold showers, the army had instilled in him an appreciation for those hours when the air is crisp and the mind uncluttered by the accumulated trivia of daily business.

He opened the front door and stood on the top of the steps leading up to the house, fists on hips, bouncing up and down on the balls of his feet, smiling at the pre-dawn darkness. Except for the automobiles gleaming on either side, the road could have been mistaken for an eighteenth-century street with white-painted window frames set in red-brick Regency facades, each doorway surmounted by a shell-shaped canopy.

Badel took a deep breath. The air was remarkably clean and would remain so for another hour until the wind wafted stinking exhaust fumes down from the King's Road. Right now, though, it smelled of the river, as it must have done at the time when Chelsea was a small village on the outskirts of London.

Badel bounced up and down a few more times, noted with a twinge of annoyance that his copy of *The Times* had not yet been delivered, and went back inside. He headed down the hall to the kitchen where he prepared himself a pot of tea—Indian, of course—then returned with a cup to the front of the house. Badel had given the maid a few days off, so it was back to self-catering for a while.

He opened the twin white doors leading into the sitting room and switched on the lights. Rich leather furniture glowed dark red. The walls of the wide, elegant room were hung with heavily varnished oil paintings and assorted examples of historical weaponry.

In front of the curtained main window stood a small walnut bureau where the second Mrs. Badel wrote endless, dreary letters to endless, dreary friends. Short, sharp phone calls took less time. Writing, Badel felt, was not a medium of communication to be squandered on trivialities.

He sat at the desk, reached into the bottom left-hand drawer for a black leather diary with his own name gold-embossed on the cover, and opened it. Attaching a pince-nez to the bridge of his nose he read his entry for the previous day, nodding now and then in agreement with himself. His writing had been a lot sounder recently. With increasing age his pontifications on life in general, backed up with examples from his own experience, had begun to take on a mellow, scholarly tone. He wondered for a moment, pen poised in mid-air, whether any of it would ever be published. A slim posthumous edition, perhaps? Not that he was any great philosopher, but in an age when civilization seemed to be on the point of collapse, people might like to read the reflections of a sensible, forthright chap whose life had been spent in the service of his country—which was more than could be said for the trend-conscious left-wingers who constantly assailed the traditional values in which he had always believed.

He was wondering which topic to devote himself to that morning when his eyes lit on the date at the top of the page. November 23rd. He put his pen down and sat back in his seat, his ramrod posture abandoned for the moment. For some reason, the date struck him as significant, almost as if someone were standing behind him and whispering it in his ear.

He turned his head sharply. Nothing. Feeling slightly foolish, Badel sighed, got up, and began pacing the room, taking occasional sips from the cup of tea in his hand. He just couldn't seem to get his thoughts in order.

He stopped below the life-size portrait hanging above the Adams fireplace. He studied it, his lips in a tight smile.

Jaqueline, his first wife, smiled back down at him co-quettishly. The artist had captured her perfectly; the tilt of her aquiline nose, the flaming red of her hair, the inviting fullness of her lips, and the wildness in her green eyes. It was that hint of wildness that had attracted Badel to her in the first place. It was what he had noticed the first time he had met her at one of his father's grand parties at their country estate. His love had been instant and all-consuming, and Jaqueline had responded with seeming eagerness to his ardent approaches. The match was straight out of a romantic novel—the only son of one of the district's wealthiest landowners and the belle of the county. Everything should have been perfect, but Badel's father refused to agree to the proposed marriage, arguing that the timing was wrong. Badel would be going off to fight soon in his father's old regiment. Besides, the boy was too young, only nineteen, and Jaqueline was at least six years his senior. Badel was suspicious of the smokescreen of flimsy excuses his father sent up every time the subject was broached. It was as if the old man knew something about Jaqueline he didn't want his son finding out.

Badel and Jaqueline carried on a clandestine courtship—secret meetings in romantic locations, full of protestations of love and passionate yet curiously chaste kisses. Jaqueline promised she would wait until marriage became possible. She didn't have to wait long. Badel's father died in a riding accident before a year had passed and the young couple were married a month after the funeral. They spent a few blissful, carefree weeks as master and mistress of Badel Hall before Badel was called abroad to fight for his country. Before he left, he commissioned a portrait of her. After playing a distinguished part in the North African campaign against the Germans, Badel returned home for a fortnight's leave. He remembered how the cold had bitten into his lungs as he was driven home through his snow-shrouded estate and how he had felt seeing Jaqueline standing at the top of the steps of the great hall, crying, her arms open, beckoning him to her. Only the thought of her had kept him sane through the long months of misery and bloodshed.

Standing before the portrait, Badel could almost feel Jaqueline's arms as they had encircled him then, her breath hot and urgent in his ear, her tears burning against the coldness of his cheeks. Badel wanted to turn away from the portrait, to forget it all, but the memories were too powerful.

Jaqueline had organized a party for his return. The prominent figures of the district came to welcome the young soldier back. Badel was one of the heroes of Alamein. The guests eulogized him to such an extent that Badel would hardly recognize himself as the subject of their praises. He soon became impatient with these well-wishing intruders. He was tired. He had been away from his wife for too long and all he wanted was to be alone with her. He caught tantalizing glimpses of her all evening, laughing, her cheeks flushed with exuberance, drinking champagne, entertaining groups of guests, dancing with other men. Around eleven o'clock, when Badel had suffered one hearty pat on the back too many, he decided to find Jaqueline and tell her it was time to bring the party to a close. He circulated through the ground-floor reception rooms searching for his wife, but without success. He asked a few of the more sober guests whether they'd seen her, but they just shrugged or mumbled in a somewhat embarrassed fashion. When he had searched the ground floor, including the kitchens and the servants' quarters, he proceeded upstairs, thinking Jaqueline might have lain down for a while to recover herself. From what he'd seen of her she had been drinking quite heavily—rather more than was decorous for a young lady. Badel didn't mind, though. It was a sign of spirit in a woman.

She wasn't in the master bedroom. Badel searched several of the other rooms until he came to the bedroom in the east wing that had been his as a child. He was about to open the door when he heard a strange scuffling noise. He pressed his ear to the door. A rhythmic slithering sound was counterpointed by short, panting breaths. Slowly he turned the handle and let the door swing open. It was a full ten seconds before the occupants of the bed registered his presence. The boy, who could have been no more than eighteen, was sitting up in bed, his back against the pillows. His eyes were closed and small, ecstatic grunts issued from his open mouth. The boy's hands were clutching Jaqueline's hair, moving in rhythm with her head as her mouth engulfed his erect penis with slow, languorous strokes.

Badel made a low moaning sound. The boy's eyes opened. Panic-stricken, he jumped off the bed and stood staring at Badel. Jaqueline raised her head slowly. Her eyes were glazed and her lips were glistening. When she saw him, she began to laugh. Badel backed out of the room slowly, his body stiff, his stomach churning. In the hallway he laid his forehead against the cool wall and whimpered. He was vaguely aware of the youth scurrying past him. Badel somehow managed to stumble to one of the spare bedrooms, where he lay down and wept like a child. It was several hours before sleep came to him.

By the time he was awakened by his manservant the

next morning, the world had changed for Badel, his perception of it forever warped by the hideous animal scene he had witnessed on the previous night. As an officer, he had often heard the men under his command discussing the whores they went with and he had listened with mild disgust to graphic descriptions of the sex acts those degraded creatures were willing to perform. But now his wife, his own dear Jaqueline . . .

He spent the next morning dazedly studying the household accounts. Jaqueline had spent lavishly during his absence. Badel Hall had been the site of more entertaining during the past six months than during the previous two centuries of its existence. Badel shuddered at the thought of what sort of "entertainment" might have been provided. He lunched in his room. When Jaqueline made a request to see him, Badel informed his manservant that his wife was not to be allowed access to him. That went for all other callers. In the afternoon Badel went riding. He galloped for miles over his estates until both he and the horse were quite exhausted. After dining on his own he retired to what had been his father's study and drank himself into a stupor. His manservant had to help him up the stairs to bed. Punishing physical exercise followed by heavy drinking bouts became the pattern of his life for the next two weeks. He could think of no other way of getting through the days. Not once did he so much as catch a glimpse of Jaqueline. He preferred not knowing where she was or what she was up to. His imagination provided enough lurid answers. After a few days her requests to see him died out, much to Badel's relief. What could they possibly find to say to each other? He would never be able to look at her again without recalling that revolting scene, and yet divorce was out of the question. The Badel family name would never recover from such a scandal. Badel guessed that Jaqueline's unfaithfulness was public knowledge anyway, which was bad enough. A court case would be unbearable. The most horrible aspect of the whole ghastly mess was that Badel still wanted her, still needed her. Inside him there was nothing but a terrible aching emptiness.

On the eve of rejoining his regiment, Badel downed a whole bottle of brandy before being helped to bed. He fell asleep instantly. The nightmares came thick and fast. That scene played over and over again in his head—the tendrils of Jaqueline's hair around the boy's fingers, her head moving up and down, her mocking laughter, those eyes . . .

"Aa-ron!" A chuckle. Badel awoke. The room was dark. His mouth was dry and he felt sick. The nightmare had awakened him. He glanced at the clock on the bedside table. Three in the morning. Long, long hours before dawn.

"Aa-ron!" He sat up with a jolt. It was Jaqueline's voice, coming from the direction of his bedroom door. The door opened slowly. She was standing in the doorway swaying slightly, silhouetted against the hall light. There was an empty champagne bottle in her hand. Badel wanted to shout at her to get out, but found it impossible. The words wouldn't come.

"Do you know where I've been, Aaron?" She giggled. Her voice was an insidiously caressing sing-song. "Oh, Aaron! Surely you know." She moved toward the bed on unsteady legs. "I've been with another man. A *real* man. It was marvelous." She tripped and fell across the foot of the bed, near his feet. Badel felt trapped, unable to move. She stared up at him, her wild eyes glinting in the hall light. She was grinning.

"Have you been lonely, Aaron? Hasn't my soldier-hero husband been just a teensy-weensy bit lonely without his Jaqueline?" She reached out a hand and caressed Badel's legs. He flinched at her touch.

"Oh dear, are we still upset?" Jaqueline lay on her back, stared up at the ceiling, and sighed. "I've slept with so many men while you've been away, Aaron, and do you know why?" Jaqueline propped herself on her elbow and contemplated him drunkenly in the half-light. "Hmm? Can't you guess?" She let the fingers of one hand travel suggestively along the shaft of the champagne bottle, then she gripped it fiercely. "Because you're so *boring!*" She let go of the bottle and placed her hand on his leg once more. He didn't move away this time. Her hand began to move upward.

"So dull. I married you because I wanted to be the lady of the manor, to live in some sort of style. Did you think I loved you? Did you seriously believe that? Poor, silly Aaron. How sad! Or maybe you thought it was your wonderful lovemaking.' She laughed harshly. 'Aaron, you're so bad, so clumsy, so *unsatisfying*." She dragged out the syllables of the last word. Her hand was traveling along the inside of his thigh. "And there's nothing you can do about it, is there? Would you like a divorce, Aaron? Would you like it all to come out in court? I can just picture it now, an endless parade of my glorious, handsome young lovers. Wouldn't the press love that, Aaron?" Her hand had reached his crotch. Her fingers cradled his testicles. "You might be a brave man, Aaron, but there's something lacking *here*." She gave his testicles a squeeze.

Despite everything, Badel felt his penis stiffening. Jaqueline's fingers began masturbating it. A bleat escaped from the back of his throat. Nausea swept through him. The woman he loved had turned into some vile, loathsome animal. Jaqueline crawled farther up the bed. Her head descended toward his penis and her lips opened. He could feel her breath against his shaft and he shuddered. At that instant something snapped inside Badel. For two weeks his emotions had been damned up, forming a reservoir of hatred. At last, the damn burst. With one swift motion he clasped the empty champagne bottle, hoisted it above his head, and brought it crashing down against his wife's skull. Jaqueline's body quivered for an instant after the bottle had shattered, then went quite limp. Her head collapsed into Badel's lap. He stared down stupidly. He could make out the gaping wound in her skull by the light from the hall. Blood began to spread over his loins like red semen.

His manservant found him the next morning still lying there, the remains of the broken bottle in his hand, Jaqueline's body slumped across him. The local doctor and chief of police were summoned, both long-standing friends of the Badel family. There was no doubt in their minds as to what had taken place; like everyone else in the district they had heard rumors of Jaqueline's infidelity. The cause of death was recorded as a fractured skull resulting from a fall on the main stairs. At the inquest, the coroner, another friend of the Badel family, decided to spare Badel the ordeal of questioning on compassionate grounds. Jaqueline was buried within a week and Badel immediately left to rejoin his regiment.

Badel left the running of the estate in the hands of a cousin and moved into his London home after the war. After ten years of celibacy he married a kind, plain, mousey woman from a good family and settled down to a quiet, uneventful life. The first thing he had done in his new home was to hang Jaqueline's portrait above the mantelpiece as a constant reminder to himself of the inherent danger of loving and trusting too much. It had served its purpose. His life, he liked to tell himself in smug moments, had generally been a pretty decent affair. Not many high points and blessedly few low ones since his first wife's demise. And never once since then had he allowed himself to be taken in by anyone. Every now and then, when his thoughts turned to Jaqueline, as they had that morning, or when the sporadic nightmares from which he suffered became too intense, he would think about having the portrait taken down, but something always stopped him. Keeping it in place was one method of atoning for his sin.

Badel stepped back from the portrait. For some odd reason his heart was beating quite hard. He frowned. Jaqueline could still reach out from the grave to affect him. Badel walked back to his desk and sat down to study the blank page again. His thoughts were still twisting and turning. A few words on the subject of marriage might be appropriate. He began to write.

"Aa-ron."

The clarity of the word caused Badel to drop his pen. It rolled off the desk onto the carpet. He swung round in his seat. That voice had often come to him in nightmares, but now he was fully awake.

"Aa-ron!"

Badel brought his hands up to rub at his eyes. The memory was strong, too strong. The portrait would have to go.

"Can you guess where I've been?"

Badel gasped. This was no product of his imagination. He half-rose from his seat, eyes on the door.

"Aaron, I've come back to you." The insidious voice seemed to be coming from the top of the staircase in the hall. It tinkled like wind-chimes through the house.

Badel stumbled toward the door. He heard footsteps on the stairs.

"Aaron, I've come back *for* you." There was a threatening undertone to the light, mocking quality of the voice.

Badel stood with his hands on the door, ready to open

it. He heard footsteps tripping across the marble floor of the hall, coming toward the living room. He could almost see Jaqueline's long, slender hands reaching for the twin door-handles on the other side. Badel twisted the key in the lock and staggered back. He could hear her throaty chuckle, could *smell* the champagne fumes. The door began to jiggle, gently at first, rising to a rattling crescendo.

"Can you guess where I've been?" The voice was close, hushed, almost conspiratorial in tone.

A massive crash followed. A terrific force pushed against the door. Splinters of wood fell on the living room carpet.

A savage, enraged scream. *"CAN YOU GUESS WHERE I'VE BEEN!"*

Badel retreated across the room, a cold sweat of terror on his body. Another crash; the door almost split in two.

"I'VE COME FOR YOU, AARON!"

Badel was back against the opposite wall of the room. A few items of weaponry scattered around him. There was a momentary pause. Jaqueline was preparing for her final assault. Badel bent quickly to retrieve a two-foot-long bayonet from the metal shapes at his feet.

Wood scattered over the room as a fist slammed through the door panel. Badel heard a chilling laugh from outside. He froze. A figure was discernible through the hole in the door. He was in the presence of evil.

Jaqueline's face was thrust into view. Her skin was death-white. Her full lips glistened. Her hair lay in garish red strands across her face like streaks of blood. It was as Badel remembered it from that awful night. Her lips opened wide. The voice, softly menacing at first, rose rapidly to a scream:

"Can you guess where I've been? *I'VE COME FOR YOU!*"

Badel raised the bayonet, clutched in both hands, high above his head.

Kiley sat in the Cortina, watching the front of Major Badel's house. It was a pleasant road, he reflected—opulent without being ostentatious. He shivered. His clothes clung to his body. His fingers were stiff and aching.

He cursed himself again for failing to wake up on the previous evening in time to call Badel. Consciousness had only returned to Kiley twenty minutes earlier with the leaden light of dawn. Rather than phone Badel, he had decided on the direct approach. It would be as well to meet with the Major before he had a chance to catch Kiley's photograph in the morning papers.

A light was on in the main downstairs window, shining palely from behind a drawn curtain. Either the maid was at work or the Major was an early riser. Kiley allowed himself another spasm of shivering, got out of the car, and stepped across the road on stiff legs. He eased himself up the steps to the front door, wondering how to approach the interview, and pushed the bell.

The door opened a few inches. A nervous, birdlike woman peered up at him. Her lips were trembling.

"Who are you?" she demanded. Her voice cracked on the last word.

"My name is Kiley, private investigator." He wondered what was upsetting the old woman. "I'm sorry to trouble you this early, but it's important that I speak to your husband."

There was a brief pause. The old lady stepped back, opening the door wide. She pointed a wizened finger across the hall at a pair of doors. "He's in there, I think. I heard noises. I'm so frightened . . . !" She began to sob. "The doors are locked. He won't answer me."

Kiley ran across the hall and thudded into the doors with his shoulder. They flew open. At first the brightly lit room appeared empty as Kiley walked into it. Then he heard shallow breathing behind him and turned.

Badel was slumped in a large leather chair facing away from the door. His lips were slightly open, hands resting comfortably across his stomach, back curved in a lazy, relaxed posture. His eyes were closed. He seemed to be dozing.

"Major?" Kiley stepped forward. The old man's eyes flickered open and he gave a strange smile.

Kiley decided on a straight approach. "Major Badel, I think you might be in some danger . . ."

The old man gave a hoarse laugh and shook his head. When he spoke, it was so quietly that Kiley had difficulty in making out the words. He placed his hands on the arm of the chair and bent over, putting his ear close to the Major's mouth.

"No danger now, quite safe. Cheated her you see. She wanted me, but I cheated her . . ."

Kiley stood up and looked down, puzzling over the words.

The corners of the Major's mouth went slack. There was a rattling in the back of his throat. A thin sliver of blood trickled down from his lips over his chin to drip onto his robe in sticky strands. Kiley clasped the old man by the arms and shook him.

The Major's hands slowly unfolded to drop limply by his sides. His stomach was a mass of seeping blood. From the center of the darkened area a blade stuck out with a small metal loop at right angles to the top. A bayonet.

Kiley felt for his pulse. The Major was close to death, but he was not lost yet. The possibility of recovery rested on whether the blade had pierced any vital organs and on whether the shock would prove too much for the old man's system. Kiley comforted himself with the thought that the Major looked like a pretty strong old bird.

He stood up straight, breathed deeply, and walked out into the hall. Mrs. Badel's thin fingers were playing nervously with the frilled edges of her nightgown. Her slim shoulders slumped even farther when she took in Kiley's expression.

"Your husband's had an accident, but I think he'll be all right." She tried to walk past Kiley into the living room, but he caught hold of her thin arms and guided her to the foot of the stairs. "Go upstairs. I'll get help." She moved up slowly, like a somnambulist, making odd, fluttering motions with her hands. Kiley waited until she had disappeared into a bedroom, then phoned an ambulance and put a call through to Withers.

"I'm pleased you're in early, Withers. This is Kiley. I've got something . . ."

"Kiley, you bastard! You'd better give yourself up. You're in deep enough trouble already . . ."

"Shut up, Withers, and listen for once! I'm at 47A Chester Row. There's a man dying here, a Major Badel. He tried to kill himself. I saw his name on a phone pad in Benson's apartment. You've got to make sure this guy lives, because he might be your only chance of sorting out the stinking mess you've been trying to ignore. It's about time you did something right!" Withers tried to interrupt, but Kiley wouldn't let him get a word in. "Don't bother calling out the heavy mob, because I'll be long gone by the time you get here. I'll be in touch."

He dropped the receiver back onto its cradle and ran back out into the street just as an ambulance, its siren sharp in the morning air, appeared at the end of the road.

Chapter Eleven

The phone rang for almost half a minute before it was answered.

"Hi, Benson. This is an old pal of yours."

There was a moment's pause before the American answered. "That was a neat disappearing trick you managed yesterday."

Kiley smiled to himself. "I'm pleased you enjoyed it. I should imagine that my being on the loose screws up your plans."

"Not really. You can't do much harm while you're busy evading the clutches of the law. Things are going pretty well at my end. How about you?"

"Top of the world, Benson. I've just heard a fascinating story about a research scientist called Hiroko."

"Hiroko?" Benson said, apparently puzzled. "Ah yes, I remember. Working too hard by all accounts. My managing director gave me a report on the incident. Unfortunate."

"Unfortunate? Is that what you usually say when someone dies? Must have been all that overtime he was putting in." Kiley paused. "On Project Alpha."

There was an almost imperceptible pause. "Kiley, why don't you just lie low for another twenty-four hours or so. That way you'll live. Interfere again and so help me Christ . . ." Benson halted, as if trying to get himself under control. The remark about Project Alpha seemed to have struck home. "I'm a little busy this morning anyway, and now I'll have to phone Inspector Withers and inform him about our little chat."

Kiley had a moment of savage pleasure. It was time for a below-the-belt blow. "Don't hang up on me, Benson. I thought we might have a chat about another friend of yours. Name begins with a 'B.' Can you guess?"

Benson sighed. "Really, I'm surprised you have time for word games. I suppose you're referring to poor Dr. Blake. Such a nice woman. That was a dreadful thing you did to her. Perhaps she'll offer you a course of psychiatric treatment when they let you out of prison."

"I wasn't talking about Mary—I'll make sure you pay for that, you bastard—I was thinking more of a certain military gentleman."

There was silence at the other end of the line, except for air whistling through Benson's nostrils. Kiley could imagine the American's supercilious grin disappearing.

"A major to be precise. Got it yet? Hey, don't you want to play this game any longer?"

"Get on with it!" Benson growled.

"Aaron Badel. Mean anything to you?"

"I don't know of anyone called Badel." He fluffed the pronunciation carefully. There was another pause. "How the hell did you find out?"

"My little secret." There was a sharp rap on the door of the phone booth. Kiley felt his stomach sinking. He turned slowly, expecting to see a helmeted policeman. He had become so engrossed in his conversation that he had forgotten to keep a lookout.

He let out a sigh of relief. It was the same woman who had been outside the same phone booth the day before, her face a study in exasperation. Kiley wondered what the hell she used the phone for, as he turned his back on her.

"Okay, Kiley, I'm waiting. Are you finished?"

"Not quite, Benson. I've got some bad news for you. Badel's alive." Kiley could imagine the American's fingers tightening around the elegant gold phone. "He's alive, Benson, and he's getting ready to talk." The phone clicked down.

Kiley pushed the door of the phone booth open and ran to his car. Within two minutes he was parked outside Waterbury Towers. He was counting on the fact that Benson would refuse the offer of police protection. After half an hour he began to fear that his news about Badel would not flush the rat from its lair, and he was just getting ready to drive off when Benson's BMW pulled out from the side of the building, headed around the driveway, and butted out into St. John's Wood Road, almost colliding with a taxi.

Kiley grinned and followed. The news had forced Benson into some positive action, as it had been intended to do.

Benson drove east for twenty minutes, then, after doodling around for a while searching for a parking space, pulled in front of a meter on Drummond Road, opposite Euston Station. Kiley waited until Benson, still dressed in his blue safari suit, crossed the road and entered the underground passage into the station, before double-parking the Cortina so it blocked the BMW.

He ran across the road, past the underground passage entrance, and entered the station through its main doors. The vast concrete-and-glass hall was packed with early-morning commuters. Kiley noted the position of four policemen strolling amid the crowd. The sound of conversation and announcements echoed around him half-heard, dreamlike.

Anyone entering the station by its underground passage had to come up a set of stairs that led into the center of the main concourse. Kiley remained about forty yards away from the spot, keeping his eye on the police and the exit at the same time. He hoped that Benson had not doubled back to the car and was relieved when he saw the American's large head, with its distinctive peppery hair, appear out of the exit.

Benson headed straight for the platforms, past rows of ticket-selling booths and bookshops, without looking around. The phone call had made him careless. Kiley felt a stab of panic. What if Benson were to get on a train? Should he get on with him? In the end he wasn't forced to make the decision. Benson turned right into a corridor, following a sign reading "Luggage Lockers/Toilets."

Keeping his head low in case the police spotted him, Kiley approached the end of the corridor down which Benson had disappeared. He peered cautiously into the long, narrow passageway. A few travelers were busy getting their luggage into or out of the metal cabinets that hugged the walls on either side. Benson was about two-thirds of the way down, fiddling with a set of keys. He found the right one and opened a locker door. He reached his arm deep inside and came out with something in his hand.

Leaving the door open, Benson turned and began walking away from Kiley down to the end of the corridor where the toilets were located. Kiley was relieved to see that there were no exits down there.

The detective waited until Benson had disappeared into the gent's toilet, then walked down after him. He paused at the open locker and looked inside. It was empty. Kiley noted the number and returned to his former position. Whatever Benson was up to, he decided, it had nothing to do with natural functions.

The American exited from the toilet five minutes later. He walked back up to the locker, replaced whatever he had taken from it, locked the door and pocketed the key.

Kiley slipped back into the main concourse and stepped into a bookshop. Through the display window he watched Benson cross the hall and reenter the underground passage. He, in turn, retraced his own steps back to the cars.

As he turned the corner into Drummond Street, he realized that Benson must have run all the way. The Cortina was gone—being towed away by the police. Benson was already behind the wheel of the BMW and pulling out into traffic.

Kiley watched in frustration. There was no point in making a bid to halt the BMW. It was already moving too fast. He waited until Benson was out of sight, then walked back into the station and headed for the luggage lockers. One of the cops eyed him suspiciously but showed no sign of recognition.

The corridor was empty. Kiley walked to the locker, got a strip of celluloid out of his inside jacket pocket, and inserted it. The lock gave way easily. He reached inside with one arm. Right at the back, propped up in a corner, he found a tubular object. He brought it out and studied it— a six-inch-long glass vial. In the bottom were a few drops of clear liquid. Kiley shrugged and pocketed the tube after checking that the cork stopper was securely in place, then clanged the locker door shut.

"Does that belong to you, sir?"

The uniformed policeman was standing right behind him.

Turning, Kiley gave a nervous laugh and patted his own chest. "You gave me a bit of a turn there, Officer." He wondered whether he had been recognized.

"I said, does that belong to you, sir? Would you mind answering?" The policeman inclined his head slightly forward in a menacing fashion. Kiley could tell that his body was tense, waiting for action.

"What? Oh, this!" Kiley laughed again and patted his right-hand pocket. "Yes, it does. Medicine." He shook his head, smiling, as if the idea that he might have stolen it was amusing.

By the time the cop said: "Then why didn't you use the key for the locker . . . Mr. Kiley?" the detective had already contemplated a whole series of attacking moves. An untrained combatant would have lashed out with his fists. Kiley stuck them firmly in his trouser pockets, affecting a nonchalant air. The cop relaxed. Kiley caught him at the right moment. He lifted his foot with ferocious velocity, and by the time he had reached the end of the row of lockers, the cop was on all fours, gasping.

Kiley slithered out into the main concourse. Another cop was heading in his direction. Keeping his hand across his face as if he had just been hit, Kiley ran toward him, shouting, "Quick, down there! One of your mates is in trouble," and pointing over his shoulder. The cop sidestepped Kiley and headed for the lockers, already detaching his walkie-talkie from his uniform.

The detective didn't stop running until he was half a mile away from the station.

Kiley sat hunched on the park bench peering occasionally over the top of the newspaper he was pretending to read. Prince had been right. The photograph of himself which had been issued to the press didn't resemble him in the least. The young, eager face stared out at him as if to say: "This is another fine mess . . ." He would have liked a cigarette, but his hands were too numb to light one successfully. The skin on the back of his hands had turned from chalk white to fierce pink and, finally, powdery blue.

A wan winter sun, which gave no heat, hung low in the sky, seeming to draw every last vestige of warmth from the earth in order to keep its pallid flame alight.

The northern edge of Regent's Park was deserted except

for a few hardy early-morning dog walkers and the occasional park keeper. Twenty yards in front of Kiley, parallel to the concrete path by which he was posted, were iron railings, beyond which was a busy main road leading up to London Zoo. Across the road was a row of detached Edwardian houses, one of which was of particular interest to him.

He glanced at his watch: eight forty-five.

He was still short of breath after his escape from Euston Station. He felt once more in his pocket for the glass vial. The news about Badel had panicked Benson into making what Kiley hoped was a serious error. The liquid in the vial might provide an important clue as to what the American was up to. Kiley had considered taking it directly to Withers and giving himself up, but something else had to be accomplished before he could do that.

"Come on," he muttered, "time you were off to work."

As if in response to his imprecation, the front door of the house he had been studying opened and a couple in their late thirties hurried down the steps with a child between them, got into a Lancia parked in front of their gate, and drove off.

Kiley watched them leave, put his paper down on the bench, got stiffly to his feet, and took off across the frosty, crackling grass. He vaulted the park railings and loped across the road. He moved swiftly through the gate and around the side of the house into the garden. He looked back once at the windows of the building, blank and glazed like dead men's eyes in the morning sun. He moved to the bottom of the garden and, grasping the top of the wall with his hands, hoisted himself up. He drew his tongue over dry lips.

Curtains were drawn in the three windows on the second floor of Mary Blake's house. It was a good sign. Mary would undoubtedly have opened her bedroom curtains on the previous day before going to work. Kiley concluded that she had come home to sleep rather than spend the night at whichever hospital Withers had taken her to after Benson's attack. One of the french windows was patched with cardboard, but the frames had remained intact despite the violence he had done to them.

Kiley slid over the wall and, crouching low, ran to the windows. Using his strip of celluloid, he pried back the lock. The doors gave with a faint click. As he stepped inside, warm air enveloped him. His skin began tingling as blood began to circulate once more to his extremities. The room showed signs of the struggle that had recently taken place there. He moved farther inside and stood listening. The house was silent. He padded over to the front window. Keeping close to the wall, he peered out at Marlin Crescent. It took him a few seconds to spot the anonymous gray Ford police car. The plainclothes detectives in the front seats were arguing about something. He could see their hands moving. Kiley felt instinctively sorry for them. They'd probably been on duty all night.

He stepped into the hall and crept up the stairs, standing stock still for ten seconds on the landing. He thought he could hear faint breathing. There was a door directly in front of him. He stepped across to it and turned the handle slowly, biting his lower lip as he pushed it open, waiting for the hinges to give a telltale squeak. It was a bedroom. The bed was untouched. Anne Warren's room, he surmised.

He crept farther down the corridor, sliding his feet along the carpet. He turned the handle on the next door and pushed. It was locked. Giving an inward groan, he retrieved the strip of celluloid from his pocket and inserted it. The lock gave without any pressure and the door swung open as if on springs.

Vapory light hovered behind the curtains facing him. A bed hugged the wall directly to his left. A quilt had been thrown back and the sheets were crumpled. An open book lay haphazardly on the floor by the bed, apparently having slipped from sleepy hands. He took a step forward. Clothes were draped over a chair half under a kidney-shaped dressing table across the room. Kiley smelled perfume and talcum powder. He took another step.

The room was warm with the heat of a living body.

The static rustle of fabric made him glance sideways to see a knife descending in an arc toward his shoulder.

Chapter Twelve

Kiley launched himself forward onto the bed, feeling a tug at his back, then twisted around and looked up.

Mary was advancing across the room, wide eyes blazing with fury. A kitchen knife with a nine-inch blade was clutched above her shoulder. She threw herself at him, bringing the knife down in a vicious loop. Kiley rolled himself onto the floor under her as she hit the bed. The knife scythed into the top pillow. He found himself staring at the pattern on the carpet. There was movement behind him. He heard his jacket ripping and there was a stinging sensation in his shoulder. He twisted his head around in time to see the knife coming down again. He was dimly aware of Mary's contorted face above him, her lips drawn back from her teeth. He managed to suppress an urge to cry out and caught at her wrist. She wrenched out of his grasp. He backed off across the floor, using his arms and keeping his legs straight out in front of him.

Mary slithered off the bed. "You bastard!" she spat out. She was getting ready to launch another attack. Kiley kicked out with one foot but missed her arm. The tip of the knife thudded into the carpet. Kiley scrambled to his feet while Mary eased the blade out of the floor with a circular, twisting motion. Her eyes studied him all the while.

Kiley knew the rules of knife-fighting—at all costs stay on your feet and keep balanced. He stood up and crouched, with his legs apart, arms circling in front. Mary got to one knee, then used the point of the blade to push herself upright. The knife was raised again to shoulder height, ready for a downward swing. Kiley counted himself lucky that she had no idea how to use the thing. She moved in close and made a few ineffectual stabs. He

133

moved his arms quickly, confusing her as he backed off
across the room. She lunged. He sidestepped and chopped
her wrist with the stiffened side of one hand.

Mary gave a tiny shriek and transferred the knife to her
left hand, holding the other arm down at her side. Kiley
stepped back toward the window as she moved in on him,
a strange growling sound coming from the back of her
throat. He dropped his arms suddenly, standing with his
back to the curtains, offering an open target. She ran at
him, eyes fixed on his welcoming chest. At the last moment he ripped the curtains open. She gasped as the sunlight flooded the room and blinded her, but kept on going.
The knife clunked into the windowframe.

Kiley caught her from behind and threw her back onto
the bed, then stood panting, hands on his knees, feeling
the sweat trickle down his face.

Mary opened her mouth to scream as soon as she realized what had happened. He was on top of her in a second, a hand clamped over her mouth. She bit into his
palm but he held steady, realizing that any cry would
bring the cops rushing in to aid her. She struggled wildly
for almost a minute, then went limp.

Kiley stared coldly into her eyes.

"I'm going to take my hand away," he managed to pant
out. "If you make a sound, I swear to God I'll break your
neck. Keep quiet and you'll be fine. Understood?"

She gave no response for ten long seconds, as if con-
sidering the threat, then nodded her head as vigorously as
his restraining hand would allow.

Kiley removed his hand slowly and examined it, still
keeping his weight on her trembling body. He became
aware of a strange animal excitement running through
him. The skin of his palm was punctured with teethmarks,
which, here and there, had drawn blood. He shook his
hand as if to dispell the pain, then got into a sitting position on the side of the bed.

Mary was lying behind him, her head leaning awkwardly against the wall. She shifted it onto the pillow.
Now that the curtains were open, Kiley could see quite
clearly the ugly bruise that Benson had left on her cheek.
There were flecks of blood on her lips, which were trembling. Her eyes filled with tears. She let out a deep, wrack-

ing sob. Kiley made as if to reach out and hold her, but her body stiffened anew when his fingers touched her arm.

He sat up straight again, fumbled in his pocket, checking to see that the glass vial was intact, then lit a cigarette and drew in smoke greedily. He wiped the sweat from his forehead and tried to assess the situation.

The woman lying on the bed behind him was obviously scared stiff. She believed that he wanted to kill her. The fear and anger which he had seen in her eyes on the previous day when Withers had awakened her was still there. He felt a sense of acute betrayal. It was as if his own mother had passed him in the street and refused to recognize him. The shift in Mary's attitude frightened him terribly, more than the knife fight had. Physical violence had been part of his life since his childhood. Mental violence, the kind that he decided Benson must have perpetrated on Mary, was far more terrifying. The confusion he felt made his guts churn.

When the cigarette was finished and Mary seemed to have cried herself out, he turned to face her.

"So I attacked you yesterday," he said matter-of-factly. Mary's eyes remained fixed on the ceiling. Her lips were compressed into a thin line.

"Okay, let's try another approach. Benson's an old friend of your, is he?" Again she made no answer. Kiley reached out his hand and caught her roughly by the chin, forcing her lips into a pout.

She bleated. "Y . . . yes," she stammered. Kiley hated to do it, but her fear of him was the only thing he had going for him at that moment.

"Listen to me carefully, Mary. You don't know Benson. You'd never met him before yesterday."

Her eyes swiveled toward him. He eased the pressure of his fingers but kept his hand in place.

"You're psychotic!" she hissed.

Kiley ignored the observation. "If you know Benson, then tell me where you first met him." She opened her mouth to say something, then stopped. She looked confused.

"Go on!" Kiley prompted. "Benson's an old buddy. Tell me where you first met. I'd love to know."

"I . . . I can't remember."

"All right, let's make it easier. Tell me any place you

met Benson before yesterday. Anywhere. It doesn't matter."

Again she opened her mouth and closed it without speaking. Kiley removed his hand from her chin. Mary shut her eyes tight and drew a hand across her forehead, as if trying to pull out the memory with her fingers.

"You've got me confused. I can't recall."

"Damn it, Mary!" Kiley said, his voice rising. "Just one bloody instance. A dinner, a scientific conference, a trip around his factory."

"I . . . I just don't know. I'm frightened . . ."

Kiley leaned in close. "You . . . don't . . . know . . . Benson," he said forcefully. "You had never seen him before yesterday."

She drew back against the pillow, her eyes still shut. "You're insane, clinically insane," she said, then added, almost thoughtfully, "It's impossible."

"Tell me one fact about him, one personal detail. What does his apartment look like, what are his favorite foods, does he have a sense of humor . . ." She was on the verge of tears again. Kiley straightened up. "Your sister died in an automobile accident last Friday. Do you remember that?" She nodded. "I came around on Saturday—stop me when you disagree—and we decided that Anne's death seemed strange; there was no reason for it that either of us could think of. On Sunday you went to the country to get away from reporters. On Monday I came around to see you at your office. I informed you about Max Bronson, the gangster who had died, and you told me about Alan Brown's death and his relationship with Anne. Remember?"

"Vaguely. It's there, but I can't get hold of it." She reached up both hands and pressed them against her temples. "There's so much going on in my mind, but none of it connects. I only know for certain that you tried to kill me . . ."

"We'll leave that aside for the moment. Look, you're a scientist, be practical. Don't fight the truth. The next day, Tuesday"—he realized with a shock that that had been less than twenty-four hours before—"I came back to your office. I told you I'd been tailed by a man called Benson. You'd heard of him. I went to interview him, then phoned you afterward. You told me that Alan Brown had handled

Benson's advertising account for a few years. You must have done some extra snooping on your own, because you said that you had something to tell me about the chief researcher at Benson Pharmaceuticals."

"No, no!" she moaned. "This is all . . . it didn't happen."

"Listen, Mary! Benson's chief researcher, Hiroko, is dead. That was what you wanted to tell me. Well, wasn't it?"

Mary opened her eyes and stared imploringly at him. "I *know* the names—they make little echoes in my mind—but I can't get anything into context."

Kiley tried a reassuring smile. "Okay, we're getting somewhere, at least. Now, tell me what happened yesterday—exactly. Take your time. If you still think I'm guilty after that, then I'll personally go and get the cops. Okay?"

Mary took a deep breath and stared blankly ahead.

"I was in my office. I was in the middle of a session. My secretary interrupted with an urgent message . . . from you. I was a little scared, but I cut the session short. I was frightened about what you'd do to me, but I knew you needed help. You'd been acting so strangely; I felt the accident had affected you badly. I needed a friend—not the police, I didn't want to cause more trouble for you— so I called Benson. He has a gun. I knew he could protect me. Couldn't think of anyone else. I drove home. You'd asked me to meet you there. I got into the house and . . . you were waiting for me. I couldn't understand why Benson hadn't arrived yet. I thought maybe that you . . ." She glanced at him nervously.

"Go on," he prompted.

"You were waiting for me in the sitting room. I asked what was so urgent that you had to see me right away and then you . . . you hit me. Across the face. I screamed. I started moving away from you, but you followed. You hit me again. You went berserk, smashing the furniture, kicking me. I tried to reason with you, but you wouldn't listen. I fell over . . . Benson raised his hand and hit me . . . Benson . . ."

Her breath was coming in short, orgasmic bursts. She repeated the American's name silently to herself, eyes wide with fear and confusion. Kiley reached out his arms and held her. This time there was no objection from her.

"That's right, Mary," Kiley nodded. "It was Benson. Benson made that phone call. He was waiting for you. Benson beat you up. Are you beginning to see the truth? Benson's been controlling your mind. You must fight his influence." He shook her slightly. "Go on, what happened then? This is the important part."

"Darkness, lying in darkness. Whispering. Someone whispering to me, but not from outside. It's as if it's inside my head." She placed a hand over her eyes. "Very soft but clear. So clear." She took her hand away and stared at Kiley. "Oh my God! What's happening to me. He's been inside my head. Am *I* going mad?"

"Is everything coming back to you now? Do you remember our phone call yesterday? The one in the morning after I went to see Benson?"

She nodded slowly. Her eyes glazed over. "It's becoming clearer . . . Oh, Kiley, what has he done to me? When I was remembering what happened yesterday, it was as if I was reading from the page of a script . . ."

"I half-guessed it. When you and Benson were telling your stories to Withers there was a similarity in the way you described the episode, almost as if you were using Benson's words."

"How did he manage it—it's impossible."

"When we've answered that question, we'll know how he managed to kill six people without being present at their deaths."

"Six?" she breathed out. A shudder ran through her body as if an icy finger had touched her spine.

Kiley rose from the bed and walked shakily to the window. "There've been a few developments since Benson got you in his power. An American singer named Clem Danaher died yesterday, and a Major Badel almost died this morning."

"Almost? How do you mean?"

"He was still alive when I left him. He'll be in the hospital by now. I hope they managed to save him. And there's another victim whose identity we don't know yet. Benson let the fact slip while he was holding a gun on me yesterday." Kiley pried the knife from the windowledge, displacing wood and paint.

"It might have been seven," Mary said hoarsely.

Kiley nodded, balancing the knife. As he did so, his

hand began to tremble, and the knife slipped from his grasp, landing on the floor. It had only just occurred to Kiley how close to death he had been.

Kiley added another cigarette butt to the mound already overflowing the ashtray on the low wooden table. Sitting across from him, Mary waved a hand in front of her bruised face as smoke wafted toward her.

"You must have been through a whole pack this morning, Kiley. I wish you'd consider what cigarettes do to your insides."

Kiley shrugged but managed to suppress the urge to light another one immediately. "Whatever harm they're inflicting, it's not as bad as all this bloody waiting around. I'll be lucky if I don't end up with ulcers."

"For God's sake, try and relax. There's nothing more we can do for the moment. Withers has it all under control." Mary bit her lower lip realizing she had said the wrong thing. Kiley frowned at her and scratched the stubble on his chin.

"That's what's driving me mad. I feel so bloody redundant. I should be out in the field helping the police."

"Remember, it was you who wanted to come here."

They lapsed into silence. Kiley lit another cigarette, Mary's admonition already forgotten. She decided it would be pointless to protest.

They had been sitting in the waiting room of the West Central Hospital's Intensive Care Unit for over three hours. The strain was beginning to tell on Kiley's nerves. It now seemed unlikely that Badel would pull through, but there was always a chance that he would regain consciousness before expiring. To be so close to an explanation of events and, at the same time, to have to rely solely on an old man's frail recuperative powers was nerve-racking.

From down the corridor came the sound of metal clattering to the floor. Kiley tutted irritably, dropped his quarter-smoked cigarette on the faded carpet, and mashed it underfoot.

Withers had listened patiently to their dual recital of events. Then, without any display of remorse, he had begun to act on their information. He was a good cop, Kiley had to admit. True, he had made a serious mistake, but he had set it firmly behind him, and now all he was interested in was getting on with the job.

Withers had immediately ordered an investigation into Hiroko's death and Project Alpha. Detectives had been sent to question the relatives and friends of the five known victims. Benson's apartment had been searched and an all-points bulletin, containing his description, had been issued. The vial that Kiley had discovered in Benson's locker at Euston Station had been sent for analysis to the forensic laboratories at Scotland Yard.

After their statements had been made, Kiley had requested that he and Mary be driven to the West Central Hospital to await Major Badel's recovery. If the old man held the secret to Benson's activities, Kiley wanted to be the first to hear it.

He stood up abruptly and began pacing the room. His clothes felt dirty and sticky against his skin, and his boots were a waterlogged writeoff. The silence of the Intensive Care Unit was oppressive. Even in the confines of the waiting room Kiley found that his sporadic conversations with Mary were being conducted in a sort of stage whisper. Through the glass window set in the waiting room door, nurses were discernible rushing past now and then in silent haste to answer another emergency light—there were no buzzers in Intensive Care.

"I'd love to have an analysis session with Benson," Mary said, just to break the silence.

"So you could provide him with a nice little loophole for his court appearance? An insanity plea?"

Mary shrugged. "I know what most policemen think about psychiatrists."

Kiley stopped pacing to look at her. "I'm sorry, I didn't mean that." He paused. "Benson didn't strike me as being crazy, but I don't suppose that means anything. He's one of the most composed, together people I've ever come across. Whatever he's doing, it's for a purpose. It's all too carefully planned to be the product of an irrational mind. Perhaps he's just evil."

"You believe in the concept?"

"Evil? All policemen do. They see it up close almost every day."

"Did you recognize it in Benson?"

Kiley frowned. "That's what's so strange. Cunning, yes. Evil, no."

Mary smiled. "You think rather deeply about things for a detective, don't you?"

Kiley decided the comment was not meant unkindly. "Strangely enough, Benson said the same sort of thing to me on the phone this morning." Kiley sat down. "Two things got to me after a while on the force—compromise and brutalization. I could never cope with the first—that's really why I left—but I soon learned that the only way of coping with the second was to develop some kind of mental life. That's what's missing in a cop like Withers. His life's his job and his job's banging the cell door on villains. All he needs to know is that Benson's guilty and he'll be satisfied. He'll want to know how, but not necessarily why." He caught himself. "Christ, *I'm* beginning to sound like a psychiatrist. Who knows, maybe Withers has got the right approach."

The subject of Kiley's remarks opened the door. Withers's massive bulk added to the claustrophobic atmosphere of the tiny room.

"Come up with anything?" Kiley asked.

"The forensic boys should have a rundown on that stuff within an hour." He brushed rain droplets from the wide shoulders of his coat. His impassive face had set like concrete. "You all right, Dr. Blake?"

She nodded. "I seem to be recovered. Any sign of Badel regaining consciousness?"

"There's a chance he might come round soon, according to the doctors. I just spoke to them."

"Anything in Benson's apartment?" Kiley asked.

"Drawn a blank. The doorman couldn't tell us anything. Seems terrified in case you come looking for him, Kiley. What did you do to him?"

"I threatened him with money."

"I've got one piece of information that'll interest you. Benson *was* in the laboratory the night Hiroko copped it. He told the security guard not to enter his name in the book."

Kiley fingered his chin. "Hiroko must have known too much. Whatever's in that vial must be the result of this Project Alpha, and Benson couldn't afford to have anyone else knowing about it."

Withers nodded. "Seems likely enough. Now, I can understand how he got close enough to Hiroko to inject him with this stuff or do whatever he did to him, but what about the other victims? If Anne Warren and Bronson and all the rest were abducted, then how did Benson manage it? He's physically powerful—and we know he's got a gun—but you can't just snatch people off the streets in broad daylight. Someone would have seen something. Do you think he was working with someone?"

Kiley was a little taken aback at being asked a direct question by Withers. "Accomplices?" Kiley arched his spine and interlocked his fingers behind his head. "No, I think he's been working entirely alone." He snapped his fingers suddenly. "Of course! Benson didn't have to use physical force, just as he wouldn't have had to with Hiroko—for the same reason."

Withers frowned. "You lost me."

Kiley grinned. "Benson knew each of his victims, well enough for him to come up to them in the street and invite them somewhere. They, in turn, must have felt some sort of obligation to him, because they went willingly—otherwise we would have heard about it."

Withers was pondering Kiley's theory when the door opened again, and a young, sandy-haired doctor beckoned them outside. When they were huddled around him in the corridor, he spoke in a low undertone: "Major Badel is conscious, but extremely weak. The shock to his system has been too great, I fear. It's doubtful whether he'll pull through. Is it really that important that you speak to him?" He gave Withers an earnest, questioning look.

"It's vital, Doctor. He might be able to give us information that could save other lives."

The doctor stared at his shoes for a while, then nodded and led them to a door some forty yards farther down the corridor, opened it, and ushered them inside. Dim light glowed from one corner of the room, casting an eerie glow on Badel's recumbent form stretched flat out on the bed. The bedclothes stopped at his midriff and a heavy wad of bandaging lay over his stomach. The Major's chest, covered in curling steel-gray hairs, rose and fell with an unsteady rhythm. His eyes were open and he was staring up at the ceiling. There was a slight rattle in his throat with each breath. His mustache, an oddly vital appendage to the dying body, bristled out from the gray pallor of his cheeks.

The doctor motioned to the three of them; Withers took up a position on the near side of the bed, and Kiley and Mary walked around to the other side. Withers leaned over slightly, his shadow falling over the Major.

"I'm a policeman, Major Badel. I'd like to ask you some questions." He had to repeat himself before Badel registered his presence. Eyelids fluttered momentarily over eyes formerly blue, now drained of almost all color. The Major's uncertain gaze shifted slowly to Withers's face.

"Major Badel, do you know why we're here?" Withers's voice was quiet but clear.

"I've been thinking," Badel began in a low whisper. "Should make a clean breast of it. Strange how I'd forgotten all about it until now. Slips into place . . . Strange . . ."

Kiley found himself straining forward to catch the feeble words.

". . . My wife, you see. She came back to get me, pay me back. Least I thought she had. Wanted to cheat her . . ."

Withers coughed nervously. "Major, are you well enough to answer some questions?"

The Major's lips flickered into a faint smile under the mustache. "Not Jacqueline at all . . . I see that now. Something to do with the American . . . Benson." Mary's arm gripped at Kiley's sleeve.

Chapter Thirteen

"I killed my wife, you know."

Withers frowned. The atmosphere in the small room was hushed. "Major, you mentioned Benson just now. Did he come for you today?"

"Don't know ... unclear ... confused."

Kiley leaned farther forward. "Major, have you heard of Anne Warren, Max Bronson, Alan Brown? Do these names mean something to you?"

Badel's eyes swiveled as he tried to locate the source of the new voice. "Yes, yes, I know them all. That's what's so strange. I know it wasn't really my wife ... something to do with Benson. I never thought he'd take it this badly ... not that I can blame him. Bad episode."

"Major," Withers interrupted, "how did you come to know these people?"

"They're dead, all dead now, I think. I read about their deaths in the paper over the last week. I thought I knew them—recognized them somehow—but couldn't pinpoint where or when I'd met them. Now I know, now ..." His eyelids closed. The doctor stepped in beside Withers to check the cardiogram above the bed. The heartbeat was still uneven but gaining in strength. He nodded for Withers to continue.

"Where did you meet?" Withers asked.

Badel's eyes flickered open again. "Long time ago—six, seven years ..."

"1974, Major?" Kiley tried.

Badel closed his eyes and gave up keeping track of the different voices. "Yes, that's it. Winter, '74. November, I think. Beautiful, snow everywhere ... I'd never skied before ..."

"A holiday resort, Major?" Withers asked.

"Yes, a hotel. Marvelous hotel near a waterfall. Cold, damned cold . . . Norway."

Kiley slapped the palm of his hand against his forehead. The one occasion on which a group of disparate, high-income people was likely to meet was on vacation. He cursed his own slowness.

"I wanted a break," Badel continued. "My wife was visiting her mother. I was bored at home. Winter holiday seemed the answer." His voice was gaining in strength. "Booked it all just a few days in advance. Flew to Trondheim . . ."

"Where exactly is this hotel, Major?"

"Trying to recall . . . difficult, these foreign names, all those little dots and lines through the 'o.' Vøringfoss, I think. On the west coast. Fossli Hotel."

"Who was there, Major?"

"Some Norwegians . . ."

"Just the English members of your party," Withers said.

"And Americans," Kiley suggested.

"Americans, yes. Benson was there with his wife and their small boy. Another Yank—that singer chap who died yesterday. Heard about it on the car radio. Danaher. Horrible little fellow, ghastly chap. Drank too much. Language was appalling. Involved in some scandal . . ."

"Anne Warren? Was she there?" Kiley asked.

"Not Warren. Blake was her name then. Good-looking woman. Television or something. She had that car accident last week."

"Blake was Anne's maiden name, same as mine," Mary interjected.

"Mrs. Anstruther and her husband," Badel continued. "Rather long-faced. Missionaries of some sort, always on about diseases. Bad dinner companions . . ."

Withers had his notebook out and was scribbling away. "Alan Brown?"

"Yes, advertising chap. Read about him drowning in his bath. Didn't remember about him until now." His voice had risen to what Kiley guessed to be its normal timbre. It seemed oddly loud in the cramped little room. The Major's chest was rising and falling at a steady rate. Color had crept back into his cheeks.

"Anyone else?" Withers asked.

The Major was silent for a while. He seemed to be asleep. Kiley was about to lean forward and shake his arm when the old man began again: "Bronson . . . what we used to call a spiv. Dreadful person. Criminal type. Still, he didn't deserve to die in that way . . . There *was* someone else. No, I can't place them."

The doctor stepped forward and whispered in Withers's ear. The policeman stretched out the fingers of one hand to show how many more minutes were required. The doctor frowned and backed off, shaking his head.

"All right, Major, forget about the last person for the moment. Something happened on this holiday, I take it. Something nasty? To do with Benson?"

"Nasty, yes. Inadequate word for it really, but it'll do. It all took place on about the third morning of our visit. Glorious day. It had been snowing during the night. The sun was brilliant, and the air . . . wonderful. We all came down for breakfast—better if we'd never got up at all." He sighed. "When we were all gathered we decided to go down and take a look at the waterfall, which could be glimpsed from the dining room window. So far we'd spent our time making fools of ourselves on the ski slopes and hadn't even visited the main scenic attraction. The Bensons hadn't come down, one of the party noticed. Someone—I think it was Anne Blake—went up to their room to see what was wrong. Benson had caught a beastly cold and was in bed. His wife and son were there with him, waiting for the doctor to arrive. Seems that Benson had a sinus condition that made even mild colds hard to bear. Needed special medicine. The boy was looking a bit glum at the prospect of spending the day cooped up in the hotel with mum and dad, so Anne Blake suggested he come with the rest of us to see the falls. It was only going to take an hour at most. Mrs. Benson didn't seem too keen on the idea, but Benson apparently said why not. So Anne brought the child down to the lobby where we were all waiting for them."

He sighed again, shook his head slightly.

"Clem Danaher had a dreadful hangover. Alan Brown was teasing him. The Anstruthers were there, all wrapped up, looking grim, as if they were about to perform some unpleasant but necessary Christian duty. Bronson was lounging around, looking nervous about something. He was on tenterhooks the whole time he was there, as if he was expecting someone to arrive. I was reading aloud from a presentation board near the reception desk when Anne and the boy came down. It was all about how the first British explorer had only been able to see the falls by having his guide hold onto his feet while he leaned over the cliff face. At that stage there was apparently no other way of seeing it. It's all different now—they've built special vantage points. By the time I'd finished reading, the child was staring up at me, obviously entranced by the story.

"We all trouped out. I think Anne had the boy by the hand. He was about five or six, I suppose, a little blond-haired nipper—huge eyes. Intelligent for his age and well-behaved. Arnie was his name. At least, that's what he was always called. Short for Arnold, I expect.

"By the time we reached the observation platform which overlooks the falls from across the canyon we were in excellent spirits. It was a beautiful sight—water crashing down all of five hundred feet. It was thundering under our shoes. The boy was jumping up and down with excitement—I don't think he'd ever seen anything like it in his life. It was a delight just to watch him. Made one feel young again. We decided at that point to ape the original explorer by proceeding to the source and seeing whether we could peek over at the waterfall from there. We tramped around to that part of the cliff where the noise was loudest. It took us about twenty minutes to reach it. A continuous spray of water danced just below the ridge. It sparkled in the sun . . ." Badel's eyes opened. "It was beautiful," he added softly, then took a deep breath.

The doctor stepped over to Withers again. "Your five minutes are up," he whispered loudly enough for everyone to hear. "I really think that the Major should be allowed to rest."

Withers spoke quietly, without taking his eyes from Badel's face. "Doctor, nothing on earth is going to stop me from hearing what this man has to say."

"But you're probably killing him!"

"You said he was going to die anyway. I don't have a legal right, I know, but if you interrupt again I'll call in one of my men and have you removed from the room. Understood?"

The doctor's freckled face flushed a deeper red. "I'll report you for this, Inspector!"

"That's fine by me, Doc. For the meantime, keep quiet!"

Kiley's emotions were mixed. Withers was definitely in the wrong and yet it would have made Kiley sick to be denied the rest of Badel's tale. Perhaps the world needed men like Withers to make the lousy decisions.

"Go on, Major," Withers prompted. "Any time you want to stop, you tell me."

Badel gave a ghostly smile. "No. Must carry on. Feel better telling it. Never even mentioned it to my wife . . . So, we were at the cliff face near the source. I got down on my knees to look over, but it was difficult. The source was too well hidden. The falls started a little below us and to our right. The cliff face starts in a fairly gentle slope which goes down for about ten yards. That section's covered in a thin layer of earth where trees and bushes have taken root. After that ten yards, though, the cliff face plunges straight down. None of us dared go farther than five or six yards down the incline. After that it became rather dangerous.

"Anne Blake was the first to suggest it. 'No one as brave as our trusty British explorer?' she asked. I know she was only joking but it made me feel, you know, not quite a man. I said I'd be quite willing to do it if two people held onto my legs. Alan Brown told me not to be so foolish and added that, besides, I was far too heavy. I was relieved in a way because I never really like heights. The child, who had been listening to our conversation, began yelling that *he* should be allowed to do it. We laughed at him, but he wouldn't desist. He began whining after a while, you know, the way children do. Danaher, rather surprisingly, suggested that he would hold onto the boy's legs. I think he was trying to imply, in a rather nonsubtle fashion, that Alan Brown was a coward. The two of them hadn't been getting on at all well. Brown remained quiet after that. The Anstruthers protested and, as I didn't like their priggish attitude toward any sort of fun, I began to support Danaher after a while. Anne sounded rather worried about the whole scheme, but I think the child's whining was getting on her nerves, so she gave in to him as well. Bronson didn't seem to give a damn what happened.

"Sounds incredible now . . . stupidity of it . . . futile. But then again, Arnie was the obvious candidate, being so light. Danaher himself wasn't very large and therefore it seemed likely that the trees would support him without any trouble. Anyway, the sight of those magnificent falls thundering away directly beneath him was the sort of thing that would stay in the child's memory for the rest of his life." Badel paused. "The rest of his life," he repeated dully.

He gave a shuddering sigh. "We should have considered the boy's parents at that point . . . but we didn't. I blame myself for that. Danaher took the child's hand and led him down the incline until they had reached the last tree; they lay flat on the earth, pointing straight down the slope. He had one arm around a tree trunk, which looked solid enough. His other hand was clasped around the boy's ankles. Directly opposite us were the granite mountains and, hundreds of feet below, we could just make out the bottom of the gorge with the river flowing along it. Danaher seemed to have a tight hold on the boy, who wriggled farther down the slope until his head was over the edge. We heard him gasp. The child started yelling excitedly. That sound made the whole hare-brained scheme seem worthwhile. Danaher had taken his gloves off and, after a few seconds, shouted up that his hands were already cold and that it was painful hugging the tree trunk—I expect it was digging into his shoulder. Although Arnie was as light as a feather he was obviously exerting some strain on Danaher, who didn't look a particularly strong chap. I stepped a little way down the slope and suggested it was time for them to call it a day. By this stage, I was feeling distinctly nervous about the enterprise."

Badel's eyes glazed over and his breathing became labored. It was as if the whole scene were taking place in front of him at that instant.

"Everything went wrong at once. Danaher pulled his arm back in an attempt to drag the boy back up. In that instant Arnie must have craned farther forward to get a better look at the falls. The earth rumbled beneath us as if the volume of water spewing out of the cliff had suddenly increased."

Tears welled up in the old man's eyes and his speech became muffled. Withers bent closer to the Major.

"The boy tugged out of Danaher's grasp. Danaher didn't seem to realize at first that he was holding nothing but thin air—his fingers must have been quite deadened by the cold. I closed my eyes for a moment. One of the women screamed behind me. When I opened my eyes again, it was in time to see Arnie staring back up at me. In the fall the child had somehow managed to grasp onto an exposed tree root just above the ridge of the cliff. His other hand was scrambling at the earth. Only his head and shoulders were visible. His eyes were bulging from their sockets. His face had gone completely white. With his blond hair, he was like a ghost-child. The tree root slowly bent. I took another step down the incline, bellowing at Danaher." Badel sucked in a huge breath. "The tree root snapped," he exhaled. Badel's eyelids closed. Tears trickled from the corners of his eyes down his drawn, pallid cheeks. "I heard the child scream all the way down to the bottom. His cry echoed along the gorge for what seemed like an eternity afterward.

"We were frozen by the horror of it all. I don't know how long we stood there, staring at the spot from which the child had fallen. It seemed a long time, but it was probably no more than a few minutes. I think I was the first to move. I went down to where Danaher was still lying—he was crying, I remember—and tried to help him up. He was as stiff as a board. Shock, I suppose. Alan Brown joined me and, between us, we managed to get him onto the plateau above the cliff. Everyone looked stunned, sick. The Anstruthers were praying. It seemed damned irrelevant to me, almost tasteless, but I suppose they were just reacting in their own way to the horror of what they had witnessed.

"We struggled back to the hotel in silence, half-carrying Danaher. I remember touching his hand—it was the coldest thing I had ever felt. About a third of the way back we stopped to rest. Behind us the waterfall emitted a steady rumble—it was ominous, like a drum roll at a funeral. I glanced over at the hotel. The sun flashed off the windows on its southern side. I imagined I could see a face at one of them. Benson's face. Might have been sheer imagination. I looked away and kept my eyes averted until we were back in the hotel."

Badel's eyelids closed against the scene. The room was

silent for several seconds. When the Major resumed, his voice was cracked by exhaustion and grief.

"The police were called, but we were all dismissed. We packed and left after lunch—no one ate, of course. We didn't see the Bensons again. The hotel took care of breaking the news to them. I made inquiries through the travel agency when we got back to England. Apparently it took searchers a whole day to locate the child's body. I wrote to Benson a year or so later. I got no reply. I couldn't blame him. I learned later, through the newspapers, that his wife had died. It was in the obituary column. I never did learn the cause of her death."

"No legal proceedings were instituted against any of you?" Withers asked.

Badel shook his head almost imperceptibly. "The agency that organized the tour hushed the whole thing up. Some of the party were well-known people, and the publicity would have done nobody any good. The only interests that might have been served were those of justice, but that has long ceased to be of much importance in the world." Badel sighed. When he spoke again, his voice had dwindled to a gruff whisper. "I've committed two appalling sins in my life—one of omission, one of commission. The first was to murder my wife; about that I feel very little guilt. My second sin was to have been present at the death of Arnold Benson and to have done nothing about it. Benson has extracted his justice . . . I'm not altogether sure I bl——"

Badel's eyes opened wide. He began twisting his head from side to side. The veins in his neck bulged through translucent skin as his face turned a paler shade of blue.

The doctor ran to his side and pushed Withers away. Badel, ignoring the medic, half-rose from his pillow, and stared at Kiley, then at Mary, as if seeing them for the first time.

"Doctor!" he croaked, then slumped back, dead.

Mary turned to Kiley and placed her face against his chest. He reached up a hand to her head and held her there for a while. She was not crying, but Kiley knew exactly how she felt. It had been a day of horrors, and Kiley was not convinced that they had witnessed the last of them.

Withers, Kiley concluded, had to be one of the stars of the Metropolitan Police to get himself a private office while he was still a detective inspector—even if it was just a small cubbyhole on the fifth floor. Gray filing cabinets were ranged along whitewashed, cardboard-thin walls on which hung charts, maps, and photographs of wanted killers. Most of them looked like bank clerks.

Withers sat behind a small desk littered with papers and telephones. Mary and Kiley were positioned across from him in uncomfortable chairs that were supposedly molded to fit the human body. Kiley shifted irritably, convinced that a hunchbacked dwarf had been used in designing the prototype. The harsh strip-lighting hurt his eyes and gave the room a stark quality.

If Withers felt any guilt over Badel's death or was worried by the consequences of an unfavorable report from his doctor, he was doing a good job of hiding it. He was working his way through a recently completed stack of reports piled high in front of him, while Kiley and Mary sat with barely concealed impatience.

From the main squad room down the corridor they could hear the mixed sounds of ringing telephones, raised voices, and unevenly operated typewriters. Kiley caught Mary's eye and gave her an encouraging smile to which she barely responded. She had been badly upset by witnessing Badel's last moments. He turned his gaze to the window. It was past four o'clock and the sun had set, suffusing London in rusty twilight, an effect that Kiley normally appreciated.

Finally, Withers shoved the papers away, leaned back in his tattered, cloth-covered swivel-seat, and stared at the map of London behind Kiley's head.

"I've got a crack squad of ten men working on this and most of their reports are in," he said after a pause. His eyes were fixed to the map. "The married couple mentioned by Major Badel, of whom we previously had no knowledge, has been accounted for. Reverend Robert Anstruther died in Malawi five years ago during a native rebellion. He and his wife ran a leper colony there. We can hardly pin that one on Benson. However, Emily Anstruther, his widow, a sixty-two-year-old alcoholic living in Enfield, was discovered lying on the floor of her sitting room last Monday, dead from a heart attack."

"That was the extra death Benson let slip about," Kiley noted.

Withers nodded. "She lived alone, so we don't know whether she went missing during the days leading up to her death. Apparently she spent most of her time in a drunken fog, so she would have been an easy target. She'd been harassed by local kids. Her doctor thought that that was what had killed her." He concentrated on the map again. "However, we do know that Clem Danaher failed to turn up for a concert about a week before he died. His manager claimed that afterwards Danaher had no idea as to where he'd been."

"What about Badel?" Kiley asked.

"His wife's under heavy sedation and in no condition to answer questions." A thought seemed to trouble him. He dispelled it with a blink.

Kiley crossed his legs and grasped his knee with both hands. "I should have made the connection between 1974 and the death of Benson's son. It was all in the *Who's Who* entry. What about his wife? How did she die?"

"Drug overdose, sleeping tablets. She was being treated for depression at a private clinic in Surrey. That's another one we can't pin on Benson."

"Good God!" Mary exclaimed. "Imagine losing your wife and only child in such a short space of time. What a ghastly ordeal!"

Withers nodded thoughtfully. "According to the staff at Benson Pharmaceuticals, Benson acted strangely for several months after his wife's death. At one stage they thought they'd have to get rid of him, but he managed to pull through after a while. Or so it seemed."

"Any more news on what Hiroko was up to?" Kiley asked.

Withers reached out for one of the brown folders in front of him and flicked it open. "The present head of research claims that Hiroko started work on Project Alpha about six months before Benson became chairman. His work on it intensified after that."

"Perhaps the two events are related," Kiley mused.

"Could be," Withers conceded. "The project might have given Benson ideas to which he needed to devote more of his time."

"Any more sightings of Benson after Euston Station?" Mary asked.

Withers shook his head. "This is one hell of a big city, Dr. Blake—it's a nightmare to police. With any brains and a bit of luck, it's a simple matter to lose yourself out there."

Kiley nodded in agreement. "And Benson just needs another twenty-four hours to complete the job. There's one more victim to go, by my reckoning. I just wish Badel had been able to remember the name. What about the travel agency? Have they been able to help?"

"Liquidated two years ago—went bankrupt. Managing director seems to have pulled a fast one. Gone abroad, I shouldn't wonder. It's the best way of dealing with debts," Withers noted cynically. "We've telexed the Fossli Hotel, but we haven't had a reply yet."

"So we're down to two unanswered questions. How did Benson get inside the heads of his victims, and who is the last person on the list?"

Mary shrugged. "Perhaps the forensic scientists will come up with something for us."

As if on cue, one of the phones on Withers's desk rang. He located it by scattering a mound of paper. One thing hadn't changed since his leaving the force, Kiley noted with wry pleasure—the inability of even the highest ranking detectives to deal with paperwork.

Withers replaced the phone. "They've completed the analysis on the substance in the vial. They're typing out a report for us." He rose and went to the door. "Let's hope for the sake of the last victim that they've produced the goods."

After he had gone, Kiley perched on the side of Withers's desk, lit a cigarette, and studied Mary. The line of her dress was riding with pleasing effect above her knees. She caught Kiley staring at her exposed thigh.

"Enjoying yourself?" she asked curtly.

He grinned. "Just studying the bruises!" He added, seriously: "Will they be able to judge the effect of the stuff in the vial just from knowing what's it's made of?"

Mary rubbed the palms of her hands together as though they were sticky. "Impossible to tell, but it might give us a lead as to the kind of area Hiroko was working in and that might prove useful in the long term. But in the short run?" She shrugged. "Don't expect miracles."

"Why the pessimism?"

Mary got up and strolled to the window. "Do you remember what I said to you a few days ago? One drug alone could not have accounted for the way in which those people died. Nor could it account for my loss of memory."

Kiley grunted an acknowledgment.

"No matter what the forensic experts have found out, I stick by what I said. There are drugs that can induce states of extreme anxiety, hallucinations, heart attacks—almost anything you care to name—but they cannot conjure up . . ." She paused for a moment as if searching for the right phrase. "They can't conjure up psychic demons."

Kiley looked across at her sharply. "Isn't that a rather melodramatic way of putting it?"

Mary turned from the window and leaned back against it. "No, 'psychic demons' describes the phenomenon perfectly. Badel's first wife was no more nor less than a psychic demon. The hallucination was so powerful, so convincing, that Badel, a soldier, a man of action, by no means a coward, gutted himself with a bayonet rather than face up to it. This is the first *positive* proof we've had that what we're dealing with is not directionless fear, but a specific fear engendered by a specific hallucination."

"What's that got to do with demons?"

"Inside each of us there's a psychic demon—that one thing, above all others, that we fear most. It's not just a phobia, like a fear of rats or claustrophobia, but something far more concrete—and it's entirely individual. Sometimes we know what it is—Alan Brown's fear of water, for instance—but we *can* go through our whole life without realizing what it is. But often the mind undergoes a type of mental paralysis and the image is automatically buried. With enough time the image can be buried entirely out of sight of the conscious mind." She paused. "What's the worst thing that could happen to you?"

Kiley shrugged. "I have no specific big fears—just about a thousand little ones."

Mary shook her head. "You're wrong. Somewhere inside you there's a psychic demon of which you have no knowledge on a conscious level. It's so innately terrifying that you refuse to admit its existence. If it were to become a reality, if you were faced with it, it would literally stop your heart or drive you to kill yourself in the attempt to escape. The horror would be unbearable."

"Are you trying to scare me?" Kiley demanded in a humorous tone that didn't work.

Mary shook her head. "I'm just trying to convey to you something of what Anne and the others must have gone through. Anne got back in the car after the accident in which her husband was killed, thinking that her fear of another such incident had been dispelled. She was wrong. It was there, but it was buried deep in her subconscious. Last Friday morning her psychic demon was released. It drove her mad with terror and ultimately it killed her. All the victims died in the worst possible way."

Kiley shivered involuntarily. He was beginning to grasp the horror, the sheer chilling enormity of Benson's revenge.

The door opened.

"I've got them," Withers said, waving a piece of paper at them. "The results of the analysis."

Chapter Fourteen

Mary rose and took the sheet of paper from him. Withers sat down behind the desk. Kiley remained perched on the edge. Both men watched her closely as she read.

After a minute, she looked up.

"You'd better translate it into English for us," Kiley said before she could speak.

Mary studied the page again for a few seconds. "The vial contained a chemical solution, as we suspected. The drug was obtained by mixing two MAOIs—monoamine oxidase inhibitors. You remember, Kiley, I mentioned them to you. They're antidepressant drugs used to treat neurotic forms of depression. Benson's company is the leader in the field. According to the report, Hiroko mixed constituent elements from two well-known MAOIs."

Mary looked up from the page and shook her head slowly. "But I don't see what's so special about this compound. I'm pretty sure such a mixture would have been tested before this stage."

"Could the compound be dangerous in *any* way?" Kiley asked.

"I don't think so. Obviously you can never be entirely positive without doing a vast series of tests on animals and, ultimately, on human guinea pigs, but I wouldn't have thought that this compound taken in the correct dosage, would have any harmful effects."

"And if an overdose were to be administered?" Kiley tried.

"Death *has* been known to occur with this type of drug, but an overdose normally merely results in a hypertensive crisis—painful throbbing in the neck and occipital area, a

157

pain that becomes excruciating. Essentially we're just talking about high blood pressure."

"How do these drugs work exactly?" Kiley asked.

Mary sat down slowly. "That's one of the problems. No one knows *exactly*. Then again, no one really knows how aspirin or Valium works. We just know *that* they do." She frowned. "You're bound to accuse me of deliberately going over your heads, but here goes. It seems likely that a person's mood is regulated in some extent by enzymes in the brain—a nervous breakdown is ultimately the result of some chemical or physical malfunction. In other words, the enzymes are affected and that, in turn, causes depression. The enzymes that seem to be most strongly connected with depression are the monoamines. MAOI drugs work by raising the concentration of monoamine enzymes in the nervous system. That seems to lift patients out of their depression. Did I lose you somewhere along the line?"

Withers looked baffled, but Kiley spoke up. "Let me see if I've got this straight. If I'm depressed, there's a lack of certain enzymes in my brain. These MAOIs work by creating more of those enzymes and getting the balance back to normal."

Mary gave a wry smile. "Right. Now all we have to decide is how this chemical compound helped Benson in killing seven people." She paused. "Let's forget about the deaths for a moment and address ourselves to specifics. How did this MAOI allow Benson to put specific thoughts in my head?"

"Perhaps it's a drug that helps to hypnotize people," Kiley suggested.

Mary shook her head. "There are far simpler ways of getting people into a hypnotizable state. To simulate a hypnotic trance in me, all Benson would have had to do was press in on the carotid artery in my neck. I wouldn't have blacked out entirely, but it would have left me confused and woozy—only that process leaves bruising, which I don't have."

"Okay, let's rule out hypnosis," Kiley suggested.

"Now that I've raised that problem, there's another one to consider: leaving aside the actual effect of the drug, how much of it would each victim need in order to respond? Drug dosage varies enormously from one person to the next. People differ widely in the rate at which they metabolize, absorb, and excrete drugs. Benson would have had no way of knowing how each of the victims would react to a specific dose."

"Maybe he administered a massive overdose to every one," Kiley tried.

"A good idea, but then I didn't suffer any of the side effects normally associated with an overdose of this type of drug."

Kiley shrugged. "Shouldn't we be trying to figure out the effect of the drug rather than how it was administered or how much of it was needed?"

Mary tapped her fingernails against the paper in her hand. She smiled. There was something triumphant about it. "There's no point in attempting to figure out the effect unless we know *who* the drug was meant to be affecting."

Kiley sighed. "The victims, naturally."

"There are no needle marks on my body." Mary paused to let the fact sink in. "I checked myself carefully this morning. I haven't been injected at all."

"Then this drug," Kiley said, pointing to the piece of paper, "is just a red herring."

Mary shook her head. "Not at all, Kiley. It's still the key to everything. If my theory is correct, then *none* of the victims was injected with it."

Kily laughed sarcastically. "How can the drug be the key to everything if it wasn't used on anybody?"

"Oh, I didn't say it wasn't used on anybody. We've been approaching this from the wrong angle. I'm sure that when Benson first took this vial out of the locker it contained more of the drug than it did when you picked it up, Kiley."

Kiley passed a hand over his mouth. Furrow lines appeared on his brow. "Then what happened to the rest of it?"

Mary smiled cryptically. "One thing's for sure—Benson didn't pour it down the toilet!" She turned to Withers. "Could you get forensic to prepare some of this solution? It shouldn't take them long. I only need three hundred milligrams."

Withers stared at her for several seconds, as if questioning her sanity. "I'll do it on condition that you tell us right now what your theory is."

Mary glanced toward the window. The world outside

was shrouded in darkness. "Benson didn't inject this solution into his victims. He injected it into himself."

There was a pause of several seconds while the two men assimilated the idea. Kiley raised his hand to his eyes as if to shield them from the harsh overhead lighting. "Have you got anything else to go on?"

Mary nodded. "The first two times you saw Benson you mentioned the fact that he was sweating heavily."

"I noticed it when I was taking his statement yesterday," Withers said. "I just put it down to nerves."

Mary shook her head. "I told you, it's a classic side effect of this sort of antidepressant. Benson has been overdosing himself. Inspector, I want some of this chemical solution so that I can perform a little experiment. I'm on the verge of an explanation. Don't hold me back."

Withers pursed his lips. "Who's going to take part in this experiment? If you want forensic involved in anything of this sort it needs the authority of the chief superintendent . . . and he's on holiday for the next three days."

"Don't worry, Inspector, *I'm* going to take part in the experiment."

"Brave girl," Kiley congratulated her.

She gave him a mischievous look. "And you, Kiley, are going to be the subject of it."

He groaned. "I knew there'd be a bloody catch in it."

Mary turned to Withers. "One more thing, Inspector. I want absolute secrecy. Apart from me, you and Kiley are the only ones who can know about it. I have an idea we're about to discover something exciting, something that might be best kept to ourselves for the time being."

Withers rose wearily from his desk, strolled to the window, and stared out for the best part of a minute. He turned to face them at length. "All right, Doctor, you're on."

The small basement laboratory was no larger than Withers's office. The lighting was just as relentless. Thick, off-white paint was peeling from brick walls. The furniture was limited to two chairs, what looked like an operating table, and a waist-high shelf attached to one wall. Withers was sitting on one of the two chairs. Kiley was propped up on the table, and Mary was standing by the shelf. The sleeve of her silk blouse was rolled up and she was dabbing alcohol onto her skin with a ball of cotton. A bottle half-filled with a clear liquid and a full syringe lay on the shelf.

"I don't know if I can let you go ahead with this," Withers said as she reached out for the syringe. "I think I was a little hasty in agreeing. If the chief super ever finds out, I'm out. Besides, there should be a doctor present."

"I *am* a doctor, Inspector." Mary squirted air bubbles from the top of the syringe, holding it up to the light, then plunged the needle into her arm before Withers had time to raise further objections. Kiley looked away, wincing.

Mary placed the empty syringe on the table and wiped at a pinprick of blood with a fresh wad of cotton. "Too late now, Inspector. Besides, it's past six o'clock. Time isn't exactly on our side. This is our one chance of gaining ground on Benson." She glanced at Kiley. "You're not looking very well. Are you sure you want to go through with this?"

"Don't worry. Injections always have that effect on me." Then, as an afterthought, he asked, "Just what are you going to do to me?" He had consented readily enough to act as a guinea pig, but now, in the claustrophobic atmosphere of the cramped, antiseptic laboratory, he was feeling distinctly nervous.

"Don't worry, Kiley. You'll be quite safe. I think it's better if you don't know what I'm up to. After all, Benson's victims couldn't have known what he was doing to them."

"Thanks," Kiley groaned. "That's really set my mind at rest. How long before we start?"

"I think we should give the drug twenty-five minutes or so to take effect."

Withers gave an enormous yawn. Mary and Kiley looked over at him. The inspector's face showed signs of extreme fatigue: dark patches had appeared under his red-rimmed eyes and his lower lips was hanging loose, as if keeping it up were too much of an effort. The scars on his face were livid white streaks against his skin.

"I suppose you were up all night?" Kiley asked. Much of his animosity toward Withers had evaporated since they had begun to work together, antipathetic personalities united against a common enemy. Somehow, the black eye Withers had left him with seemed fairly unimportant now.

"It doesn't matter. I'm used to it," Withers responded gruffly. The force of the statement was neutralized by the second massive yawn that accompanied it. "Sorry," he gasped out. He rubbed vigorously at his eyelids with his index fingers. "Don't know what's come over me."

"It's called exhaustion, Inspector," Mary noted dryly. "Why don't you go and rest somewhere? I'm sure I can handle this all right on my own. Just lock the door from the outside so that we won't be disturbed."

Withers blinked his eyes wide open. "Nonsense. I know you want privacy, but that's taking it too far. If anything goes wrong, I'll be the one who gets roasted. Anyway, I'm damned sure Benson isn't asleep, wherever the hell he is."

"Take a catnap, then. I'll wake you up before I start the experiment."

Withers nodded. "It'd be easier than arguing with you. Okay, just for a few minutes." He rested the back of his wide, squat head against the wall behind him. After a few moments his mouth had opened slightly again and the room vibrated with his snoring.

Mary, still holding the ball of cotton against her arm, sat down. Kiley lay back on the couch and closed his eyes.

"You stay awake!" Mary commanded. Kiley ungummed his eyelids and sighed. They chatted for twenty minutes, then Mary glanced at her watch. "Okay, I think we've waited long enough."

"This is the big moment, huh?" Kiley asked, feeling an involuntary twist in his gut.

"Or a terrible anticlimax." Mary shrugged. "Still, we have nothing to lose—except the life of Benson's last victim. Now I want you to close your eyes and make your mind as blank as possible." She moved her chair close in to the table. "If you feel an urge to do something, anything at all, act on it."

"Shouldn't we wake up Withers? After all, we promised."

Mary glanced over at the Inspector's slumbering form. His chin had fallen onto his chest. "No, let him rest. Unless Benson is located soon, I expect he'll be up all of tonight as well." Kiley noted the fierce determination in her face, the sudden hardness in her eyes, and decided not to make a fuss about it.

Mary closed her eyes as well, her face impassive. She

could hear the policeman's snores and tried to block them from her mind. Soft industrious noises floated in from the main forensic laboratory next door.

"Getting anything?" Mary asked after a few minutes of silence.

"Not a damn thing."

"Okay, we'll keep trying. I *can't* have made a mistake."

Kiley's initial nervousness had worn off. He was beginning to feel bored and not a little ridiculous lying there. "Maybe if you told me what you were trying to do, it might help."

Mary's voice betrayed impatience. "If you knew before hand, the whole point of the experiment would be lost."

He relaxed again. He thought of the victims. The faces of the dead floated in front of his closed eyelids.

"Do you feel an urge to do anything yet?" Mary demanded after another minute had passed.

"Yeah," Kiley responded with sarcasm, "I'd like to take a leak." He opened his eyes and turned his head to look at her. Mary's eyes were still screwed shut. Kiley noticed a movement from across the room.

Withers was awakening with a series of rapid, uncontrolled body jerks. As Kiley watched, the Inspector's eyes opened wide. With a choked yell the big man shot out of his chair. He stumbled forward onto his knees and remained on the ground for a few seconds, his face twisted in pain.

Kiley gave a nervous laugh. There was something half-comic, half-chilling about the scene. "What's up, Inspector? A cramp?" Kiley asked, propping himself up on the table with his elbow.

Mary, hearing the question, opened her eyes and looked at him for a moment. "Did you shout out just now? Did you get something?"

Kiley pointed beyond her shoulder. She turned. Withers lumbered to his feet and turned to give the empty chair an angry scowl.

"My God, it worked!" Mary whispered.

Withers shook his head slowly.

"I think the strain's been too much for you, Inspector," Kiley observed.

Mary shook her head wonderingly. "Not at all. It

worked. It actually worked." Her voice was rising with excitement.

Kiley reached out his hand to her shoulder. "Hey, Mary, take it easy. Maybe you've been doing too much yourself."

Mary turned on him. "It worked, damn you! Can't you see that?" She pointed at Withers. "That was the effect my mental signals should have had on you. I was trying to get you to imagine that the table was red-hot. I wanted to see you shoot off it like a scalded cat. It's the easiest way to get a positive reaction in hypnosis experiments. Only *you* didn't respond. Withers got the message instead of you!"

"What the hell is happening in here?" Withers muttered. "I was asleep." He bent over and reached out his fingertips to touch the seat, tentatively at first. He grasped the wood firmly, then turned to Mary. "When I woke up, the chair felt as if it was on fire. My whole back was burning up." He shook his head confusedly. "What in Christ's name is going on?"

Kiley slid off the table and helped Withers back into his seat. The Inspector pressed his fists against his temples and looked up worriedly at Kiley. "What happened to me?"

Mary appeared beside Kiley. "My experiment worked, Inspector. I know how Benson managed to get inside the heads of his victims."

Withers groaned and covered his eyes with his hands. "Let me get my own head clear, then explain it to me."

Mary walked over to the shelf and held up the glass bottle next to the syringe. Withers blinked several times. "Okay, I'm ready. How did Benson manage it?"

Mary leaned back against the shelf and held the bottle aloft between forefinger and thumb, waving it slightly. "This chemical solution," she said slowly, attempting to conceal her excitement, "probably *is* an antidepressant, judging by its constituent chemicals. More important, much, *much* more important, it allows a human being to make contact with other human beings without recourse to the normal sensory channels."

Withers looked up at Kiley questioningly. The detective shrugged his shoulders.

"Listen, both of you. Human beings relay information to each other in a variety of ways, *all* involving the senses—sight, touch, smell, et cetera. I can speak to you, make facial expressions, touch you in a certain way. In short, there are several methods of communication open to us. There is another method of communication which science shies away from because it has so far been unable to explain it—the purely mental."

Kiley snapped his fingers. "You're talking about telepathy, right?"

Withers snorted disbelievingly. "You can stop right there, Doctor. It's all fairy tales. Telepathy? It's like ghosts and astrology—garbage."

"Inspector," she went on quietly, "telepathy is anything but a fairy tale. There are hundreds of recorded instances of mental communication between human beings, sometimes when they're hundreds of miles apart. Many of these instances are well documented and scientifically verifiable. Take identical twins, for instance; it happens between them all the time. Lacking an explanation, scientists have tended to turn a blind eye to the phenomenon and their skepticism has infected the general public. Believe me, it happens. Telepathic communication is a solid fact of life."

Kiley shrugged again. "I'm willing to listen until something more likely comes along."

"It won't." Mary said forcefully. "This drug obviously acts as a telepathic agent. Hiroko cracked the secret of telepathy—probably purely by accident. Both of you know what just took place. I was sending out a mental signal. You picked it up, Inspector. I wrote nothing down, I didn't speak, I was several yards away from you when you imagined that the chair was burning up. The only way I could possibly have communicated with you was on a mental plane."

"Then why me instead of Kiley?" Withers asked. "After all, you were directing your signal at him. I was asleep."

"Perhaps only certain people are able to receive telepathic signals," Kiley suggested.

Withers shook his head. "Doesn't fit the facts of the case. *If* what Benson did to the victims had something to do with telepathy—not to mention what he did to Dr. Blake here—then all of them must have received his signals. They all acted on them."

Mary sat down slowly on the edge of the table. She stared at the clear solution in the bottle for a while with a perplexed expression. She was perspiring heavily.

Withers began pacing the room, hands behind his back. He stopped suddenly and wheeled around to face them. "I was asleep," he repeated softly. "That was the difference between you and me, Kiley. I was dead to the world." He looked at Mary.

At first she failed to respond, as if she had not been listening, then she gripped the bottle hard and returned his gaze. "Inspector, you're right. You *were* asleep—that's why you picked up my message. That's why Hiroko called it Project Alpha. It all fits into place. 'Alpha' was the key to everything. I should have guessed it sooner. I should have realized what it meant before this experiment ever took place."

"Jigsaw puzzles never were my strong point, Mary. How about explaining what you're talking about."

"Ever hear of Alpha waves, either of you?"

Withers responded after a pause. "Brain waves, aren't they? Don't look so surprised, Doctor. I was waiting for a witness to recover from a road accident once and when his brain waves stopped functioning he was pronounced dead. That's where I remember it from."

"Excellent, Inspector! Brain death is measured by an electroencephalograph. When it reveals that there's no longer any electrical activity in the brain—in other words, when there are no longer any brain waves—the patient is pronounced clinically dead. There's no longer any possibility of even partial recovery, and the doctor is no longer under any obligation to sustain life." She paused. "Now, there are four separate identifiable types of brain wave operating on different cycles. The most important are Theta and Alpha waves. Whichever type of brain wave is dominant depends entirely upon a person's mental state."

"What kind of mental state is associated with Alpha waves, then?" Kiley asked.

"Alpha waves predominate whenever a person is in a state of detachment, relaxation, sleeping—all those states that imply a reduction in the cognitive processes or a lack of alertness." Mary glanced at her watch. "If both of you had been wired to an EEG machine ten minutes ago, you, Kiley, would have shown more activity in the Theta cycle, because you were wide awake and not relaxed, while your brain, Inspector, would have had Alpha waves predominating.

"Benson's solution"—she raised the bottle aloft again—"this solution is the result of Project Alpha. When it's injected into a person this chemical mixture releases telepathic energy, and that energy can *only* be received by a person in whose brain the Alpha waves predominate." She looked at the two men beseechingly. "Do you understand?"

Kiley nodded slowly. "I'm beginning to. You've got to be relaxed, dazed, or asleep before you can receive mental commands of the person who has injected himself with the solution. For instance, you, Mary, were unconscious when Benson put the false story into your head. He made sure of that. That's what you meant when you remembered lying in the darkness, hearing whispers *inside* your head. Benson was speaking to you direct." Suddenly Kiley looked frightened. "Jesus! Can you imagine the power of this stuff?"

"I'd rather not," Mary said. "But you're right. When Benson put that new story into my head, the one in which it was *you* that attacked me, all he did was wipe my brain clean and feed in new data. It was as easy as putting a new tape in a cassette deck."

Withers scratched his head reflectively. "Is that why Major Badel couldn't remember where he had met the people whose deaths he read about in the paper?"

"Precisely," Mary nodded. "All memory of them was wiped from his mind—but the shock that Badel suffered brought it all back to him at the end. The whole process is like hypnosis, only it makes hypnosis look like a cheap conjuring trick. It's hypnosis taken to the ultimate limit."

"All right," Withers said, obviously pleased at having caught up with his companions, "so Benson met his victims on the street, got them up to his place—probably using the private elevator from the garage—put them to sleep, either by physical violence or by drugging them, then injected himself with the chemical solution. After that, he gave them a series of commands. When they got back to wherever they'd been picked up from, they had no memory of meeting Benson, or of the Norwegian holiday." He rubbed his hands together. "That just about wraps it up, then."

"Not quite, Inspector," Kiley frowned. "There's one last

victim out there somewhere who's going to go through living hell unless we get to him first."

Mary nodded. "And we've still got to figure out how Benson sets them off in the first place. The victims are primed to die on certain days. How does he manage that?"

Kiley checked his rear-view mirror as they drove by Regent's Park. The lights of the police car following them were discernible: twin fluorescent spots in the black, windswept night.

Kiley looked at his watch. The minute hand was edging toward midnight. He thought about informing Mary of this unpleasant fact, but a quick, sideways glance revealed that she was still asleep and he didn't have the heart to wake her. Her pert face was drawn with fatigue.

Kiley felt decidedly gloomy. They had waited patiently for over five hours at Scotland Yard, and had drawn a blank. The Fossli Hotel register for 1974 had been destroyed in a recent fire. All the police had been able to discover about the managing director of the travel agency who had organized the Norwegian trip was that he was "somewhere in Surrey." The first surge of elation they had felt at discovering both the motive and method for Benson's crimes within the space of a few hours had evaporated rapidly. There was little point to solving the case unless the final victim on Benson's deadly list could be saved.

Above the low hum of the car, Kiley heard a church bell strike the hour somewhere in the distance. It was the death knell for some poor bastard. He shivered at the thought that another life was about to be cut tragically short because of Benson's futile bitterness.

When they arrived at Marlin Crescent, Kiley helped Mary into the house. The day had been a long, traumatic one for both of them, and it had been her utter exhaustion that had convinced Kiley to take her home to sleep.

Two policemen—one of them Withers's top sergeant—were deputized to remain on duty in Mary's living room one at each window, while two more remained on duty in the car outside. Kiley slipped them a bottle of Scotch from Mary's drink cart. They didn't even try and refuse it. When they were all in place, Kiley led Mary upstairs to her room. They sat on the edge of the bed for a while, sipping brandies which Kiley had poured.

An assumption existed between them that needed no words. There was an inevitability about the event which did nothing to mar their mutual enjoyment of it. They undressed each other slowly, languorously, and began to make love, caressing each other with a sure, sensual tenderness. They were like lovers who had come to know each other's bodies over a long period of intimacy.

Kiley lay on his back afterward, humming. It was a long time since it had been so good; a long, long time . . . He smoked a cigarette and listened to the sharp, insistent sound of the rain drumming against the windowpane. Its urgency shattered his reverie and awoke the image of Benson in his head. Somewhere out there in the darkness were killer and victim. After a while the image faded and he became conscious of Mary sleeping peacefully beside him, her head nestled in the crook of his shoulder. He had just made love to a woman who, only a few hours before, had tried to kill him. He felt his eyelids grow heavy as he reflected upon the irony of the situation. He reached down and stubbed out his cigarette in the ashtray on the floor by the bed; then, resting a hand on the flat of her stomach, he molded his hard, muscular body to Mary's soft curves.

In the seconds before he drifted gratefully into dreamless sleep he wondered whether Benson's final victim was enjoying his last night on earth.

Chapter Fifteen

The jangling of the phone beside the bed woke him. Groaning, Kiley stretched out one hand and hoisted the receiver to his ear. By opening his eyelids a fraction he could tell that murky dawn had arrived.

He tried to speak but found that his mouth was thick with sleep. The voice at the other end of the line brought him into a sitting position immediately.

"November twenty-fourth. Today is November twenty-fourth." Benson's voice was not much more than a low whisper, but unmistakable nevertheless.

Kiley opened his mouth to speak, but something about the oddness of the message decided him against revealing his identity to the American. The receiver clicked loudly in his ear. He held the phone in front of his face for a moment, staring at it curiously.

If Benson had phoned the house, it would have been in order to speak to Mary Blake. But why should he find it necessary to announce the date to her?

Kiley swung his legs out of bed and looked over his shoulder. Mary was still asleep, her head nestled deep into the pillow, the sheet pulled up to the line of her shoulder. Kiley reached out a hand and was about to rouse her when he heard a movement downstairs.

Dragging on his pants he walked out of the bedroom to the head of the stairs. The plainclothes sergeant was standing in the front hall, frowning. Kiley tripped down toward him.

"Did you listen in on the call?" Kiley asked.

The cop nodded. He was a young man with a sharp, intelligent face. "What there was of it. I must have picked it up at the same moment you did."

"Am I right in thinking that all he did was repeat today's date?" The cop nodded again. "And it *is* November twenty-fourth?"

"Yes, it is, but why should he remind Dr. Blake of the fact? Maybe he wanted to speak to you."

Kiley shrugged—he had no answer for the cop—and stepped into the living room. The curtains were open and the room was bathed in obscure light. The other cop was sitting next to the coffee table, by the phone. "Was that Benson, sir?" he asked.

"Skip the 'sir' routine, please." He paused, standing with his hands on his hips. "It was definitely Benson. Private phone too, by the sound of it. I wonder where the hell he's phoning from."

"From what the DI told us, we know Benson's a bit of a nut, but that phone call was really weird. Does it mean anything, Mr. Kiley? Perhaps we should wake up Dr. Blake and ask her if she can explain it," the cop suggested.

A warning bell rang somewhere deep in Kiley's head. "Maybe we should just leave her alone for a while. Perhaps he'll ring again . . ." The strident buzzing of the phone cut across his last words. Kiley made a lunge for the receiver before the cops could get to it.

He held his breath and listened.

"Dr. Blake?"

Kiley breathed out with relief. It was Withers. "No, Inspector, it's Kiley. We've just had a phone call from Benson."

"Benson? What did he have to say for himself?"

"Nothing. He just repeated the date and then rang off. He must have thought he was speaking to Mary Blake. I didn't say anything. We're still trying to figure out what he's playing at."

"Save yourself the effort. Today's a significant day for Benson."

"How come?"

"Arnold Benson fell to his death on November twenty-fourth, 1974."

"Holy Christ. But why announce it to Mary?"

"We located the managing director of that travel agency an hour ago. He's living under an assumed name now. At first he wasn't willing to reveal the identity of the last person on the Norwegian trip, but I told Surrey C.I.D. to lean on him. They got him to cough it up. I think they're even rougher than us down in the country."

"So we know who the final victim is."

"Yes, we do. Is Dr. Blake awake?"

Kiley was momentarily confused by the nonsequitur. "She was sleeping upstairs when I left her a few moments ago. Why do you want to know?"

Withers paused. "Send my sergeant up to check that she's still out. If she's asleep, leave her. If she's awake, then tell him to bring her downstairs, but, whatever he does, he mustn't speak to her!"

Kiley gave the young cop the order, then turned his attention back to the phone. "Why can't he speak to her? What's up?"

"Kiley, you're going to find this hard to believe. Just take it as gospel truth."

Kiley groaned. "Come on, Withers, spit it out!"

"We *do* know the identity of the last person who was present at Arnold Badel's death." He paused. "It was Dr. Mary Blake."

A shockwave broke over Kiley. The carpet under his feet felt like broken glass, the phone was a lump of freezing metal in his hand, the room seemed airless. He brought one hand up to his forehead, trying to bring his mind back to order. "Are you sure?"

Withers's tone was cold. "We've double-checked it. At first I thought there was some mixup with the names. You know, Anne Warren was called Anne Blake at that time, but the bloke from the travel agency was right. Dr. Blake was there when Arnold Benson died. She was staying at the hotel with her sister. They went on holiday together."

Kiley's attempted laugh died in his throat. "Withers, it sounds as if Benson got to you as well. How could Mary possibly have been there? It's preposterous! Impossible!"

"Impossible's not a word that has much meaning when applied to this case, Kiley. It was impossible that Badel didn't recognize his dead companions when he read about them. It was impossible for Dr. Blake to believe that you had attacked her yesterday . . ."

Kiley shook his head to clear it. "When could he have done it? I'd already spoken to Mary about Benson before he got his hands on her yesterday. She was *sure* she didn't know him—and let's face it, that holiday would have been hard to forget."

Withers hummed reflectively. "He must have got to her before yesterday."

It hit Kiley in a flash and he gasped. "Of course! I know when he did it. She told me that she spent last Sunday with friends in the country. I bet she never got there. Benson must have used the drug on her *after* Anne Warren's death." He paused. "Hang on, there's a problem. Mary told me about Alan Brown on Monday, the day after Benson first got to her. Why hadn't she forgotten all about him?"

"Simple, Kiley. Benson just wiped out all memory of the vacation from the minds of the victims. Mary knew about Alan Brown from *after* the holiday. Anyway, it doesn't matter much now. All I know is, Dr. Blake mustn't be allowed to wake up. Is that clear? We don't yet know how he triggers his victims off, but—"

"Yes we do, Inspector," Kiley interrupted. "That phone call this morning was the trigger mechanism. Giving her the date was Benson's way of setting her off. Each of his victims had a certain date assigned for their deaths. When they realized what day it was . . . boom! Today he was taking no chances. He wanted to make sure that Mary got the message loud and clear. It makes sense. It's almost impossible to get through the day without hearing the date at some stage. Anne Warren heard it on the car radio . . . remember, it was just after the eight o'clock news when she went crazy. Bronson got up late and wandered into the Dug-Out. He must have heard it on the television."

"You're right!" Withers cut in. "Badel's diary was open on his desk and Alan Brown had just finished reading the Sunday papers. Okay, we'll leave the rest of the details till later. I'm sending round an ambulance for Dr. Blake. If your theory's correct, Kiley, we can save her life simply by keeping her unconscious for the entire day. We'll take her to the West Central Hospital and put her in Badel's old room. The doctors are used to us and my men know the layout of the place."

"Okay, but make sure the ambulance gets here *fast*."

Kiley put down the phone and ran upstairs, remembering to keep it light-footed. The young sergeant was standing outside the half-open bedroom door, peering through at the bed. He turned to meet Kiley, placing his index finger against his lip.

"She's still asleep," he whispered.

Kiley nodded. "Good. They're sending an ambulance right away. She mustn't be allowed to wake up. It could kill her."

The cop stared at him incredulously. "Are you being serious?"

"No time for explanations. Go out to the gate. Make sure they have some kind of sedative ready and that they don't make too much of a racket getting into the house." The cop glided away down the stairs.

"Kiley? Is that you?" He froze when he heard Mary's sleepy voice coming from inside the bedroom. His body tense, he put on a cheerful grin and went inside.

She was sitting up in bed, holding the sheet against her breasts with one hand, running the fingers of the other hand through her tousled hair. She returned his smile, yawning. "Thank God it's you. For one awful moment I thought it might be Benson. I heard the phone ringing. Anything important?"

Kiley knelt on the edge of the bed and leaned over toward her. "Nothing important, Mary," he said softly, trying to keep the panic from his voice.

Mary said, "I suppose this is the big day, then," still smiling. "I hope Benson hasn't got to his victim already." She turned away from him and reached out for her watch lying on the bedside table. Kiley realized it was digital. The date would be shown quite clearly on the face.

"Mary!" he said sharply. She turned back toward him, surprised. Her smile flickered.

He shook his head sadly. "Believe me, I'm sorry for what I'm about to do." Steeling himself, he balled his fist. It traveled no more than six inches to her chin. Her eyes rolled upward a split second after the punch and she fell back on the pillow.

"Sorry, kid," he muttered and pulled the sheet that had fallen from her grasp back over her naked breasts.

The hospital room was much as Kiley remembered it from the previous day; the same stillness, the same muted lighting, the uneasy presentiment of death lingering in its corners.

Mary was unconscious on the bed that Badel had occupied, her head lying on the pillow at the same angle that the Major's had at the moment of death. Except for the slight rise and fall of her belly under the sheet, she could have been a corpse.

"Are you sure this is the right place for her?" Kiley asked Withers, who was standing on the other side of the bed.

"Pretty woman, isn't she," Withers noted rather absently, then said: "Yes, this is the right place. Security might have been tighter at the Yard, but we don't have the medical facilities there, as you know. If something should go wrong, she'll have the very best medical attention immediately." He looked over at Kiley. "I *have* thought about this, you know."

Kiley shrugged. "I know, I know. I'm just scared, I suppose. It's knowing that the potential for her own destruction is locked up inside her head. It's as if that bastard Benson had wrapped sticks of dynamite around her body that'll explode if she makes one move." He paused. "Couldn't we have hypnotized her and wiped out Benson's commands in that way?"

"I checked on that. The dynamite metaphor applies to that as well, unfortunately. There's a danger that a hypnotherapist trying to counteract Benson's signals through hypnosis might just set off the trigger by mistake. It's a chance we can't afford to take."

Kiley nodded. "I suppose not. I just wish there was something else we could do."

"Listen, in some ways we've had a break. Until this morning we had no idea who the last victim was. Now we have her and she's getting the best protection available. Apart from him"—he indicated a uniformed constable visible through a wire-mesh partition set in the door—"there's another two on guard at the elevator entrance and another two in reception. They're all armed and they're all crack marksmen. They know just how dangerous this bastard is. Benson hasn't got a hope in hell of getting into this room. Dr. Blake is completely safe."

Kiley shrugged. "I just don't know. I'm beginning to suspect that Benson has supernatural powers. Imagine being able to wipe Mary's mind completely clean. It's uncanny."

"Kiley, he's like any other criminal. Take away their guns and they're powerless; take away Benson's drug and he's nothing."

"Benson isn't your average villain. He's got one hell of a brain. Let's face it, he's made monkeys of us so far." Kiley looked back down at Mary. Her jaw was slack. "I haven't damaged her, have I?"

"The doctor said she's fine. You've nothing to feel guilty about—probably saved her life."

Kiley shrugged. "What am I supposed to do now? I couldn't stand any more waiting around. My nerves are shot to hell. If I could just get my hands on that son of a bitch, I'd—"

"You could phone your mate at the *Daily Express*," Withers cut in.

"Prince? Surely you don't want to release the story yet?"

"Too bloody right I don't. I want Benson locked away before we tell the press. It's just that Prince has been on the phone to the Yard this morning pestering me."

"That early? That's not like him."

"Says he's got something urgent to tell you. Refused to divulge it to me."

Kiley frowned. "Did he say what it was about?"

"No, but at least a phone call would keep you occupied for a few minutes. He's at home waiting for you to call him. Here's his number." Withers handed Kiley a piece of paper with a seven-digit number scrawled on it.

Kiley gave Mary one long last look. He wanted to reach out and touch her but was afraid of waking her. Nodding his thanks to Withers, he moved out into the corridor past the cop on duty and headed for the waiting room, where he remembered seeing a pay phone. He got through after a minute.

"Kiley, my old dear, how are you? Most worried about you I was. I take it from Withers that you're no longer a wanted man."

"Prince, this isn't really the day for pleasantries."

"Oh, tut, tut! Less speed, more haste. From a police communiqué issued yesterday I see our old friend Benson is on the lam. The police want to question him in connection with the death of a Major Badel. I take it that this has something to do with the other deaths we discussed? What is Benson, anyway? Salesman for an undertaker's?"

"You think anything you like, Prince. I'm not in a position to give the story away yet. Perhaps by this evening."

Prince chuckled. "It's ironic that you should adopt that high-handed tone with me, old son, as it is *I* who has information to impart to *you*."

Kiley's mind, which was still with Mary back in the hospital room, snapped to attention. "What kind of info?"

"A veritable twenty-four-carat nugget, old son. Er, I take it you'd like to get your hands on this Benson character."

"Get on with it!"

"I know where Benson is hiding out."

Kiley's hand tightened on the receiver. "Okay, tell me where he is, for Christ's sake."

"Not so fast, old son. Naturally I have interests which must be served. The *Daily Express,* in whose vineyards long have I toiled, needs this exclusive. I'll lead you to Benson as long as I'm there when you pick him up. Snap! Snap! Lovely big photo for our front page. We cut out the police, you become a hero, and I add yet another illustrious triumph to my long and glorious career."

Kiley held the phone against his chest, not wishing to betray his excitement. Cutting out Withers seemed a mean thing to do after all the cop's hard work, but then Kiley reminded himself of his previous treatment at the Inspector's hands. Benson was still armed and dangerous, but Kiley just *knew* he could handle him this time around.

"Okay, Prince, it's a deal. Where is he?"

"Let's not be silly, Kiley. I'll meet you at your office in half an hour with a photographer. Can that be arranged?"

"If you insist, Prince, but you know I could just send Withers around to your place to charge you with obstructing justice. He's a bit of a brutal sod. You might need more than just a new pair of sunglasses when he's finished with you."

Prince chuckled. "I know you can send him round, Kiley, but you won't. Half an hour, then. Ciao."

Kiley angrily slammed the receiver back in its cradle. Reporters, like detectives, could be mean, hungry bastards.

Withers was walking down the corridor from the direction of Mary's room with the shambling gait of an exhausted man when Kiley stepped out of the waiting room.

"Well, Kiley, did he have anything interesting for you?"

"Wouldn't give me details on the phone. I'm going to see him anyway. As you said, it'll take my mind off things. I can't see I'm doing much good around here."

"Where are you meeting him?"

"My office."

"Want a lift? I'm going back to the Yard to check on whether there are any developments in the Benson search. It's on my way."

"No, thanks. I'll take my Jag." Kiley was finding it difficult to look Withers in the eye. Behind the Inspector's shoulder he could see the constable in a stiff-legged, hands-behind-the-back pose outside Mary's room. A Colt .38 Police Special was hanging from a holster on his hip, the uncovered butt jutting out from his body to allow easy access. British cops only got issued guns on special assignments, but even then it didn't look quite right.

"You hiding something from me, Kiley?" Withers asked suddenly.

Kiley mustered an innocent look. "Are you kidding? What could I be hiding?"

"Okay, forget it. This case is getting to me."

"I suppose you've been up all night again?"

Withers shrugged. "I couldn't sleep if I tried, just knowing that Benson's out there somewhere."

"Maybe he'll turn up. You never know."

They walked down the long, windowless corridor to the elevator. Armed policemen stood on either side of it, hands resting on their guns. As he left Withers in the hospital courtyard and headed for his car, he couldn't help feeling that he was abandoning Mary. He shrugged off the uneasy sensation as he gunned the car into life.

Kiley parked the Jag across the street from his office. The drunk woman he had seen giving the girls in the massage parlor a hard time a few nights before was doing an impromptu John Travolta impersonation farther up the street. The derelict's spastic gyrations finally brought the traffic to a halt and Kiley managed to slip across. The atmosphere was surprisingly close and he could feel droplets of sweat eddying down his forehead. He promised himself a bath in *eau de cologne* when Benson had been taken care of.

He dragged himself up to his office, plonked himself down in his desk seat, and switched on the lamp. Outside, a massive storm was brewing. When this was over, Kiley reflected, he'd use whatever money was left in his dwindling bank account on a holiday in the sun. California, perhaps. With the comforting image of sandy beaches in his head, he lounged back in his seat, stuck his legs out straight in front of him under the desk, and interlocked his fingers over his stomach. Perhaps Mary could be persuaded to come with him. She'd need a break after her ordeal. Unless the ordeal was death, he reminded himself. He yawned. The Prince was late and that was unlike him. He yawned again.

"I'm not surprised you're tired, Kiley. You've been a busy boy." Benson's voice was like a knife stabbing into his brain.

Chapter Sixteen

Benson was by the hat-stand, in the darkest corner of the room, one hand resting on one of the curved pegs, the other holding a .32, which was pointed at Kiley.

"I had an idea I'd be seeing you again," Kiley said, mustering as calm a tone as he could manage in the face of the crawling sensation in his stomach.

Smiling laconically, Benson moved into the pallid light cast by the desk lamp and sat down opposite the detective. The American's blue safari suit was showing signs of having been slept in. His beard was unkempt and a few strands of stray hair lay over his forehead. There was a streak of dirt on his broken nose.

"I congratulate you on not losing your nerve so far, Kiley. It's a good performance."

Kiley shrugged. "What did you expect? Hysterics?"

Benson smoothed the strands of hair back into place. "Not really. Believe it or not, I've come to feel quite a bit of respect for you during our short acquaintance. If it hadn't been for your intervention, my plans would have been executed by now." The word was apposite, Kiley thought. Lamplight shimmered off the sweat on the American's face. Benson's direct, hound-dog eyes reflected pain. He brought up a hand and rubbed lightly at his temple.

"Headache, Benson? I believe the side effects of MAOI antidepressants can be pretty bad. That accounts for the sweating as well."

"You *know* about that?"

"Everything there is to know, Benson." Kiley decided that playing for time was his best bet. If he could string Benson along until Prince arrived, he could conceivably take him by surprise and overpower him.

180

Benson shook his head slowly and managed to restore the smile to his face. "My respect for you increases all the time." He shrugged. "Very well, then, you know why I'm here."

"Mary Blake."

"Quite. I saw her being carried out of her house earlier today. I could tell she was just unconscious. I decided against following—either someone in the police car or you would have spotted me soon enough. I take it that someone else answered the phone this morning?"

"That was me."

Benson grinned humorlessly. "You certainly display a remarkable talent for getting in my way. I won't ask you whether or not she's alive. You would only lie, and I think I know the answer anyway."

"How did you know that Badel was dead?"

"I phoned the hospitals until I found out where he had been admitted, then pretended to be his family doctor. I doubt if you'd make the same mistake with Dr. Blake. Now just tell me where she's being held and I'll let you live."

Kiley barked out a laugh. "Like you let Hiroko live?"

Benson frowned. "Hiroko reacted badly when he discovered my plans. He was threatening to go to the police. I had no choice."

"You could have abandoned the whole mad scheme."

"Oh no, Kiley, that was the one alternative that I was unable to contemplate. Do you know how long I've waited for this opportunity?"

"Six years to the day," Kiley responded quietly. He shivered, noticing how cold the room had become. Either the temperature had dropped rapidly outside or his own fear was producing a physiological effect.

Benson ran the tip of his tongue along his lips. "Good Lord, you know about that as well!"

"Badel told us the whole story before he died."

"Is that how you knew about Dr. Blake?" He spat her name out venomously.

"No, Badel couldn't remember her name. He recognized her just before he died, but we misread the signs."

"I'm glad to hear you've made at least one mistake."

"Withers traced the managing director of the travel agency through which you booked the trip. He had her name. It was your phone call this morning that provided us with the triggering device you used to set your victims off."

Benson paused. "You're being remarkably open with me, Kiley. I notice that your eyes keep straying toward the door, almost as if you were expecting someone."

Kiley shrugged. "No one knows I'm here."

Benson grinned wolfishly. "You surprise me. I thought your reporter friend was due for an appearance."

Kiley tried to choke back a gasp but was too slow.

"What's his name again?" Benson continued. "Prince?"

"How the hell did you know?" Kiley growled.

Benson rubbed at the underside of his beard with the gun barrel, producing a rasping noise. "I'm disappointed in you, Kiley. Can't you guess?" He waited for a response which didn't come. "I paid your friend a little visit last night. We had a little 'chat'—without speech, of course. I was with him when you phoned this morning. In case anything went wrong I wanted to make sure I had an opportunity of seeing you this morning. I phoned Dr. Blake from his place, drove around in time to see her being driven away in an ambulance—a cover, I suppose—then I went back to Prince's house. He was in my power when you were speaking to him!"

"You fucking . . ."

"There's no need for that kind of language, Kiley. Whatever happened to the British tradition of the good loser? Your friend is safe, I assure you. Confused, but safe. Hiroko is the only 'innocent' whom I have been forced to kill so far." He paused. "Whether your name goes on that list depends entirely on your response to my questions."

Kiley gulped back his panic and forced himself to remain cool. "How did Hiroko get onto the secret of the drug?"

Benson narrowed his eyes. "Playing for time, Kiley? I suppose I should do the same in your position." He glanced at his watch. "Not even midday yet. Very well, I'll explain it to you." Benson sucked in his breath suddenly and a tiny groan escaped from his throat.

Kiley tensed as if to throw himself out of the seat. Benson stabbed the gun in his direction. "One more move and you're *very* dead." Kiley wondered how bad a headache it had to be to faze a man of Benson's iron self-control.

Kiley displayed the palms of his hands. "Anything you say, Benson. You're holding the gun."

Benson took a deep breath and resettled himself in his chair, seemingly recovered. "Like most great scientific discoveries, it was accidental. Hiroko was testing a new antidepressant on some patients. One of those taking part in the experiment reported that he had been watching television on the third night of treatment when his ten-year-old son, sleeping in the next room, came through to his father to complain that he was being awakened by peculiarly vivid dreams. When asked to describe the dreams, the boy gave a fair résumé of the program the father had been watching. Hiroko, a brilliant man, began researching the telepathic aspects of the drug. It took two years to perfect. He gave me a report on it during the early stages of research. I was immediately alive to its potential."

"Potential for what?"

Benson's eyebrows arched. "Why, for justice, of course."

"You're confusing revenge and justice. Justice is a moral concept, revenge isn't. Anyway, didn't you feel that the people who saw your son die had been through enough? Can you imagine the feeling of guilt they experienced?"

"Bronson? Danaher?" Benson laughed softly. "You talk of feelings of guilt, Kiley. Arnie was, literally, my whole world. My family . . ." Benson's eyes wandered momentarily to the desk top. He looked wistful. "My life was devoted to my family, Kiley. You should have met my wife and son. You might have understood me better, I think. My wife and I were still very much in love after ten years of marriage. Not many couples can claim that these days. We tried so hard to have a child. My wife suffered two miscarriages during that period."

"I didn't know that, I'm sorry."

Benson looked over at Kiley. His drooping eyes contained a terrible sadness. "Yes, you can imagine how we felt when Arnold was born. I awoke every day with a new sense of purpose, a deep contentment I'd never felt before. And Arnie? Well, he was the kind of son most men dream of having. Not some sugary, pampered rich kid, but a real 'little man.' The vacation in Norway was to be a treat for all of us—the first time the three of us had been away together since Arnie was a baby. I'd been working too hard for too long." His voice was thick with emotion. Tears brimmed in his hound-dog eyes. "It was supposed to be the happiest week of our lives." His voice cracked. Benson snorted suddenly and sat ramrod-straight. There was hatred in his gaze when he looked at Kiley again. "They killed my son, Kiley. They took my little boy and they dropped him to his death."

"Benson, I can understand how you feel, but surely it was just carelessness, stupidity . . ."

Benson was on his feet, leaning across the desk.

"THEY KILLED MY SON!" he bellowed. Kiley considered making a grab for the gun. It was no more than a few inches from his face, but Benson's trigger finger was so shaky he didn't dare try it.

Benson moved back a pace and stood, hunched over, taking deep breaths. "I beg your pardon," he croaked, then sat back down. He wiped the perspiration from his forehead with one shaking hand. Sweat patches were visible under his armpits. "I apologize for my outburst." He paused. "They killed my son," he repeated. "That's all there is to it. And then they killed my wife." Benson shook his head slowly from side to side. "She took her own life nine months later. She just couldn't live with it—she would have died of a broken heart anyway. Not a day went by when she didn't relive that dreadful moment in her own mind."

"But *you* managed to live through it."

Benson smiled grimly. "I had a purpose in life. I had a mission. They all had to die, of course, that was obvious. I could have arranged it in the conventional way. I could have taken out contracts on their lives. I had the money, but"—he shrugged—"that wouldn't have been true revenge." Benson leaned forward on the edge of his seat. "You see, I wanted them to experience what Arnie had experienced. I wanted them to die in terror—raw, naked terror. I wanted their deaths to be unimaginably horrible. I wanted them to walk through the valley of the shadow of death . . ." He looked up at Kiley suddenly. "Do you think I'm mad?"

"Morally insane, yes. You're dangerous, that's all I know."

Benson seemed to consider Kiley's response for a few moments, then carried on as if he hadn't heard it. "I waited a long time until I discovered a method whereby I could achieve my aim. I knew, from the moment that Hiroko informed me of his experiments on Project Alpha, that here it was at last. Unfortunately, Reverend Anstruther had already died, but his end was violent enough to satisfy me. As a bonus, his wife, Emily, had decided to settle here. Danaher came to live in London when his recording career fell apart. That meant they were all right here in London, within reach. Nothing could have been easier. It was as if the fates had taken my side. There was one minor flaw—Hiroko. Through lax security on my part and an overly curious nature on his, he got wind of my plans—not the complete picture, but enough to make him threaten to go to the police. I killed him. He was the final part of the experiment."

"Frankenstein destroyed by his own monster." Kiley paused. "There's one last detail I'd like to know, Benson. It can't make any difference to you now. Tell me what you put into the minds of your victims."

"I made it simple, beautifully simple: 'On such-and-such a date you will suffer the most horrible of deaths.'" He grinned triumphantly.

Kiley whistled softly between his teeth. "Very neat."

Benson shrugged. "I like to think so, Kiley. I then wiped all memory of myself or the vacation from their minds and set them free . . . with a time-bomb in their heads."

"What now, Benson? There's no way the police will let you escape. Half the cops in London are looking for you."

The American smiled easily. "I know that, Kiley. As soon as Dr. Blake dies, I will take this gun I'm holding, place it in my mouth, and blow my brains out."

"Why not do it right now? You've had enough blood. Your son's death has been avenged six times over."

Benson shook his head. "You still don't understand, do you? It was all or none. If Mary Blake lives, then everything will have been in vain. Kiley, she has to die! Surely you can see that? Tell me where the police have taken her and I'll let you live."

Benson rose from his seat and began moving around the side of the desk. Kiley felt his throat constricting. He closed his eyes.

"Benson, you'll get nothing out of me, so get it over with."

Benson was standing directly behind him now. Kiley shifted his feet so that the soles of his boots were pressed against the legs of the desk. He tensed himself, ready to throw his body backward.

"Tell me where Mary Blake is, Kiley, and I promise you'll live." Benson was standing right behind him now, no more than a yard away.

"What is it with you, Kiley? Have you formed a romantic attachment to the woman or do you have a 'white knight in shining armor' complex? Get wise, Kiley. The age of chivalry is dead!"

Summoning the last reserves of strength in his bruised, exhausted body, Kiley shoved backward, in a gamble for his life. He heard Benson yell. There was an explosion inside Kiley's skull, and the carpet rushed up to meet him.

In a last flash of consciousness, he thought: I gambled. I lost.

"Kiley, wake up, damn you!"

Kiley was dimly aware that someone was holding the lapels of his jacket and shaking him vigorously. He opened his eyes. The room was a moving blur.

"Thank Christ!" he heard someone mutter. The shaking stopped. Kiley blinked hard. His mind was a fog. Withers's massive slab of a face was no more than a few inches from his eyes.

"Withers, what're you doing here?" he slurred.

"Kiley, concentrate! What the hell happened to you?"

"Happened? To me?" Kiley stared around the room with a puzzled frown. Withers delivered a stinging slap to his cheek. Kiley sucked in air. Another blow shook his head.

"Hey!" he yelled, waving his hands in front of his face as if to fend off a wasp. "Cut that out!" Withers's hands grabbed the front of his jacket again and he felt himself being hoisted out of his seat. The big cop's piglike eyes bored into him.

"Concentrate, damn you! What the hell happened here?"

"Here?" Kiley's eyes traveled once more around the office as if he had just realized where he was. The sergeant who had been on guard in Mary's house during the night was standing by the door. Withers's grip relaxed and Kiley subsided back onto the seat. He brought his hands up to cover his face. It was as if patches of mist were hanging in his mind, obscuring his thoughts. Withers's hand gripped his shoulder hard.

"Kiley, has Benson been here?"

Benson! That was it. Benson had been in his office, waiting for him. Benson had spoken to him. Benson . . . the mist began to clear.

Kiley's hands parted. "Benson *was* here."

Withers groaned. "Did you tell him where we were holding Dr. Blake?"

Kiley looked up at the Inspector. "No, at least, not as far as I know. I refused to speak. He said he'd kill me if I didn't tell him. He got behind me. I was ready to push back against him, then . . ." He reached round to feel the lump on the back of his skull. With a wince he brought his hand back to examine it. His fingers were running with blood.

Withers stooped to examine the wound. "Nasty one, but you'll live."

"I thought he'd shot me. It's coming back now. I know I didn't tell him anything. Wait!" A whisper echoed somewhere deep in the recesses of his mind. "Oh God! He's found out! I know he has."

"How do you know?" Withers's tone was urgent.

"I can feel it . . . him. He's been inside my head." He traced an index finger over his temple. "I can feel the bastard. In here! He must have used the drug to get it out of me while I was unconscious. All he needed to do was get me to talk—no problem for him. But why did he let me live?"

"We don't need to worry about that at the moment." Withers stepped around the desk, picked up the phone and dialed quickly. "Yeah, is that the West Central Hospital? This is Detective Inspector Withers. Two of my men are on duty in your reception area. I want to speak to one of them. I don't give a shit if you're not allowed to leave the desk. Get one of them to the phone right now." He paused for a few moments, tapping his foot and glancing nervously at Kiley. "That you, Bishop? Good. Benson knows where Dr. Blake is. That's correct. Keep your bloody eyes peeled! We'll be there in fifteen minutes. Warn your men!" He turned to Kiley when the receiver had been replaced. "What happened to the reporter?"

"Benson got to Prince. He did the same thing to him that he did to Mary. Benson was with him when Prince made the calls to you and then to me. It wasn't Prince's fault. He didn't know what he was doing."

Withers nodded. "Okay; if you're feeling well enough to move, let's get to the hospital."

Kiley struggled to his feet and took a few steps toward the door. His legs hardly obeyed his commands. It was like walking in a dream. One of his knees buckled. Withers, walking behind, caught at his elbow. The sergeant opened the office door and Kiley was guided down the stairs and out into the waiting police car.

They were moving within seconds, the siren blaring. Kiley, lay at an angle across the back seat, swinging helplessly from side to side as the car swept around corners. "How did you know to come to my office?" he shouted to Withers, who was sitting in the front seat.

"We got a reported sighting of Benson in your area. I phoned you a few times. When there was no reply, I put two and two together."

"Thank God you did!" Another thought struck Kiley. "If Benson got all his info from me, he must know exactly how well the hospital's guarded. How the hell does he expect to get in?"

"He's desperate enough to try shooting his way through. I hope he tries it. He'll be cut down as soon as he shows his face. My men'll be taking no chances."

"Look, Withers, Benson is absolutely desperate." Adrenaline had washed Kiley's mind clear. "If there's a way of getting to Mary, he'll find it."

Withers twisted around in his seat. "Are you trying to cheer me up or something? There's no way he can get past my men. Understood?"

Kiley studied the policeman's grim face. They rode in silence for five minutes. Behind the car the tires were creating miniature tidal waves. The windshield wipers flailed uselessly at the water flooding against them. At several points Kiley wondered how the sergeant could see anything at all ahead of him.

It was only when the hospital loomed into view that Kiley realized how Benson could have got into the building without meeting the cops on duty in reception. He decided to remain silent until his suspicions were confirmed.

"Wait out here, Sergeant!" Before the car had skidded to a halt, Withers was already out and running for the hospital entrance, Kiley on his heels. Inside the reception area, patients were huddled along the walls, waiting for treatment. Withers's squat head twisted from side to side, like a clockwork doll whose mechanism had ceased to function properly.

Two uniformed constables approached from either side of the hall.

Withers turned to Kiley. "I told you Benson wouldn't get past them."

The first policeman was standing in front of them. "Everything's quiet here, sir."

"When did you last check with your men on the sixth floor?" Kiley asked.

The cop looked at Withers uncertainly before responding. "About five minutes ago. They had nothing to report."

Kiley ran over to the reception desk. A dark-haired girl behind it finished a telephone conversation, then turned to him, smiling.

"Can I help you, sir?"

"Yes, I'm with the police. Have any patients been admitted to the Intensive Care Unit during the last half hour? It's very urgent."

"I'll check for you, sir," she answered brightly and began flicking through sheets attached to a clipboard in front of her. "I don't think so . . . Wait a minute. Yes, here we are. About ten minutes ago. A middle-aged man was picked up from Portobello Road—apparently suffering from a heart attack. The doctors should be working on him at this moment."

Kiley looked up at Withers, who had joined him. "Give your boys on the sixth floor a call. Tell them they've got a visitor."

Withers swung around on his heels. "Radio up!" he barked. "Tell them Benson's on their floor somewhere. He feigned a heart attack. Tell them he's been admitted as a patient."

One of the constables unclipped a walkie-talkie. "Able Baker Seven, this is Tango Delta Three calling, over." He waited a few seconds, then repeated the call sign. Static crackled back at them.

Chapter Seventeen

Kiley realized with a start that there was only one gun among the three men who were riding up in the elevator; it belonged to the young sergeant whom Withers had called in from the car. He mentioned the fact to Withers, who dismissed it.

"If Benson's up there, I won't need a gun. I'll kill him with my bare hands. If he's harmed Dr. Blake . . ." He let the threat trail off.

Kiley silently applauded the sentiments, but the lack of firepower worried him. Withers had deliberately left the constables down in reception in case Benson should somehow manage to slip past them; in addition, a back-up unit had also been radioed for.

Kiley and Withers moved to the back of the elevator as it inched its way to the sixth floor. The sergeant snatched the .38 Police Special from his coat pocket, and stepped toward the doors, holding the gun by his cheek, pointed at the ceiling. A trickle of sweat was coursing down his forehead and his hand was shaking.

The doors whispered open with agonizing slowness.

"Easy, Sergeant," Withers warned him. "Nothing rash. Just take a look down the corridor . . ." As the doors opened fully, his voice trailed off. Legs encased in blue serge trousers were visible lying on the ground a little to the side of the elevator.

"Jesus!" Kiley groaned. "Benson's shot them!"

The sergeant gulped and readjusted his grip on the gun. There was a muted buzz of excitement from the far end of the long corridor, coming from the direction of Mary's room. The sergeant edged forward, one hand against the side of the elevator door to stop it from closing. His head shifted forward until he could see down the corridor.

"Both dead," he muttered, staring down. He turned his head to peer up the corridor in the direction of the noise. The sergeant's gun had moved in a blur. There was a sharp crack of an automatic firing, then a sound like a hammer hitting a melon nearby. The sergeant's body shuddered and began to slide down, the nails of one hand grinding into the metal of the elevator doors, the gun still clutched in the other. Withers moved forward to support him, but was too late. The sergeant fell forward so that the top half of his body was lying in the corridor. Withers grabbed his legs and began pulling him back inside the elevator. When he turned the sergeant over, there was a bullet hole spewing red pulp below his open but sightless left eye. He was dead. Withers clenched his fists. Averting his eyes from the dead cop's face, Kiley leaned over and disengaged the .38 from his hand. He grasped Withers's shoulder. The big cop looked up through tear-filled eyes. Most older cops work with younger men whom they come to regard as sons and successors. Withers obviously felt that way about the sergeant, Kiley realized.

"All right, Withers," Kiley growled. "We've got the bastard now. Let's take him!"

"What are we going to do?" Withers demanded. The abrogation of responsibility was a gauge of his shock.

"Just do as I say. There might still be time to save Mary. If Benson's in the corridor, he might not have got to her yet—he told me he'd shoot himself the moment he'd taken care of her. He's probably killed the constable on duty outside her room and is trying to get the door unlocked."

Withers stood up as if in a trance. Kiley hoped he wasn't going to do anything stupid. "Just stay in here, Withers. Don't move unless I tell you. I'm going to try and pick him off." Kiley moved to the front of the elevator stepping over the sergeant's corpse. If he showed his head in the same place as his predecessor, Benson would no doubt blow it off. Kiley remembered with a shudder that the American had told him he was a marksman. He dropped down on his haunches and listened. There was another shot down to the right. Benson had disposed of the lock. This was Kiley's only chance.

He launched himself along the ground out into the corridor, his stomach on the polished linoleum. The bodies of the two dead cops provided a cover of sorts. He slithered behind the first corpse.

Benson was standing outside the door to Mary's room, his hand on the handle. In the wood where the lock had been, there was a smoldering gap. Beyond Benson, Kiley saw the body of the cop who had been standing guard over Mary. At the far end of the long corridor two doctors and three nurses were clustered in white-faced terror.

"Benson!" Kiley shouted as he tightened his grip on the Colt's trigger.

Benson wheeled, hunched over, and fired before Kiley could get off a shot. The detective felt a stinging pain in his right hand. A neat red furrow ran from knuckle to wrist. The gun fell from his grasp. The searing pain made him wince and twist his head. He looked up at Withers, who was framed in the elevator doorway. Kiley edged his left hand around toward the fallen gun.

"Freeze!" Benson shouted. "Withers, I know you're in the elevator. If you don't come out, I'll take Kiley with one shot."

Kiley's mouth formed a silent "no." The big man stepped out into the corridor and turned to face the American. An eerie calmness had settled over the massive cop. Kiley gasped as Withers began walking slowly up the corridor toward the American.

"Benson, this has gone far enough," he began in a quiet, reasoning tone. "You can't get away from here. I want you to give me the gun. I've got men waiting downstairs. Just throw the gun away and start walking toward me."

"Withers, you crazy bastard! Come back here!" Kiley shouted.

Benson took careful aim, his right arm extended, his left hand grasping his wrist. He waited until Withers was some twenty yards away before firing.

The huge cop stopped walking suddenly, then turned slowly to face Kiley. The Inspector's expression was infinitely calm. There was a neat bullet hole a few centimeters above his left eyebrow. Withers's mouth opened as his eyes fixed on Kiley. He took a few steps toward the detective, then fell forward stiffly onto his face, without making a sound. He lay quite still on the floor, arms out by his sides, ankles crossed, in a crucifixion pose, his neck twisted at an odd angle.

Benson lowered the gun to his side and shook his head.

"I wish he hadn't made me do that," he remarked conversationally. He was speaking just loud enough for Kiley to pick up what he was saying. "All these dead bodies . . ." Benson shook his head and looked around. "Like the last scene in *Hamlet*." He barked out a laugh. His drooping eyes shifted to Kiley.

The detective was staring at Withers's corpse, wondering what had made him walk to certain death. The cop must have known that Benson wasn't going to give himself up. Was it his way of making up for his early mishandling of the case? A last bid for glory? An emotional reaction to the sergeant's death? Kiley's mind was reeling. With an effort he managed to focus his attention on what Benson was saying.

"I let you live, Kiley. I gave in to sentimentality, and now look where it's got me."

"Why didn't you kill me back in the office?" Kiley shouted back. He wondered how long it would take for the police back-up unit to arrive. Deep in his gut he felt it would not be soon enough.

Benson shrugged. "Respect for a valiant adversary. There was really no reason for you to die."

"What about these poor bastards, Benson, these cops? Was there a reason for them to die?" Kiley was trying hard to keep the hysteria from his voice. Each second that Benson was kept away from Mary was a minor victory.

"Nobody had to die, apart from the animals who murdered my son. Nobody," Benson repeated in a tone that came close to regret. "All I wanted were the lives of those six people: Anne Warren, Bronson, Emily Anstruther, Danaher, Badel . . ." He chanted as if it were a litany. He turned to stare through the glass partition set in Mary's door. "And Dr. Blake."

Kiley struggled to his feet. Benson turned to look at him again. The American's face was running with perspiration. His blue safari suit was black with sweat. Clutching the wrist of his wounded hand, Kiley took a faltering step toward Benson, then halted. The American emitted a squeal of pain and brought his free hand up to his head. There was no point in trying to rush him. Kiley had seen how quickly the man could recover from these devastating migraine attacks.

Kiley's gun was lying within his reach, but his chances of getting off an accurate shot with his left hand were nil, and the dull throbbing in his right hand told him that it would be useless to him. Besides, there was always a possibility that a stray bullet might hit one of the medical staff still hunched at the end of the corridor. Kiley looked down at Withers's corpse. The policeman's eyes were open. They seemed to be staring up at Kiley. The Inspector's lips were slightly parted as if he had died trying to say something important. Perhaps he had died trying to save Kiley. Maybe his advance had been designed to act as a shield for the detective's retreat.

When Kiley looked up, Benson was staring at him once more, the gun held loosely at his side. He had strayed a few feet from Mary Blake's door.

One of the doctors standing in the group behind Benson made a move forward. Benson turned and fired a warning shot into the ceiling. The group froze.

"Stay where you are!" Kiley warned them.

Benson wheeled back toward him. "Now, Kiley!" he bellowed suddenly, "it's time to bring our brief but fascinating duel to its conclusion. I told you opposition would be useless against the drug. I can feel the power pulsing through me right now." He raised the gun and aimed it at Kiley. The detective shut his eyes. Several heart-stopping moments later he opened them. The gun was back down by Benson's side. The American was smiling laconically.

"No, Kiley, you'll die by the drug."

Kiley frowned. "How? I'm wide awake. There isn't an Alpha wave in my head." He heard the elevator doors closing behind him. The back-up unit had arrived. The sergeant's corpse would provide an eloquent warning for them. "How can the drug affect me now?"

"You've only just discovered what it is. You haven't yet realized its full potential, Kiley. I'm going to demonstrate its full power." He chuckled softly. "You probably imagined that it could only be used to affect one person at a time. Not so. You're about to get your name in the scientific textbooks, Kiley, next to mine and Hiroko's"

There were ten doors set in the walls on either side of

the corridor between himself and Benson. The first one to his left opened slightly.

"Get back inside," Kiley said, quite quietly.

"Mass telepathy, Kiley," he heard Benson call down. "It's never been done before. Appreciate it while you can. You won't be around too long to enjoy it."

A gray, pallid face appeared out of the dark crack. Dull, listless eyes stared out of white skin covered in brown blotches. The ICU patient stepped out into the corridor on sticklike legs.

"Back inside, for Christ's sake," Kiley growled. "It's dangerous out here."

The patient stared at Kiley uncomprehendingly. The old man appeared to be so close to death that Kiley was convinced that another few steps would kill him. An extraordinary change came over the patient's features. His eyes took on a quality of blazing anger. He stepped forward again. His lips curled back from his teeth and he let out a surprisingly powerful growl.

"Please go back inside!" Kiley pleaded.

An intravenous tube was attached to the patient's arm, coiling under the sleeve of his gown. As the old man took another step, Kiley heard a clanking sound in the room he had just vacated. The tube was attached to a contraption like a hat-stand with an inverted bottle of clear liquid hooked onto it. The old man was dragging it behind him as he moved forward.

Kiley looked down the corridor at Benson. The American was grinning, toying with his beard, watching the scene with evident amusement. Beyond him, the doctors and nurses had taken Kiley's advice and remained stock-still.

In confusion, Kiley looked back at the still-advancing patient and saw that all the doors along the corridor were opening. Other patients were beginning to move out of their bedrooms, like zombies.

"This is just the start of the demonstration, Kiley," Benson shouted. "There's more to come, much more." He chuckled again.

Kiley began backing away from the dozen or so white-robed ICU patients who were heading toward him, hatred burning in their eyes.

"Benson, what the hell is this?"

"Can't you guess, Kiley? Can't you see what I'm doing?"

It all clicked into place. This procession of half-dead somnambulists shuffling hideously toward him was under Benson's mental control. This was the experiment in mass telepathy. He had to admit there *was* a certain gruesome fascination to it.

The old man from the first room made a feeble lunge at Kiley; he batted him aside with the back of his uninjured hand.

Kiley turned toward the emergency exit, some forty yards behind him. He knew that the police had had it locked, but there was always a chance he could batter his way through.

He gasped. Patients were descending on him from that direction as well. There was an extra twist in his gut when he realized that some of them were carrying vicious-looking surgical instruments. Steel blades gleamed under the overhead lights.

These people, most of whom looked to be on the verge of death, had either been sleeping or under heavy sedation. Benson's message of destruction had been received loud and clear by their Alpha wave-dominated minds. The power of the drug seemed almost unlimited.

Kiley waited until the walking dead were arranged in a semicircle around him, pinning him to the wall. Now he wished he had picked up the gun.

"So long, Kiley!" he heard Benson call. Kiley looked over the heads of his attackers toward the American. Benson was engrossed in the scene. Kiley was dimly aware that the door behind Benson was opening slowly, but his view was cut off by the patients surging in on him. Bony hands began pummeling his body. Sticklike legs rammed into him. He felt himself going under as he attempted to fend off the blows. Blades ripped into the material of his jacket. There was a sharp pain in his left leg.

With a struggle he managed to get to his feet, and he began lashing out wildly with his fists. It was like hitting phantoms. The light bodies crumpled on impact, but there were so many of them now that no sooner had one fallen than another had taken his place. Kiley dropped to the ground suddenly. Before his attackers could react he began burrowing frenetically though their legs. He had reached the edge of the group before enough of them had thrown themselves onto his back to halt his progress.

Some thirty yards away, Benson, his back to the still slowly-opening door of Mary Blake's room, gave Kiley a laconic shrug.

An icy sensation ran down the detective's back. He realized dimly that a scalpel blade had slit the skin open in a neat line near his spine. With a yell he twisted onto his side, displacing several of his attackers. There were no cries, no shouts, just growls and a few grunts. The eerie semi-silence of the encounter merely added to Kiley's intense fear.

He gave a last, despairing yell! "Save me, for Christ's sake! Save me, Benson, damn you!"

Benson frowned and began to turn away, apparently satiated by the horror he had wrought. Kiley tried to rise but was forced back. His strength had all but disappeared. He glanced at the floor indicator above the elevator. He could see that it was ascending; now at three, now four. It was his only hope. He caught sight of a knife blade descending toward his arm. He fended it off with a tired, defeated punch.

He looked back up the corridor. Benson was immobile, lost in thought, staring at the ground, as if his conscience were finally putting up a struggle.

Kiley opened his mouth to scream again, but stopped himself. Mary Blake was visible now standing in the open doorway of her room, directly behind Benson. She was dressed in a regulation hospital robe, her eyes narrow slits of hatred. Clenched in her hand, which was raised to shoulder height, was a scalpel.

Something thudded into Kiley's back. There was no more fight left in him. He slumped against the floor. As he did, he vaguely registered the elevator door swooshing open. Heavy boots sounded on the linoleum near his ear. The blows on his body and the pressure on his back lessened. He twisted his head to look up and saw cops scattering the patients aside. Someone hauled him to his feet.

He immediately began to stagger toward Benson. As the American raised his gun and aimed it carefully at Kiley, the blade in Mary's hand came swinging down in a vicious arc. It took Kiley a split second to comprehend; Mary had received Benson's signals for violence along with the rest of the patients.

The blade scythed into Benson's back. His whole frame shook and the gun wobbled in his grasp. Mary pulled the scalpel out and brought it down again. The blade glanced off Benson's skull, but the force of the blow sent him tumbling to his knees.

Mary brought the knife up for another blow. Benson dropped his gun and turned his head to stare up at her. Kiley could see the American's mouth opening. Benson was trying to say something. The date! He was trying to tell her the date!

Kiley began running, followed closely by the cop who had helped him up.

Mary stood, the blade held high, her eyes fixed on Benson, as if transfixed by the dying man's gaze. As Kiley reached the prone American, he heard the word "November" quite distinctly. His boot caught Benson in the side of the head and sent him sprawling. The cop with Kiley launched himself at Mary, caught at her wrist before she could stab, and brought her crashing onto the floor. Her head hit it awkwardly, knocking her unconscious. Kiley felt like crying with relief. One of the doctors who had been huddled at the far end of the corridor ran to Mary's side. He examined her neck, felt for her pulse, then nodded at Kiley. "She'll be all right."

Benson moaned softly. Kiley knelt beside him and stooped over until his ear was close to Benson's mouth. The American was still trying to speak.

"Is she . . . is Dr. Blake . . ."

"No, Benson," Kiley said harshly. "She's alive. She's going to be fine."

Benson shifted his head so that his pain-filled eyes were staring into Kiley's. "You . . . you won, Kiley," he coughed out in a strained whisper. Blood gushed from one corner of his mouth and dripped down his beard and onto the floor.

"Nobody won, Benson," Kiley said softly. "A lot of people lost."

Benson's head jerked as if he was trying to nod. "I did it for Arnie—just for Arnie. They had to die."

"Sure," Kiley sighed.

Benson's body stiffened suddenly. He groaned and more

blood welled from his mouth. His last breath escaped with a soft hiss that turned into a chilling death rattle.

Kiley stood up slowly, dimly aware of the pain in his own body. He watched as two nurses helped a policeman carry Mary back into her room. He turned to stare down the harshly lit corridor.

Most of the patients were being led back to their rooms. Some lay dead. Two cops were carrying Withers's body toward the elevator.

Kiley patted his pocket with a bloodied hand, found a cigarette, lit it shakily, and dragged smoke deep into his lungs.

All in all, he reflected, it had been one hell of a week.